CW00666240

Reluctantly Alpha

The Barrington Billionaires
Book Eight

Ruth Cardello

Author Contact
website: RuthCardello.com
email: ruthcardello@gmail.com
Facebook: Author Ruth Cardello
Twitter: RuthieCardello
Goodreads
goodreads.com/author/show/4820876.Ruth_Cardello
Bookbub
bookbub.com/authors/ruth-cardello

New York Times and *USA Today* bestselling author Ruth Cardello returns with a hilarious addition to the Barrington Billionaire series.

Connor Sutton never had a problem attracting women. Tall, blond, easy-going . . . all he had to do to get them into his bed was to stop saying no. He never wanted to be rich or famous, but when his sister married a billionaire, he became both. To fit into the Barrington clan, he had to make a lot of changes and although being rich is nice. . . all it takes to make him happy is a loaded pizza and a cold beer.

Until he meets Angelina Kroll and discovers what it's like to want someone he can't have. Then she's all he can think about.

As a hardworking, single mother, the last thing Angelina is looking for is a fling with a movie star, especially gorgeous, broody Connor Sutton. She gave up believing in happily ever after a long time ago. When she's unexpectedly fired, Connor offers her a job that's impossible to refuse.

He's not the man she thinks he is.

She's not the woman she'd hoped to be.

They've both left behind more than they wanted to.

Will they discover fitting in doesn't have to be all or nothing?

Can they be rich . . . and happy too?

Copyright

Dedication

This book is dedicated to Joanna and Aly. Both real life examples of the kind of heroines I write in my books— strong, intelligent women who make the world a better place.

And little Betty, the mini-therapy horse Joanna rescued from a kill pen. She's real and you can read about her here.

ruthcardello.com/news-and-ponderings/2019/11/26/the-real-story-behind-betty-the-mini-therapy-horse

Chapter One

"**W**ELL LOOK AT who slipped in while I was counting the register," a woman in her late fifties called out as soon as she spotted Connor Sutton in the corner booth of her family-style pizza restaurant in Queens, New York. She made her way to him through the otherwise empty restaurant, whistling as she did. "You look more important every time I see you."

Connor loosened his tie and stood to greet her. "And you, Ada, just keep getting more beautiful." He held out his arms for a hug that she walked into.

"Don't let my husband hear you talk like that." She was blushing when she stepped back.

"He can have you," her husband, Joel, called out from behind the counter. "Connor, tell her just because the doctor told me to eat better doesn't mean I have to cut everything with any taste out of my diet."

Connor walked over and shook Joel's hand. "I'd listen to Ada. She's only trying to keep your sorry ass alive."

Joel nodded toward his wife and sighed. "Figures he'd take your side."

Ada gave her husband's back a flick with a rolled towel. "Because I'm right."

He spun her around, dipped her over his arm, and said, "What did you say? Can't hear you."

She clung to his shoulders, laughing. "I said I hope my next husband has the sense to listen to his doctor."

"Your next husband?" Joel growled something into her ear that had her laughing and swatting him after he righted her.

The scene warmed Connor's heart. His mother had died when he was a child and had been sick before that for as long as he could remember. Had his parents ever been as light-hearted and happy? He liked to believe so, although that was a time no one in his family spoke of.

Behind Connor, the door of the restaurant chimed, announcing the arrival of another patron. All amusement left Joel's face. Ada gripped his arm. Connor tensed at the heavy silence and spun on his heel, prepared to face down a gang leader or early afternoon drunk.

He instantly relaxed as he recognized the friend he'd ask to meet him for lunch. "You made it."

"You know him?" Joel asked in a strained voice.

Connor nodded. "Absolutely. Bradford get on in here and meet two of my favorite New York friends. Joel and Ada Fetter, this is my good friend, Bradford . . ." It was only then he realized he didn't know his last name.

Bradford removed his mirrored glasses and placed them into the breast pocket of his dark suit. He didn't smile as he joined them.

Beside him, Joel appeared small and intimidated. Connor flexed his shoulders. He didn't like to see either of his friends uncomfortable. Bradford was what Claire would call socially challenged. People should be able to look past his scars and tattoos, and they would if he stepped out of his "I'm a hitman" persona long enough for them to get to know him.

To lighten the mood, Connor gave him a hearty welcoming punch to the arm.

Bradford didn't so much as flinch, but he did give Connor a warning look.

Joel's arm tightened around his wife and they took a step back.

Their nervousness only encouraged Connor. He held open his arms toward his glaring friend. "Don't make me hug you."

"I would drop you to the fucking floor," Bradford said in a tight voice.

Connor chuckled. He'd only hung out with Bradford a few times over the past year, but the man had a dry humor that really cracked Connor up. "You could try, or you could smile and show my friends that you're really a good guy who is here because you care about me."

Bradford looked from Connor to Joel and Ada and back. He flashed a smile that wasn't reflected in either his eyes or his tone as he said, "I flew in from Bulgaria because you said there was a situation you couldn't handle on your own."

"Bulgaria?" Connor waved a hand in Bradford's direction. "Do you see why I love this guy? Bulgaria. I don't even know where that is, but I said I needed him and he flew all the way back from there. That's a good friend."

"That *is* a long way," Ada agreed in a forced friendly voice. "You must be hungry, Bradford. Why don't you have a seat and we'll bring out some . . ."

"Pizza. Plain," Connor suggested with enthusiasm. "It's kosher. That means—"

"I know what kosher means," Bradford said.

Of course he would. Bradford was well-traveled. Connor had needed Joel to explain it to him. "Well, then you know how challenging creating an authentic New York kosher pizza can be. People take food very seriously in this area. Ada makes her own mozzarella."

"Everything here is produced from scratch," Joel added with pride.

"Sounds delicious," Bradford said. This time his smile held a bit more sincerity.

"It really is," Connor said. He took a seat once again in the corner booth. "Ada, two draft beers. Your choice."

"You got it," Ada said. She delivered them in chilled mugs almost as soon as Bradford sat down.

Connor took a good swig of his.

Bradford did as well. After lowering his mug, he demanded, "What do you need?"

Asking for help wasn't something Connor was accustomed to, but ever since his younger sister, Viviana, had married a billionaire, he hardly recognized his life. In the small town of Cairo, Upstate New York, his family had been kind of a big thing. Confident. Well-liked. Not so much in the circles the Barringtons ran in. Especially not in the beginning. His plaid shirts and jeans hadn't been good enough and almost all of his humor had been lost on them.

After a year of working with Claire Wendell, accountability and life coach, he and his brother Dylan understood that they laughed too loud, drank too much, and often didn't pick up on social cues. She was too kind to ever say it that bluntly, but Clay Landon had been brutally honest about why Viviana was constantly apologizing for Dylan and him.

They needed to change or they'd always be the butt of everyone's jokes.

It was tough love not everyone could have handled, but both Connor and Dylan had been grateful for it. The last thing either of them wanted was to diminish any of the happiness their sister had found with Grant Barrington, especially since they'd started a family together. Little Sean would be raised very differently than the Suttons had been, but Connor wanted to be part of every bit of his journey.

Clay's blunt assessment of what would make that difficult had been a wake-up call, but it had been accompanied by an introduction to a film producer who had changed Connor's and Dylan's lives once again. *Danger Doubled*, a romantic comedy about two brothers who had fallen in love with the same woman, had made them household names.

They were now both featured in articles as big-screen heartthrobs. Dylan as a badass. Connor as a genius doctor.

Neither could be further from the truth. Over the years they'd indulged in a fair share of bar fights, but Dylan had never thrown the first punch. He didn't like confrontation.

Unfortunately, confrontation liked him.

And Connor? Reading was a new pastime to him. He could recite complicated medical terms like a parrot, but understood very few of them. Claire had done a thorough job of creating a version of him that the public loved. Too good.

Every new person Connor met assumed he was brilliant like the doctor he'd played. To maintain the illusion, he kept more and more of his thoughts to himself. Public perception was important if he didn't want to embarrass Viviana again.

Part of him craved the simplicity of his life before the Barringtons. His family had been easier to please, and he'd felt good about himself back then. Nothing he did now brought the same satisfaction as a hard day of manual labor on a construction site followed by downing some beers with his friends.

There was no going back, though.

As his family's company had grown, it had changed. So had the way his old friends treated him. Relationships that had once been effortless were now . . . complicated. Some accused him of changing too much while others wanted him to suddenly have all the answers.

I don't have answers.

I'm still just—me.

If anyone understood what it was like to not fit in, it was Bradford. Connor cleared his throat. "This weekend I have a speaking engagement in New Jersey."

"And?"

"Dylan accepted a role in a movie set in Iceland. He's already on location."

Bradford simply held his gaze.

Connor added, "Claire is preoccupied with wedding shit this week."

Nothing.

Connor swirled his beer in his mug before saying, "I shouldn't go alone."

"Because you're receiving death threats?"

"No. No, nothing like that."

Bradford frowned. "Then what's the problem?"

Connor leaned closer and lowered his voice. "It's too dangerous."

"What?" Bradford lowered his own voice in a mockery of Connor's. "I have no fucking idea what you're talking about."

"Speaking at Reemsly Preparatory Academy. It's a private school. Those people are smart. They'll ask me questions I won't know the answers to. I can't look like an idiot."

Bradford's hands fisted on the table. "That's your emergency? I flew back for this?"

"I didn't say it was an emergency. I said I had a situation I couldn't handle on my own."

A low guttural sound was Bradford's only response.

Connor continued, "I'm a public figure now. I don't want to be. My goal was to make enough money so the Barrington staff would stop thinking I'd steal the silverware."

"I doubt they believe you'd know how to use it."

"Don't be a dick. I'm serious."

"*I'm* the dick?" Bradford rubbed a hand over his forehead. "Why am I here?"

"I know you won't judge me, and I need help."

"Oh, you definitely need help. I'm trying to figure out, though, why you thought I was the one you should call."

"You're here, aren't you?" Connor asked with a shrug.

"I am. Can't even argue that one." Bradford chugged the rest of his beer then set it down with a thud. "What do you need, Connor?"

"Advice. How do I get out of this without making Claire look bad or making a fool of myself?"

"You probably can't unless you let me put you in the hospital," Bradford joked, even though his tone remained serious.

Connor shook his head. "I'm looking for something less extreme. Plus, I like my face the way it is."

"Then you're shit out of luck." Bradford's gaze was cold steel dipped in indifference.

Impressively impossible to read.

"I could use that." All those acting lessons might actually pay off.

"What?"

"Your expression." Connor sat up straighter. He narrowed his eyes at Bradford.

"Are you fucking with me?"

"No," Connor assured him as he brought his brows together in a deep frown. "Tell me when I get it right."

Ada appeared at the table with a pizza and some plates. "Everything okay, Connor?"

Instantly, Connor's smile returned. "Perfect. Thanks, Ada. Looks great. I'll have one more beer. What about you, Bradford?"

Bradford's only response was another of his dark looks.

"He'll have another too," Connor said cheerfully.

She was back in a flash with two fresh mugs. Connor thanked her again.

"Your problem is you're too fucking nice," Bradford said once she was out of earshot.

"Me? No. Ada and Joel are the nice ones. Dylan and I found this place the first week we were in the city. They made us feel like we were old friends even though nobody knew our names yet. They're good people."

"Joel is jumpy because his son hung with a bad crew before they shipped him to Rhode Island to live with Ada's brother. He's in college now, but Joel's had a few run-ins with his old friends. Seems that his son left without settling all his debts."

Connor's mouth dropped open. "How do you know that?"

"I make it my job to. The more you know about people the more prepared you are to deal with whatever shit they start."

"I can't imagine the Fetters starting shit with anyone."

"But now if they do, you know where their jugular is."

Connor mulled that while digging into the pizza. He didn't agree with how Bradford saw the world, but it also wasn't the first time Connor had been told he was too nice. No one messed with Bradford. No one apologized for him or said he embarrassed them. Like a character study, Connor decided to borrow a little badass for the school function. "I'm going to say a few things I might be asked. Show me how you'd respond."

Between taking bites of pizza, Bradford said, "Shoot."

"What's the planet that was downgraded to a dwarf?"

"No one is going to ask you that."

"It's just an example. I know there was a planet that was. I can't remember the name of it. There's a lot of stuff I don't know. What do you do when people ask you a question you can't answer?"

After downing some of his beer, Bradford sat back and tapped his fingers on the table before saying, "Do you see the irony of someone like you speaking at a preparatory school?"

Connor's smile dimmed. "Claire set it up for me. The drama department requested my visit."

"You are quite possibly the least intelligent person I've ever met."

Connor frowned. "Hey, if you don't want to help me, just say it."

"What's your actual IQ? Can you tell me or is that another term you don't know?"

Sitting up straighter, Connor leaned forward. "Fuck you."

"Don't say it out loud. Think it."

Fuck you, Connor thought before it sank in that Bradford was deliberately goading him to help him and his smile returned. "Got it. *Think* badass. Less is more."

"If you're outgunned in a battle, you've got only two

choices . . . run like hell, or keep them guessing what you'll do. In a conversation, silence makes people uncomfortable. Use it to your advantage. Given enough time, smart people talk themselves into sounding stupid, and assholes give up because they prefer easy marks."

Connor nodded. "Thanks, Bradford."

"Don't call me for this shit again."

Fair enough. "How about deep-sea fishing? Grant has a hundred-foot yacht he doesn't use. I promised I wouldn't party on it, but he never said I couldn't fish off it. It has its own crew. All we'd have to do is bring poles, some bait, and a cooler. I hear there are thousand-pound bluefin tuna off the coast of Nova Scotia. Imagine the size of the sandwich we could make with that much fucking tuna."

Bradford laughed and finished his beer. "Tell me when you go. I'm in."

Connor picked up another slice. "I might need to modify Grant's yacht. I'm sure he won't mind."

Bradford only smiled and shook his head.

Just before biting into his pizza, Connor paused. "The Fetters are nice people. Is anyone still messing with them?"

"Not recently."

"Back home I would have found the address of whoever was, and we would have had a good talk. It may or may not have involved using my fist. I don't know the rules around here, and since my name is linked to the Barringtons, I can no longer do whatever I want to. I have to stop and think things through."

"They've got you on a short leash, don't they?"

Connor frowned for real this time. "It's not like that. They've been good to my family. I don't want to cause trouble for any of them."

His nod said he understood. "Things are different in the city. Don't try to talk to these guys. You'll get yourself shot. Or arrested. Or both."

Suddenly not hungry, Connor sighed and sat back. "So, what do people do—nothing? That doesn't seem right."

"A lot of people would prefer to look away than get their hands dirty."

"Isn't that worse?"

Bradford took a moment to answer. "In my book it is, but I've got nothing to lose."

A heavy silence hung in the air. "That's not true. You have people who care about you. The Barringtons would practically adopt you if you let them. I know Sophie is disappointed you won't stay with her and Dale."

"I do better on my own."

Sad. "Everyone feels like that until—"

"Do you ever shut up?"

Yep. Connor bit into his pizza.

The silence that followed would have made many people uncomfortable, but Connor used it as a chance to perfect his technique. *Square shoulders. Steady, dead eyes. No hint of humor or patience.*

Reemsly Preparatory Academy, don't fuck with this badass.

BEING CALLED INTO the office of the headmaster was rarely a good thing. Angelina Kroll sat with her back straight in a chair in front of his desk, wondering if this was how the students felt when they were asked to do the same. Mr. Svete hadn't looked up since she entered. He was reading the screen of his computer and frowning.

She would announce her arrival, but she was reasonably certain he knew she was there. This was a power play. He wanted to unsettle her. She retained her composure as well as her confidence. People she cared a lot more about had tried to tear her down with no success. She never missed a day of work, and she had the numbers to back up the quality of her job performance. If he had an issue with something she'd done, she'd deal with it and keep moving forward.

That was her secret to survival—keep moving forward. Don't look back.

Don't waste a moment on regret.

"Miss Kroll," Mr. Svete finally said as he removed his glasses and laid them on his desk. "Thank you for meeting with me on such short notice."

"Of course. Not a problem."

He picked up a paper from his desk, looked at it, then raised his eyes to her. "Reemsly took a chance on you. Fresh from college. Your most persuasive qualifications I'm sure were your aunt's endorsement, her generosity as an alum, and your prior attendance at the school as well as your son's current enrollment."

Ouch. So it wasn't that I graduated summa cum laude with a business degree from Rutgers? Since there wasn't much she could say in response, Angelina held her tongue and waited. She wasn't about to defend herself before she knew what his concern was.

Mr. Svete stood and moved to the side of his desk. "We all miss your aunt."

"Thank you," Angelina answered, although she was sure they missed her for different reasons. When nothing in the world had made sense to Angelina, Aunt Rudi had brought order back from chaos. Strict, but loving, she hadn't judged Angelina for getting pregnant at sixteen, but she had required that she stay in school and had enrolled her at Reemsly. She said there were two things no one could take away from a person: a good education and their dignity. Both were personal commitments that were an individual's responsibility to maintain.

Angelina could still hear some of their conversations echoing in her head.

"I messed up, Aunt Rudi. You don't know the horrible things people say about me—to me."

"If you respect yourself it doesn't matter what anyone else says. Mistakes don't define a person. How they handle themselves through them does. Go home and cry to your parents, or stay and prove everyone back there wrong."

"I miss her every day," Angelina added. Even after two years she sometimes went to call her aunt only to remember she was gone. "So much."

Mr. Svete cleared his throat. "I spoke with Whitney's teachers. Your son is having a difficult year."

Breathe. "Nothing he can't handle."

"Not every flower blooms in every soil."

"What are you saying, Mr. Svete?" Her aunt had paid

Whitney's tuition, but Whitney had been on an employee scholarship since her death. Although Angelina had been named in Aunt Rudi's will, it hadn't been a large sum. Aunt Rudi had been so generous with her money while living that there hadn't been much of an estate to leave anyone. Isn't that how it should be? She'd often said gifts are best given from a warm hand.

Mr. Svete moved to sit on the edge of his desk. "Nothing yet. Just expressing a concern. Are you prepared for Connor Sutton's visit?"

Don't overthink this. Stay focused. "Absolutely."

Leaning forward, closer to her face, close enough for his breath to nearly gag Angelina, Mr. Svete said, "I cannot stress enough how important it is that he leave with a good impression of our school. I don't need to tell you that, although endowments are up again this year, there are areas of need we can't yet afford to address."

She met his gaze directly. "Our revenue from annual donors is solid. Outreach to alumni is ongoing and the response remains positive. If you have time to look over our latest capital campaign you'll see we exceeded our goal. The new computer building will be fully funded next year."

"I fear your background limits you to seeking short-term solutions and not cultivating the relationships that will ensure Reemsly's future for generations to come."

Angelina almost said, "My background?" but she held her temper in check even though she had a pretty good idea what he was referring to. Her job not only paid her bills, it also allowed her son to attend one of the most prestigious prep schools in the country. The instant gratification she'd glean from telling Mr. Svete off was outweighed by how much she loved her son. "I understand."

He straightened, looking straight down his nose at her. "I don't think you do. Mr. Sutton is the type that many women lose their heads around. He must leave this campus raving about it, but he's not the one who matters. One Barrington enrolled at our school would change everything. That should be your goal. Make that happen and my job is secure . . . as is yours."

Angelina rose to her feet in response to the threat as well as the insult. His opinion of her might not matter on a personal level, but it did when it came to remaining employed at the school. "I assure you that Mr. Sutton will leave impressed, and my goal has always been to secure the future of Reemsly."

"I will concede that asking Mr. Sutton to speak to our drama department about his sudden success was brilliant."

And not my idea. The head of the drama department, Mary Kleplin, has a crush on him and encouraged her students to write to him, but I'm not about to say that. "It certainly opened the door for new opportunities. I look forward to hearing what Mr. Sutton has to say on the subject."

"This is an opportunity that cannot be taken lightly."

Angelina straightened her skirt. "It won't be." She walked toward the door.

"Miss Kroll."

Angelina stopped just outside his office. "Yes?"

"Keep Miss Kleplin in check. I'm well aware of that situation."

"Yes, sir." She waited, but he'd returned to his desk and was once again looking at the screen of his computer. She closed the door behind her and sighed.

As she walked by the secretary's desk, the woman looked up and waved for her to approach. "Was it about Whitney? I heard about what happened on the soccer field yesterday. Boys can be brutal at that age."

"The soccer field?"

Mrs. Tellier had been at Reemsly as long as anyone could remember. Her welcoming smile had put Angelina at ease on her first day at the school and many times since. Mr. Svete was the third headmaster she'd worked under. Nothing happened at the school Mrs. Tellier didn't know about. She grimaced and lowered her voice. "He didn't tell you? In PE class the Keaton boy knocked him to the ground *after* he made a goal. You should encourage Whitney to join the team. The coach turns a blind eye to anyone but his stars, and your son is good."

"Whitney doesn't like sports." Angelina wrung her hands together. "Nothing happened to Keaton?"

"He blamed Whitney for stealing the shot from him. You didn't hear it from me, but one of the kids saw Keaton kicking Whitney while he was down. I heard about it this morning. I'd suggest you speak to the coach, but that's like talking to a wall."

"Oh, I will speak with Mr. Hamilton, but I'll talk to Whitney first. Thanks for telling me. Whitney hates it when I get involved, but that's not right. The school has a zero-bullying policy."

"Policies don't work unless they're enforced and sadly this problem is top-down. Mr. Brennan would have never tolerated such things, not even from our legacy children."

"I remember." Under Mr. Brennan's reign neither the students nor the faculty had made Angelina feel unwelcomed even as a teen mother. The culture back then had been about academics, personal growth, and inclusion. His retirement had been a sad day for everyone at the school, and unfortunately the climate on campus had changed along with its administration.

Mrs. Tellier snapped her fingers. "I have an idea. I know Mr. Sutton is coming to the school to give a talk about his movie, but you could have him say a few words about good sportsmanship to some of the boys as well. There's always the wow factor of meeting someone famous, even for these children. The problem isn't just Keaton or Whitney. Watching nothing happen and feeling voiceless affects every child in this school. I'd say it, but I'm helping my granddaughter pay for her college loans. Otherwise I'd already be retired."

Mr. Svete calls firing anyone who disagrees with him "cleaning house." She's right to lie low. And how sad that this is our new normal. Angelina leaned over and gave one of Mrs. Tellier's hands a comforting squeeze. "You don't have to say anything, I'll handle this, but thank you for telling me."

A smile returned to Mrs. Tellier's face. "Don't frown like that when you meet Connor Sutton. He is one fine-looking man. And single. I wonder if his taste is slightly overweight women in their late sixties? I used to do some things with my husband that had him smiling for days."

With a laugh, Angelina straightened. "Let's keep that story to ourselves."

"You'll bring him by to meet me, though, won't you?" Mrs. Tellier wiggled her eyebrows. "I promise I won't throw myself at him unless he begs me to."

Angelina wagged a finger at her. "Should I invest in a whip to keep you all in line when he's here?"

Mrs. Tellier fanned her face. "Child, if you don't already own a whip, you have no business being the one who gets to spend time with a man like that. I watched his movie ten times. He was sent down from heaven for no other reason than to be enjoyed."

With another laugh and a shake of her head, Angelina backed out of the room. "Promise me you won't talk like that when he's here."

"Promise you'll bring him by to meet me."

"Deal." *I think.* She paused. "I have to do this well, Mrs. Tellier. There's a lot riding on his visit."

Suddenly serious, Mrs. Tellier said, "It'll be fine. Just be yourself, Angelina. Remember, all the dark does is help you see how bright you can shine."

"Mr. Brennan used to say that." Angelina looked back at Mr. Svete's closed door with a longing to see his predecessor walk through it. "And he was right. Thank you, Mrs. Tellier."

It wasn't until Angelina was back in her own office that she was able to close the door and let out a shaky breath. *There's no reason I can't do this.*

I just have to keep moving forward and show Whitney how to do the same.

We'll figure out the Keaton thing.

Whitney and I aren't going anywhere.

Connor Sutton, hold your hat, because I'm about to impress the shit out of you.

Chapter Two

CONNOR DROVE A shiny new blue Mercedes Benz GLS up the long tree-lined entrance to the school. It wouldn't have been his first choice, and his large frame barely fit inside it. Still, it was a Mercedes and it was free. Funny how easily things were sent to people who didn't need them. Everyone wanted him to wear their clothing, drive their cars, visit their clubs. No one would have given him shit before he could afford to buy it for himself. The world had it backward.

The morning rain had cleared and after he parked he took a moment to admire the rainbow arching over the tall brick main building. *Did they order it or does even nature provide the wealthy with extra little perks?*

He lowered the visor and met his gaze in the mirror, narrowing his eyes as he did. *You've got this. Silence is your armor. Give the speech Claire wrote, smile only when you have to, and get the hell out.* He put on a pair of mirrored sunglasses. *Keep them guessing, and maintain the advantage.*

He flipped the visor up and adjusted his jacket sleeves. The more he wore suits, the less he felt like a fraud in them, but he missed the comfort of broken-in jeans and faded plaid shirts. No, they hadn't been tailored to him, but they'd fit him better. Most of Connor's current clothing had been purchased by Clay Landon as a welcome-to-New-York gift. Men still commented on the quality of his single piece leather dress shoes. When did men start caring about shit like that? They were nice, but in Connor's opinion, not as impressive as his favorite pair of steel-toe work boots. *I don't even know where those are anymore.*

He checked the time on his black Octo Finissimo watch—a gift from Viviana. Modern. Expensive. A statement of power and wealth. *Who even needs a watch anymore? I used to check the time on my phone and that worked just fine.*

Watches are statement pieces, Claire says.

Look at me, everyone, I can afford a watch.

Big fucking deal.

He sighed.

I can't believe Bradford wouldn't come with me. I would have gone with him.

As Connor sat there without opening the door, he conceded that Bradford likely hadn't come for the same reason: he didn't want to be there. Neither of them belonged at such a place with its immaculately manicured lawn and three-story glass building entrance. Security probably routinely threw people like them off the sprawling campus.

He'd come before the start of classes because he didn't want to put himself in a situation where he'd have to interact with students before his speech, but realizing his was the only car in the front lot he began to think he'd played this wrong.

I should have strolled in right before my scheduled talk—kept things rushed—and pretended I was late for another engagement. Now I have time to think about all the ways this could go badly.

A silver car, Connor recognized it as one of the subcompact electric base models, pulled up beside his. Hopefully it was the woman Claire had arranged for him to meet . . . Angelina . . . *Oh, shit, I forgot her last name. Not Jolie. Crust? Crawl? I should have written it down.*

He stepped out of his car and turned to greet her.

Then time slowed. Angelina Whatever-the-fuck-her-last-name-was emerged from behind her car and knocked all the breath clear out of Connor.

Light shone down on her between passing clouds, darkening her glasses but not before he had a glimpse of striking blue eyes. She was dressed in a long-sleeved, two-tone knit dress some might call conservative, but the term *heavenly* floated through Connor's mind. It hugged her in all the right places but left some delicious areas to his imagination. Long blonde hair was tied back in a loose knot, adding a softness to an otherwise starched style. Oh, hang on . . . as his gaze moved down her long legs, her shoes brought a flush to his cheeks. Normally he was amused by how otherwise intelligent women chose torture devices for their feet when barefoot was just as sexy, but he had to admit hers completed his fantasy that she was all business at the office but one wild ride in the bed.

"Mr. Sutton. I hope you haven't been waiting long." Her voice tickled over him, sending enough of his blood heading southward for him to need a moment before answering her.

He swallowed hard. Even before he was legal age, women had wanted him. He was a healthy man in his prime. Sometimes he said yes. Sometimes he said no. He had nothing against the idea of commitment or relationships, but for one reason or another things had never progressed that far. Either he broke things off or the woman did. Often his partners became friends over time. They said he was too nice to stay upset with even when things didn't work out.

None of them had ever affected him like this.

He was feeling anything but nice as she stepped closer. His heart thudded in his chest; his cock was prepped and ready. His response to her was primal, left over from a time when a man could see a woman, decide she was his, toss her over his shoulder, and run off to his cave with her.

Fuck, it felt good to want someone that way.

"Mr. Sutton?" she asked, a small frown wrinkling the skin between her brows.

"That's me." He closed the door behind him with more force than he'd meant to.

She held a hand out in greeting. Heat spread through him as he wrapped his hand around hers. Small, delicate, but with a firm, confident grip. Too many images of where he'd like that hand to wander flashed through his mind. He released her hand and told himself to calm down.

"Everyone is so excited about your visit. Since you're here early, would you like a tour of the campus? As an alumni myself, there's a level of personal pride I feel whenever I introduce someone to it."

She can introduce me to whatever she wants to. Consider me all in.

There was a time when he would have shared his thoughts with her, but he'd received a year of tutelage on how and why to keep them to himself. What would Bradford say? "If we have the time, I see no problem with that."

She gave him the sweetest smile. "Speaking of time, I was wondering if you'd be willing to squeeze in some for our school's soccer team. They are equally thrilled you're here and there is very little crossover between the drama and athletic departments."

"Meet them or give a speech?" One he could do. The other he wasn't prepared for.

She searched his face before saying, "Nothing formal. Just a little motivational talk. Like any other group of children, they could benefit from hearing about good sportsmanship and the importance of taking pride in the gifts of others as well as their own."

"I can't see that happening today." *Yeah, no. It's not like I never went to school. Sounds like you have some douchebag kids in need of reining in. I would love to help you with them, but you should have called ahead so Claire could have written an appropriate speech. You do not want the one my high school football coach used to give us. Something tells me no one has ever threatened to run these kids into the ground so hard their nuts get grass burn.*

Her lips pressed together in a straight line. It shouldn't have been a sexy move, but it made Connor want to kiss all that starch right out of her. "Of course. I shouldn't have asked. Let's start the tour in the main building. If we're quick we can get out before the hallways fill with students."

Her tone was polite, but her body language was screaming something much less friendly. Not the reaction he was used to from women. He couldn't have offended her, he'd barely spoken.

The smile she gave him as she opened the door to the building was forced. If he knew her better he would have said something funny or acted the idiot until she relaxed and laughed. This wasn't the place for that, so he followed her without speaking.

The tour felt a little like a sales pitch, which was odd since he was too old to enroll and didn't have children. Still, the classrooms were nice. The cafeteria was bright and clean. She went into great detail about the anticipated improvements to the technology department.

Just as she'd promised, they were out of the building before the first bell rang. He followed her down a winding park-like path to a hill with a bronze statue of children playing. His attention wandered as she gave him an unabridged history of the school. She'd talked long enough that his initial boner was a distant memory.

Yes, she's beautiful.

Her ass—perfection.

Her voice . . . addictive to listen to.

The topics she chooses to discuss? Total snore fest.

"There's a test at the end of this," she joked as if realizing his mind had wandered.

"Sorry, I can only remember facts about things I'm interested in." *Oh, shit, did I just say that out loud? I mean, it's true. And if she knew me, she would be laughing because she'd know I said it mostly as a joke aimed at myself because of my painfully short attention span.*

She is not fucking smiling.

This is where I'd normally roll over and apologize—like a Labrador offering my belly up for a rub.

Because I'm nice.

Too nice.

Not today, lady. Today I'm badass.

It's not my fault you think a forty-five-minute monologue about people no one has ever heard of is a good choice of how to spend our time together. I thought you might be the one, but my cock has been wrong before.

It once thought dating Mary Ellen was worth testing how well her father could shoot. Luckily he only took out the tires of my car.

There was also the time it convinced me a pro boxer would understand that his little sister was neither a virgin nor shy about what she wanted. All I did was say yes and give her a fun night. Did that really merit the ass-kicking he tried to give me?

So, sure, you're incredible.

Sexy as all hell.

And pissed at me now.

You know what? Get in line. People need to relax. I'm not that bad.

You could have had an amazing time with me.

Possibly life . . . I mean, for a second there, I imagined the adorable kids we'd have together. But if you're looking for an apology, you're not getting one.

I've got a speech memorized, and you've just reminded me why that's all that will come out of my mouth today.

WOW, WHAT A *dick*.

A lot of what she did to fundraise for Reemsly involved interacting with wealthy people. Some of them were down-to-earth, no different than they would have been if they had much less money. Some thought what they had was due to divine intervention or proof that they were more deserving of it. Very few were crass enough to show how superior they felt.

Not Connor Sutton.

If the Barringtons were anything like him, no financial gift would be worth having them enroll. *There has to be a better way to get the kind of funding Mr. Svete thinks we need.*

She would have loved to tell him that, but she was working on very little sleep, and if she started to say what she was thinking she wasn't sure she could stop.

On the drive home from school the day before, she'd asked Whitney about what had happened to him during PE class. He'd claimed nothing had happened. She'd told him she knew about the soccer game, his goal, and what Keaton had done.

"It won't happen again," Whitney had said in a quiet tone that had broken Angelina's heart.

"I'm not saying you did anything wrong, Whitney. I'm saying I know what happened. You can talk to me about anything. You know that, right?"

"I know," he'd said before taking out his tablet and popping in his earbuds.

She'd tried to talk to him one more time after dinner. He'd gone to his room to read. After knocking on his door, she'd walked in and sat on the edge of his bed. "No one should ever touch you. I'll make sure it doesn't happen again."

He'd shaken his head. "Don't say anything, Mom. I already don't fit in. You'll just make it worse."

His comment had rocked through her. "Make it worse? And what do you mean you don't fit in? Your grades are excellent. Your test scores are some of the highest. There's no reason you couldn't be valedictorian if you apply yourself. That's what all of your teachers tell me."

Without meeting her gaze he said, "Stanford has an online high school. That's my goal."

"No, it's not," she'd said. She'd known he was having a rough year, but he had friends at Reemsly. Didn't he? He used to. "You can't want that. You love Reemsly."

He'd turned away from her, pulling a blanket up and over him as he did. "Promise me you won't say anything to my teachers, Mom. And don't talk to the coach."

When she hadn't answered immediately, he'd lowered the blanket and glared at her.

"I always do what you say, Mom. Even when I don't like it. When do I get a say in what I want?"

Her breath had caught in her throat then because what he wanted and what she wanted for him were directly at odds. She wanted to protect him. How could she promise not to?

She'd blinked back tears and given his leg a pat. "We're both tired. We'll talk about this again tomorrow, okay?"

He hadn't answered.

She'd leaned down and given his head a kiss. "I love you."

His expression had softened. "I love you too, Mom."

"We'll figure this out."

He'd nodded and turned away again.

So, yeah, she hadn't slept.

And, sure, she might have talked nonstop about the history of Reemsly because her nerves were shot, and she'd wanted to say something . . . anything that would change Connor Sutton's mind about talking to the soccer team.

Why would I have thought for one minute that I could make this man care about anything beyond himself?

The longer they stood there without speaking, the more her temper rose. Just who did he think he was? Yes, he was good-looking. Not her type, but a lot of women found his square jaw, wide shoulders, and towering physique sexy.

Sadly, he'd only reinforced her opinion that the better looking a man was the less attractive his personality was. She wasn't drawn to flash. Muscles? Flat abs? Overrated. His short blond hair and beard looked low maintenance, but he probably spent hours in front of a mirror admiring both.

If one was in doubt about what was important to him, all they had to do was look at the kind of car he drove. Total compensation vehicle. Sure, he looked amply endowed below the belt as well, but probably stuffed his tighty-whiteys with a sock.

And his watch? A six-figure vanity purchase. Not original, but it went with his overpriced suit and look-at-how-rich-I-am shoes.

A person could have money without shoving it down everyone's throat.

Lost in her thoughts as she was, she didn't realize Mr. Svete had approached them until she heard his voice. "Mr. Sutton, it's a pleasure to welcome you to Reemsly."

Connor turned to face him, but neither smiled nor greeted him. He simply looked at him as if he had no idea who he was.

Mr. Svete seemed put off by it for a second, then held out his hand and introduced himself. "Mr. Svete. Headmaster."

Connor shook his hand, and nodded once before pocketing his hands.

Mr. Svete cleared his throat. "I see you're getting the grand tour. I hope Miss Kroll has shown you our state-of-the-art gymnasium. Not only have we added an indoor track, but the pool is up to Olympic standards."

"Fascinating," Connor said without emotion.

Watching Mr. Svete uncharacteristically at a loss for what to say would have been amusing if Angelina's job couldn't be terminated at his whim. She stepped in to say, "We were just about to make our way to the drama building."

Just then a man caught Angelina's attention. Dark suit. Mirrored glasses. Standing off by himself watching them from about a hundred feet away. "Is that your security detail,

Mr. Sutton?"

Connor's head snapped toward where she'd pointed and he smiled. "Oh. Yes. Sure. He's with me."

"He's welcome to join the tour," she said.

"Hold on, I'll ask him if he wants to." With that, Connor jogged away.

Mr. Svete's indrawn breath was audible. "I'm not impressed, Miss Kroll, and it doesn't appear that Mr. Sutton is either."

Shit.

"The day isn't over yet, Mr. Svete."

"Don't disappoint me, Miss Kroll," he said before he walked off.

Angelina took a deep breath, told herself she'd faced tougher challenges, and found her smile again. *This isn't the world's shittiest day. It's an opportunity to shine.*

I can do this.

Chapter Three

CONNOR COULD HAVE hugged Bradford, he was that happy to see him. He didn't though. Badasses don't hug. Instead, he kept his hands at his sides and his voice low. "I'm totally fucking up already, Bradford. You have to get me out of here. I'm going to raise my voice—tell you off. You take your best punch at my head. Make it count. I want to leave in an ambulance."

The corners of Bradford's mouth twitched like he was holding back a smile. "It can't be that bad."

"It is. See that woman over there? She already hates me, and I've been careful to say next to nothing to her. The guy with her gives me the creeps. You know how some dogs can sniff out cancer in people?"

Bradford ran a hand over his face. "Sure."

"I have a super fifth sense that tells me when someone has a sick, twisted soul. That man is a horrible person who should not be around children."

"You mean *sixth sense*."

"You have it too?"

"No, forget it. And he's harmless, not so much as a parking ticket. I wouldn't put too much stock in your supernatural ability since it hasn't warned you off of me."

Connor frowned. "Not today, but soon, we have to talk about your self-esteem issues. But for right now could we focus on figuring out how to get me out of here?"

"Twisted-soul-man just walked away, you're safe."

"Good." Connor glanced over his shoulder to confirm it, then relaxed a bit. His gaze lingered on the woman who looked uncertain if she should wait or join them. "I didn't know I had a type until I met her, but isn't she perfect?"

Bradford clapped a hand on Connor's shoulder. "She's out of your league, pal."

"Is that even a thing?" Connor looked her over again. "I'm sure I'm not, with my looks and your personality."

"You just said she hates you."

Did Bradford not understand women? "The kind of hate that always ends with sex, yes. But there's a problem: I can't have sex with someone while I'm being you. What if she fell for me? Would I always have to be you? No offense, but it's not much fun."

"So, you just assume that no matter how she's acting now she'll end up wanting to have sex with you?"

Connor shrugged. "I can't explain women."

Bradford laughed. "I need to watch this play out. In your mind every woman wants to fuck you?"

"Nooooo, but I sense when one does."

"Like a dog sniffing out cancer."

"Exactly."

"Another fifth sense."

"Sixth sense," Connor corrected, finally getting the joke. "I get it. People already have five senses so my soul detector is a sixth sense which would make this a seventh sense . . ." He started counting off on his fingers the other senses he credited himself with.

"Tell me about it later." Bradford gave Connor's shoulder a shake. "Time to shut up; your friend is walking over."

Connor turned his head away and stretched out his facial muscles, schooling them as he'd been taught to before a tough scene. By the time Angelina was standing in front of him again, his face was carefully expressionless again. "Angelina Kroll, this is my . . . bodyguard, Bradford."

Bradford's greeting was a curt nod.

Unlike most people, Angelina didn't seem intimidated by the scars or the tattoos. She smiled at him with the openness she'd shown Connor when they'd first met. "Would you like to join us? We'll be heading to the drama building now."

"I'd like that," Bradford said with a charming smile.

Hang on.

Bradford could be charming?

And she was smiling back?

Oh, hell no.

"You should probably stay outside to keep an eye on the cars," Connor said.

"The area is secure," Bradford assured him without taking his eyes off Angelina. "I didn't go to college so I have to admit I'm a little intimidated to be here."

Her face softened and she put a hand on his forearm.

"You shouldn't be. Education is a lifelong journey, not a race. Yes, these children are lucky to be receiving a good foundation, but it's what a person does with what they're given that matters."

"I'm always worried I'll slip up and say something that reveals what I don't know."

Bradford, I'm going to kick your ass for this.

Seriously. You do not get to be me while I'm you.

Angelina's hand remained on Bradford's forearm. "I remember feeling the same way when I first came to this school. I was sixteen and had made more bad choices than good. We had the most incredible headmaster back then. He taught me that no one is better than anyone else. Peel back the layers of differences . . . whether they're financial, racial, cultural, or sexual . . . we're all the same. Everyone is simply trying to do the best they can, and Reemsly's mission statement is about helping all of our students see that and become the best version of themselves rather than trying to make them all the same. You would have fit in perfectly here."

"That's kind of you to say. You've really put me at ease, thank you." *Oh, my God, could Bradford lay bullshit on any thicker?* "I'd love to see the drama building."

"Fantastic." Angelina dropped her hand and turned to Connor. All warmth left her eyes. "Ready?"

Connor grunted.

When Angelina turned to start walking, Connor pointed a finger at Bradford then fisted his hand.

Bradford flashed a smile.

He's testing me. He doesn't think I can get Angelina to want to fuck me. Connor laced his fingers in front of him and stretched in anticipation.

Watch and learn, Bradford.

They were about to enter the drama building when Connor would have sworn he heard Angelina swear under her breath. "Mrs. Tellier. You caught us just in time. We're heading inside to meet Mrs. Kleplin's class."

An older woman in a perfectly pressed dress suit and flats walked up with a huge smile on her face. "Mr. Connor Sutton. It's a pleasure to meet you. May I call you Connor?"

"Sure," Connor said just before she enveloped him in a hug.

"I'm a huge fan."

She shook Bradford's hand, but didn't take her eyes off Connor as she did.

No creep vibe, though. Connor was picking up that she thought he was hot, but a lot of women did, and he didn't hold it against them.

"Could I have a moment?" Mrs. Tellier asked.

"We're running late," Angelina said in a rush.

"This will only take a second," Mrs. Tellier said as she grabbed Connor by the arm and dragged him several feet away. In a low voice, she said, "Pretend I'm gushing about how much I like you."

Was there something in the water at Reemsly? In a loud voice, Connor said, "How nice of you to say so."

"Did you agree to speak to the soccer team?" she asked.

"Flattering, but I must decline," he answered, impressed

that his response was both true and fit their improv session.

Mrs. Tellier laughed like they were flirting and yanked on his arm so he lowered his head. "Angelina's a single mom. Her son is being bullied by a boy on the soccer team. If you are half the man you were in *Danger Doubled* you'll help stop it."

Angelina has a son?

God, I hate bullies.

He didn't need to ask why it couldn't be handled by the administration. He'd met their excuse for one. He straightened. "Okay, I'll do it."

Angelina was at his side in a flash. "Wow, look at the time. We really have to go."

Mrs. Tellier fanned her face. "I hope to see you again, Connor."

He looked from her to Angelina and back. "Never know what the future holds."

"Mr. Sutton. Please. They're waiting for us," Angelina said.

"Coming." He winked at Mrs. Tellier.

She winked back.

Angelina held the door open. As Connor walked through it, she said, "Whatever she asked you, know that she was just joking. The older she gets the more questionable her sense of humor becomes."

He stopped, leaned down until his face was just above hers and lied. "She said you're single. Are you?"

Angelina blushed, her eyes dilated and her breathing changed. *Bingo, she wants me.* "My personal life is none of your business, Mr. Sutton."

"Yet," he said and almost whooped in victory when she swayed on her feet. "I changed my mind about speaking to the soccer team."

She swallowed visibly. "Thank you. I think it'll be beneficial for them."

"I'll make sure it is."

They stood there for a long moment, simply looking into each other's eyes. The attraction he'd felt for her earlier was back—full force. Part of him wanted to crack a smile, confess that her entire impression of him was wrong and suggest they start over. Another part of him, the same appendage that had been sure Mary Ellen's father wouldn't actually shoot him . . . was certain he should wait until she knew him better before she . . . well, knew him better.

"Okay, so let's do this." Her voice was deliciously breathless.

"Yes, let's," he echoed in a low growl women had told him melted their defenses.

She gave him another long look, then turned to lead the way through the building.

As they walked, Bradford said, "I believe I have underestimated you, Connor."

"I'm used to it," Connor said with a smile that he wiped from his face when Angelina opened a door that led to a stage.

"You got this?" Bradford asked.

"This one yes," Connor said. "I may need a little help with the soccer team."

He walked past Angelina and fell into the role he'd played over the last year. Claire would have been impressed with his pacing, the naturalness of his movements, the way he used the stage but also connected with the audience.

He spoke about the importance of learning the craft, the dedication required as far as memorizing scripts, and the long hours during production. He delivered every appropriate joke effortlessly. He paused after each motivational comment to ensure it was delivered with impact. When he wrapped up the talk, the students were applauding enthusiastically.

The drama teacher came over and gave him a grateful hug that became awkwardly difficult to extricate himself from, but Angelina had thankfully intervened. Always a gentleman, he complimented the teacher on her class and left her smiling and gushing about how much pleasure he'd brought the drama department.

Angelina was still speaking to that teacher when Bradford said, "A seventh sense isn't required to see that women get stupid around you."

Connor's gaze went to Angelina, and he sighed. "They don't stay, though. It never really bothered me before. I can make her want me, but you're right, she's out of my league. She has a son too. That's a big responsibility. And some asshole on the soccer team is messing with him. That's why she wants me to speak to them. Don't let me screw that up. We don't leave until we know her kid is safe. That's the stuff that matters."

"You mean that."

"Of course I do."

"This isn't all about fucking her?"

"Dude, how hard do you have to try to get someone to have sex with you? I just have to stop saying no."

ANGELINA HADN'T EXPECTED to be impressed, but Connor Sutton had a stage presence that was undeniable. He might only have one movie under his belt, but she could see a long career for him. Reemsly students were notoriously difficult to impress, yet all those who'd packed into the theater to listen to him seemed to fall under his spell.

After peeling Miss Kleplin off Connor, it was no easy feat to convince the single teacher that her place was with her students rather than in his arms. Not that Angelina could blame her. All he'd done was flirt a little and Angelina was finding it difficult to breathe normally around him.

He was deep in conversation with his bodyguard as she approached. She took advantage of the opportunity to soak in the perfection of him in his suit while remembering what he looked like beneath it. Along with almost every other woman with a functioning set of eyes, she'd watched *Danger Doubled* more than once simply to see him answer the door in just a towel. The heroine had made a huge production about having him put on clothing, but every single one of Angelina's friends thought she was crazy. And when he dropped the towel and walked away bare-assed? Who hadn't watched that scene a thousand times?

That woman was a fool.

I guess it would have been a short movie if he'd opened the door and she'd said, "Yep, let's do this."

Angelina blushed as she'd remembered saying those very words to Connor. Not in that context. Definitely not with that intention, but she had to admit when he'd looked deeply into her eyes "Yes" was a word that would have come easily to her.

Sex. No wonder commercials used it to sell everything.

Angelina wasn't a prude, but her early pregnancy had made her cautious when it came to men. She'd dated since having Whitney—even had sex a few times. The men she'd been with were very nice and had understood that her priority was her son. None had been in her life long enough to meet him.

Nor had they made her feel all wound up the way Connor did. He was exciting, irritating, arrogant, sexy on a fantasy level. She told herself he was the opposite of her type, but there was no denying that her body had a very different opinion.

She found it easy to stand there looking up at him mindlessly, simply returning his smile, savoring the heat in his gaze. He probably looked at every woman in that very manner. Likely practiced that charm in front of a mirror for hours.

"Are they ready for me?" He had the most adorable crooked smile.

"Who?" she asked.

"The soccer team."

Bradford's audible groan pulled Angelina back to reality—the one where her son needed her and nothing mattered more than that. "They're in different classes, but I'll call them to assemble in the gym."

"Here is fine," he said, referencing the grassy area with picnic-style tables. "Let's keep it casual."

I'm sure he says that a lot. "Of course. I'll gather them up and be right back. Can I get you anything? A bottle of water? Anything?"

"All set," he assured her.

"Okay, so plan to start in about fifteen minutes."

"I'll be here." His smile promised that and so much more.

Angelina spun on her heel and strode back to the main building. The farther she got from him, the easier it was to focus. By the time she was in the office asking the secretary to call the soccer team for an assembly, she was able to laugh at her own strong reaction to Connor.

After making the announcement over the intercom, the woman said, "I'm so jealous. Mrs. Tellier was in here earlier. She said Connor Sutton is even sexier in person than he is on the big screen. Is he?"

"He's good-looking," Angelina agreed. She didn't want to think about his attributes, though. She needed to remind herself about all the reasons why following him right back to his car and home was not an option. "If you're into that type. I'm not. Someone like that is fun to watch in a movie, but can you imagine how disappointing it would be to date him? First of all, he's not the intellectual, caring doctor he played in the movie. He's just another highly paid actor with a huge ego who thinks . . ."

The look of horror on the secretary's face stopped Angelina midsentence.

"Is he behind me?" Angelina asked in strangled voice.

"I am." His tone was cold as ice. "I thought I'd take you up on that bottle of water."

She turned slowly, with a grimace on her face, but was saved from having to say anything by the arrival of the soccer team. She wished she'd had a moment to apologize, but all warmth was gone from his expression, and she had a feeling it wouldn't have been well received.

Looking as flustered as Angelina felt, the secretary leaned over the counter and offered Connor a bottle of water. "This one is even chilled, Mr. Sutton."

"Thank you," Connor said smoothly, bestowing a smile on her that brought a flush to the secretary's face.

He's not that good-looking, Angelina thought with irritation. She asked the soccer team to head outside and meet them at the picnic tables. Happy to simply be out of class, they made their way without protest.

This time Connor held the door open for Angelina . . . but he didn't meet her gaze as she walked past him. She felt horrible. "Mr. Sutton—"

"Don't," he said abruptly.

Don't what? Apologize? Lust after you?

Make an idiot out of myself while pretending not to?

Something had to be said. "I was out of line."

He shrugged. "You didn't say anything that's not true. I'm not the character I played in *Danger Doubled*."

Once outside there were too many students within earshot for them to continue the conversation, so Angelina fell silently into step with him. A moment later they were standing next to five tables of fourth- and fifth-grade boys.

Bradford stood off to the side beneath the shade of a tree.

Angelina glanced at Connor, but he was once again wearing his sunglasses, and he looked as closed off as when she'd first met him. *Me and my big mouth. I'm lucky he decided to stick around. No one would have blamed him for leaving after hearing me.*

She turned back to the students. "Mr. Sutton is here by request of the drama department, but I thought you'd also like to meet him." Most of the boys looked excited—even Keaton, and he was normally too cool to look excited about much. "Thank you, Mr. Sutton. Kids, let's give him a warm welcome."

The boys clapped enthusiastically. The gratitude in her voice was sincere. What he was about to say might directly affect her son's academic future at Reemsly. He didn't know that, but he'd still graciously agreed to speak to a second group of children. She was disappointed with how unprofessionally she'd behaved and for what she'd said. It wasn't his fault her brain went a little haywire around him.

A lengthy silence followed the applause. It lasted long enough that Angelina began to wonder if he was waiting for her to say something else.

She was about to, when he started.

"Soccer. I can't say I know a whole lot about it beyond that it's not football." His joke fell flat. He visibly tensed as he seemed to sense it as well.

The coach joined the group, choosing to stand behind the table that was full of all of the star players. He didn't apologize for being late nor did he look pleased to see his team gathered.

Connor removed his mirrored glasses and pocketed them in his jacket, then scanned the group. She wanted to shake him and tell him to say something.

He finally did. "A team is a team, though. Mr. Billings, my old coach, used to say there is no I in team unless you write the word in block letters and then you'll find it right there in the A's hole. Only he said it a little cruder than that."

A few of the boys high-fived each other.

Bradford rubbed a hand over his eyes and the coach frowned.

Where was the smooth speaker from the stage? This man seemed far less relaxed, and Angelina was beginning to regret asking him to do this, especially as a few teachers arrived and one began filming with her phone.

"I could talk to you about how football taught me how to work with people. I could tell you that soccer will probably do the same for you." Connor pocketed his hands and looked up at the sky for a moment before continuing. "I'd rather tell you a more personal story."

Angelina closed her eyes briefly and prayed it was one that was appropriate for the children to hear. *Please. I said something stupid, but this is for Whitney. Please let it go well.*

Connor loosened his tie. "I wasn't born this size. I remember what it was like to be small. So small I was pushed around." He walked over and stood next to the smallest member on the soccer team who was sitting off by himself. "Looked over. Never chosen first for any team."

He moved to stand next to another table. "I had a late growth spurt. I was so small that when I was in third grade my little sister had to come to my recess to deal with the boy who was making it so I didn't want to go to school anymore. I'll repeat that part in case you didn't hear me. *My little sister,* a first grader at the time, came to my recess and faced down a boy who'd made third grade a living hell for me."

Some of the boys laughed. Some remained politely quiet.

Keaton made a joke to the other boys at his table who laughed along with him. The coach didn't discourage them.

Again, Connor took a moment before speaking. He walked between the tables until he came to where Keaton was seated. "Now, my brother Dylan likes to razz me by asking how that kid could have been all that bad if he could be taken down by our little sister. That's the thing about bullies, though. They aren't bigger, faster, smarter, braver. They're just mean enough to make people afraid of them."

He looked right at Keaton until the boy looked away. Only then, did Connor turn his attention to the other children. "I've never asked myself why my sister was able to scare Keith Bacon into leaving me alone. Viviana is one tough cookie. But I have wondered many times why my older brother didn't step in. His growth spurt had already hit. He towered over us and wasn't afraid of anyone. I only asked him once, and it didn't go well. I couldn't understand his anger. Then I realized it was because he felt bad he hadn't stepped in. My brother loves me."

Another round of laughter erupted from the group.

This time, Connor arched an eyebrow. "Oh, I'm sorry, are you all too cool to say the word love? You'll outgrow that. If you still have your mom, you'd better hug her tonight and tell her that. I lost mine a long time ago, and I still miss her every day."

Angelina gasped in the strained silence that followed. His gaze met hers briefly, and she glimpsed a sadness that shook her. *Have I completely misjudged him?*

He turned his attention back to the students. "Why do you think my brother wasn't the one to help me? He's not a bad person, but he did nothing. That happens more than you'd think. Good people see something they know is wrong, and they don't step in to stop it. Ever wonder why?"

No one spoke at first.

From the sidelines, Bradford said, "They're afraid the bully will come for them next."

"Maybe," Connor said. "But I don't think Dylan was afraid."

As the talk connected with how she felt about Mr. Svete, Angelina found herself speaking her truth. "Being the first voice is scary."

Connor's attention riveted back to her and she regretted her outburst. He was supposed to leave Reemsly so impressed with the school that he encouraged the Barringtons to enroll their children. *He's not supposed to see issues that need fixing. What am I doing?*

Andy Monroe, one of the larger boys who had struggled

with his weight the year before said, "Maybe they don't care because no one helped them when they were picked on."

Another silence.

Connor moved to stand next to Andy. "Now that is one I understand, but let me pass on to you a little something I learned from my father. He gave me a lot of advice I didn't take, but this one bit stuck with me. He said, 'Don't let the worst person you know be the one who influences you the most.' I didn't know what that meant when he first said it. I get it now. In your life, you will meet countless amazing people, but almost everywhere you go there will also be one wing-dinger of a jerk. Sometimes more than one. The one you become the most like depends on which one you spend more time thinking about. Ever hear the tale of two wolves?"

Andy shook his head.

Connor sat down next to him. "I just read about it. Some people say it's a Cherokee legend. Honestly, everyone wants to claim the genius of it. Essentially, there are two forces inside of you that are constantly battling. One is negative and angry. That's the voice in your head that remembers every awful thing people have said or done to you. The other is positive and hopeful. That's the voice that believes people are essentially good and worth defending even if they weren't brave enough to defend you. Which wolf wins? The one you feed."

Rising to his feet, Connor looked from one table to the next. "Back to Keith Bacon. What do you think happened to him after my sister woke him up to how he was behaving?"

Timmy Edwards raised his hand. "He switched schools."

Connor shook his head. "I'm from a small town. We only have one school. Our graduating class had fifty people in it. His parents were dirt poor. They weren't going anywhere. No, we became friends."

A general sound of disbelief echoed through the group.

After shrugging and walking from table to table again, Connor said, "I know. I know. But this was before people recorded everything. No offense, but we had some things easier. Back then, we made mistakes and if we learned from them everyone moved on. Before social media, we weren't all defined by the stupidest thing we've ever done."

Connor returned to the table where Keaton was. "I don't like the word bully because I don't like labels. They trap people into thinking they can't do better. When Keith and I became friends I spent time at his house and it was not a happy place. He needed intervention as much as I did. And once he saw what he was doing, he stopped. All it took was one person to tell him that there might be a better way."

"What college football team did you learn all this wisdom from?" the coach asked in a snide tone.

Several of his students snickered.

A few looked away, seeming embarrassed.

"That's about all the time we have for today." Angelina rushed to Connor's side, prepared to bring a quick end to this.

Connor closed the distance between himself and the coach, until he was towering over him. Next to him, the coach looked neither intimidating nor confident. Collectively the teachers and students held their breaths.

For what felt like an eternity, Connor simply stared the man down. The coach went white, then red, then some angry shade between. Still Connor said nothing, merely arched an eyebrow.

The coach's fists clenched.

Bradford took a step out of the shade.

Angelina joined them, unsure of what she'd do if fists started flying. *No. No. No. This is not how the talk was supposed to go.*

Connor held out his hand and flashed those perfectly white teeth of his. "Feed the right wolf, my friend. Few will have as big of an impact on these young men as you will. You'll be the one they're quoting when they're our age. What do you hope they'll say?"

Cornered and aware the exchange was being recorded, the coach had limited options. He shook Connor's hand. "That I taught them how to win."

After dropping his hand, Connor looked around at the boys who were enthralled by the exchange. He smiled. "And hopefully to never be the block letter version of a team."

Just like that the soccer team was won over. Their laughter was much lighter.

Angelina wished her son had been there to watch the transformation, but he wasn't a member of the team. She could have called for a school-wide assembly, but that wasn't what had been in the plans.

Not that this was either.

"Does anyone have a question for Mr. Sutton?" Angelina asked the students.

"No questions," Connor said in a harsh tone. "I'm already late to my next engagement." Connor's reaction took her by surprise. So approachable one moment—so closed off the next.

"Of course." Angelina was quick to smooth the situation over. "Why don't we all give Mr. Sutton a big thank you for coming out to see us."

The boys clapped and cheered.

Connor leaned forward and said something to the coach that made him relax a bit. Angelina wished she'd been standing close enough to hear. It couldn't have been a threat. Every time she thought she knew what to expect from the famous actor, he zigged when she thought he'd zag.

She dismissed the students back to their classes while Connor spoke to the handful of teachers who had gathered to meet him. His smile was full-blast charm, but the sparkle that had been in his eyes earlier was gone.

I did that. Me and my big mouth.

When he started to walk away with his bodyguard, Angelina trotted after them. "Mr. Sutton."

He stopped.

Bradford said something then nodded to Angelina and continued walking away.

Angelina came to a skidding stop beside Connor. "Thank you for speaking to the soccer team."

He raised and lowered a shoulder. When their eyes met she found it hard to breathe. "I hope it makes a difference."

"Me too," she said then gave herself a mental smack for being so honest. He needed to leave with a better impression.

"They're good kids. Historically Reemsly has a one hundred percent college enrollment and predominantly to Ivy League schools."

He cocked his head to one side. "I don't have any children."

She smiled brightly. "I'm sure you know people who do."

"People," he mulled the word as if it were a new one to him then he frowned. "Oh, I get it now. This isn't about me. Asher warned this would happen, but I admit I thought he was being paranoid. Are you disappointed I didn't bring a Barrington with me? How much of today was real? Do you even have a son?"

Angelina gasped. "How do you know about my son?"

His smile was devoid of warmth. "You're good. I'm glad I came. This was educational. I'm not used to women flirting with me for any reason other than sex." He leaned closer, so close Angelina's body began to hum for his. The bastard knew it too. His mouth twisted a bit. "Well, at least I wasn't wrong about that."

As the reality of how poorly she'd handled his visit began to sink in, she reached out and grabbed his forearm. "You can't leave like this."

He looked down at her hand. "If you're about to offer to have sex with me if I introduce you to a Barrington, I regretfully have to decline, sweetheart. Although I admire your dedication to your school."

She gasped and released his arm. "You're disgusting."

He raised two splayed hands. "Hey, easy on the insults,

Miss Grabby. I said no."

"To something I never asked for. I wouldn't have sex with you if you were the last man on earth and we were humanity's final hope." She groaned as she heard her own words. "I'm sorry. I shouldn't have said that."

He studied her face for a long moment. "What are you afraid of? It's not me."

Oh, my God. I don't even know how to salvage this. I can't tell him. "No, it's not you."

His expression darkened. "Is it that bad here?"

I should deny it. But it was impossible to lie while looking into his eyes. Just about a whisper, she said, "Lately. It hasn't always been like this."

"Quit."

"It's not that simple."

"Because your son goes here. The headmaster has you by the balls."

"You could say that."

In the silence that followed she wondered if he would offer to take care of the situation for her. Like some hero, charging in on a white horse, slaying her dragons.

Would I even want that?

"Funny," he said slowly, "I didn't take you for someone who'd put up with crap like that. I guess none of us are who we appear to be."

Ouch, but perhaps I deserve that one. "I'm sorry about what I said in the office."

He bent closer, so close she was sure he would kiss her. Her lips parted in anticipation even as she told herself it would be a mistake. "So quick to apologize even when I'm being a dick. I liked you better when you were calling me disgusting. Where's your son's father?"

The mention of Whitney's biological father jolted her out of her daze. She snapped, "That's none of your business."

He hovered over her a moment longer, long enough for a shiver of need to lick through her. Did he feel it?

The fire in his eyes was laced with something else— concern? "Very true, but when I needed help, my little sister kicked ass for me. If you've already given up the fight, who'll do that for your son?"

With that, he turned and strode away.

Apparently not him.

She hugged herself as she watched him make his way to the parking lot and exchange a few words with Bradford. She wanted to rush after Connor and tell him her son didn't need help because he had her and she was his champion.

"If you've already given up the fight . . ." She muttered the words he'd thrown at her. *I haven't given up the fight. I'm right here, working my ass off so my son has the opportunities I only found when I left Oklahoma. That's how I fight, buddy. I make sure there is food on the table, a roof over our heads, and that my son has a better education than I could ever afford to give him.*

You know what I didn't need today? A big movie star spouting opinions on things he knows nothing about.

If my son needs saving, I'll do it myself.

Chapter Four

B ACK AT HIS car, Connor refused to look over to see if
Angelina was still watching him. Being a badass was
exhausting, and stepping off the emotional roller coaster of
the last few hours was a relief. All he'd wanted to do was
fulfill a commitment and not embarrass himself or his family
by doing so.

He hadn't expected to meet a woman he wouldn't want
to leave behind—someone so beautiful he couldn't get the
image of her out of his mind, so complicated he couldn't
figure out if she wanted him to stay or go.

He didn't belong there, but he hated that he was leaving
without fixing the situation for her son. "That is one messed
up school, Bradford."

"How about the woman? She doesn't look very happy
with you."

"She'll get over it. She actually seems like a nice person,
but she's scared. I wonder what her kid is like. Is he as
uptight as she is? And I'd put money on Keaton being the
one who's messing with him. He's only doing it to impress
the coach."

Bradford sighed. "If you want, I'll look into the situation."

Now that's a good friend. "When you say 'look into it' that doesn't involve anything that could get either of us arrested, does it? I promised Viviana I'd stay out of the news."

Bradford removed his glasses long enough to say, "Depends on what we find." He flashed a cold smile. "But nothing I do is ever reported."

"Don't you have to get back to Bulgaria?"

"It can wait." After replacing his glasses, Bradford said, "I remember what it's like to be little and scared. It's not a good place."

Connor glanced back at Angelina who was walking into a side entrance of the main building. "Look into the headmaster. My guess is he's patient zero when it comes to whatever ailment this school has."

Bradford nodded. "Sounds about right. Just so you know, your talk to the soccer team wasn't half bad."

"Thanks! I hope it helps." A weight lifted from his shoulders. "I didn't know what to say when the coach asked me what college team I'd played on. It was like he knew I never attended one."

"You shut him right down. I'm curious. What did you say to him at the end?"

"I asked him if he wanted to grab a beer sometime."

"Interesting."

"Yeah, it's like they say: Keep your women smiling and your enemies drunk."

"No one says that."

"I do."

Bradford threw back his head and laughed. "The world would be a better place if everyone saw it the way you do."

"Truth." Connor turned to open the door of his car, then stopped. "Angelina was trying to hard-sell the school to me because of my affiliation with the Barringtons."

"So, she was doing her job."

"Yeah. And she might not want to fuck me." Not everyone got his sense of humor, but Bradford did.

He shook his head but was fighting back a smile.

Connor slid into his car then opened his window to say, "No, hang on, she doesn't want to fuck *you*. Today I wasn't me. Had I been, she'd be calling in sick for the afternoon . . . possibly tomorrow morning as well."

"Goodbye, Connor. I'll tell you if I discover anything useful."

"Thanks for today, Bradford. It meant a lot to me that you came."

Bradford didn't answer, but Connor hadn't expected him to. Everyone had issues left over from childhood—Bradford more than most.

Flashing a thumbs-up at Bradford, Connor peeled out of the parking lot and sped down the driveway.

ANGELINA RELUCTANTLY MADE her way back to her office. It was tempting to flog herself over every misstep she'd taken that day, but Aunt Rudi had taught her to focus on the wins instead. The drama students would go home and rave about

Connor Sutton's visit. Things like that often brought the school spontaneous financial gifts. So the day wasn't a complete wash.

The soccer team had heard a speech about responsibility toward each other. Would it make a difference? She wanted to think so. There had been a sincerity to it that had made it ring true for her as well.

She'd probably never see Connor again and that was for the best. What had Mr. Svete said about him? "He's the type many women lose their heads around." She could see that. Was it his size? His perfectly rugged features? He'd definitely been born with more than his fair share of good looks.

And he wasn't a complete asshole.

No more than I am, anyway.

As Angelina was about to step into her office, she heard Mr. Svete raise his voice. "No you can't leave early. And don't bring me a note from your doctor and think it will change anything. I have been more than patient with you, but I could have someone do twice the work you do for half the price. Tired? We're all tired."

"I didn't say I was tired," Mrs. Tellier said in a much lower tone that had Angelina stepping closer to hear better. "I said the office called with test results they thought I should hear immediately. It might be nothing, but when you're my age and the doctor says it's important . . . you go."

"Last week it was a family issue that couldn't wait. This week it's the doctor. If you want to stay employed here, Mrs. Tellier, my suggestion is you schedule your emergencies for after four p.m."

"I'll see if I can get a later appointment," Mrs. Tellier said, her voice cracking with emotion.

"Please contain yourself. It's not a mystery why women don't make it far in business. Especially not one your age."

Unable to stand another moment of it, Angelina stepped into Mrs. Tellier's office. "Is everything okay?"

Mrs. Tellier reached for a tissue and nodded without looking up from her desk.

"Do you need something, Miss Kroll?" Mr. Svete snapped.

Angelina looked from him to Mrs. Tellier and back. Connor Sutton's speech echoed through her thoughts. *Why does a person remain quiet in the face of what they know is wrong? Is it possible all Mr. Svete needs is to be reminded how to behave?* "It's been a stressful day for everyone. I'm sure when you have time to stand back and look over all Mrs. Tellier does for the school you'll see that it far outweighs a request or two to leave early."

Mr. Svete rose to his full height and a flush reddened his cheeks. "Is that all?"

"No." Angelina squared her shoulders. "Kindness and civility are things we can only teach our students by modeling them. It's not okay to speak to any woman the way you just spoke to Mrs. Tellier. It's not okay to use your position of power to intimidate those around you. We all want this school to succeed, but we also all deserve to be treated with respect."

A sneer twisted Mr. Svete's mouth. "A bit full of yourself today, aren't you?"

"Not at all. I just believe if we are entrusted to shape the minds of the next generation, we need to hold ourselves to a higher standard."

"If you're not happy with the way things are at Reemsly, Miss Kroll, maybe it's time you resign your position."

Mrs. Tellier rose to her feet and rushed to say, "Oh, I'm sure that's not what she's saying."

He turned and glared at the older woman.

While his attention wasn't on her, Angelina shook her head and motioned for Mrs. Tellier to sit back down. She mouthed, *Remember your granddaughter. I've got this.*

Angelina cleared her throat. "I have no intention of resigning."

"Then let me make this easier for you. You're fired."

"You can't fire her for having an opinion," Mrs. Tellier said.

"Say another word, Mrs. Tellier, and you'll have all your afternoons free. All your mornings as well," Mr. Svete said in an ugly tone.

Mrs. Tellier's eyes filled with tears that she blinked back, but she sat back down. A much younger Angelina would have right-hook-punched the smug expression right off the headmaster's face. She wasn't that person anymore, and she refused to become that person again. "There is a standard of behavior that even you are held to, Mr. Svete. Fire me for no reason, and you'll have quite a legal fight on your hands."

The look he gave her was pure evil. The kind of look that makes a person want to clutch their children and their purse closer to them. He leaned down and pressed a button on

Mrs. Tellier's phone. "Mrs. Quinn, call Whitney Kroll to the main office. He'll be leaving early today. And prepare his school records. I was just informed that his mother will be transferring him to a public school."

Angelina hadn't felt such cold fury since Whitney's father had eagerly signed off his parental rights. She went nose to nose with the stork of a man. "Don't involve my child in this."

There it was—that look that made the hair on the back of Angelina's neck stand on end. "I'll give you a choice. Go quietly and we're done, or see if any good school will consider your son when I'm done explaining why we had to ask him to leave."

"You can't do that."

"Watch me." He leaned closer and Angelina hated that she took a step back.

It all felt so unreal. Her eyes flew to Mrs. Tellier's for confirmation that this was some nightmare her alarm was just about to wake her from. She looked on helplessly. Angelina didn't want her to get involved, but she also hated to see her spirit crushed.

Angelina spun on her heel and snarled. "You're destroying everything Reemsly stands for. Why? What do you get out of being so cruel?"

"Goodbye, Miss Kroll. Security will escort you and your son out."

"No security needed. I have no desire to be here a moment longer." There was a temptation to threaten him again, but responses that felt good in the moment were often the ones a person regretted later. She needed time to think. Would he actually smear her son's reputation? Was she willing to risk testing if he would?

Oh, God, what am I going to tell Whitney?

I'll have to tell him something.

She hesitated at Mrs. Tellier's desk. She wanted to reassure her that everything would be okay, but she was still in shock. The only thing she was certain of was that she didn't want to make things worse for the older woman. There had to be a way to win, but something told Angelina that was a battle for another day.

Right then, her son was being pulled out of class and likely being told he was leaving the school. No warning. No explanation. She needed to be there when it happened.

Without another word, she strode across the hall, grabbed her purse, then in a controlled but quickened pace made her way to the main office.

Whitney was already seated on the bench outside of it with a manila folder in his hand. He stood as she approached. "You okay, Mom?"

She pulled him to her and simply hugged him. He was tall for his age, nearly eye-to-eye height when she stepped back. "I'm fine. We're fine. Do you have everything?"

He nodded. "Yes. I don't keep much in my locker. Did you withdraw me from the school?"

"We'll talk about it in the car, okay?"

He followed her out of the building without protest. "I can handle Keaton, Mom."

Deep breath. She opened the passenger door for him

then went around and slid into the driver's seat. To give herself time to collect her thoughts, she started the car engine and drove away from the school. For several moments neither said a word. They simply drove. She stopped at a small park with the bridge she and Whitney used to throw twigs off to see which would float away faster. Together, they stepped out of the car and walked to look over the bridge as they had so many times before. "First, I'm sorry, Whitney. I'm so sorry about how today went down. I'll fix it. You may need to miss a few days of school, though."

He pulled a leaf from a tree and released it above the rushing stream. "What happened?"

"It's not something you need to worry about. Just know that although we left today that doesn't mean I'm giving up. Sometimes a person's best strategy is to back up and gather information before acting."

"Were you fired?"

She gripped the railing of the bridge. "Yes."

"Good."

Her gaze flew to study his profile. She expected him to be sad, scared, maybe even angry with her. He looked a whole lot calmer than she felt. "It's not good, Whitney. You're at Reemsly on a scholarship based on my employment there. I either need to get my job back or empty our savings to re-enroll you."

"I don't want to go back."

"You don't mean that."

"I do." He released another leaf over the water below. It floated gently down then disappeared beneath the turbulent current. "I'm good at soccer, Mom. Really good. I bet I could have been one of the best players on the Reemsly team."

"I thought you didn't like soccer."

"I love soccer. I just didn't want to be on that team."

Angelina turned more toward her son. "Why?"

"I don't like the way they think they're better than everyone else. I didn't want to be like that, and I didn't want to fight with any of them about it because—"

He stopped abruptly and Angelina's heart clenched. "Because?"

He kept his eyes on the water below. "I didn't want to get in trouble and get you in trouble. Everyone knows Mr. Svete is an asshole."

Angelina gasped at the first swear she'd ever heard come out of her son's mouth, but didn't correct him. It was too accurate. She hugged him and realized he wasn't a little boy anymore. At thirteen, he was her height and growing up so fast. Part of her hated that she'd put him in a position where he'd felt he needed to take care of her. Another part was so proud of him for wanting to. "Thank you, but don't worry, Whitney. I can handle him."

He stood taller and pressed his lips in a straight line before saying, "Don't go back there, Mom." He hugged her this time and her heart broke as she realized he was afraid for her.

I thought I was protecting him, but what was I teaching him?

To be quiet? To accept a kick without complaint?

She hated that Connor's questions were still so fresh in her thoughts. *"When I needed help, my little sister kicked ass for me. If you've already given up the fight, who'll do that for your son?"*

I've always seen myself as a fighter.

A survivor.

I wanted better for my son.

Life didn't come with an instruction manual. She'd made the best choices she knew at each step, but that didn't mean she didn't wonder if she could have done better.

"Mr. Svete doesn't scare me." Angelina cupped her son's face. "I'll get you back into Reemsly."

He pulled his head away. "I'm not going back to that school, Mom."

Angelina took a deep breath. She adjusted the collar of his shirt. "I want you to be happy, Whitney, but school is something I can't be flexible on. There are two things in life no one will be able to take away from you—"

His shoulders squared and finished for her, "A good education and my dignity. I know, Mom. That's why I don't want to go to that school. I want an education, just not the one that school is serving."

How could she argue with that? She'd never heard education referred to in the same terms as a school lunch, but somehow it was fitting. Honestly, she wanted a job, but not the one that school was serving her, either. She nodded. "We have a little time to figure it out. I have some money saved. I'll see what's online and homeschool you until we find a place where they're serving something better. How's that?"

Her son cocked his head to one side. "How will that work when I'm already better in math than you are?"

"The hell you are." She chucked her shoulder against his. They shared a laugh.

When hers ended in a shaky sigh, her son turned to look down over the water. "It's going to be okay, Mom. You'll see."

She took a place beside him. "How could it not be when I have you for a son?"

They took in the view without speaking for a moment, then he asked, "Why did he fire you?"

Before they'd decided he wouldn't return to Reemsly, she wouldn't have told him. Now though, she was beginning to think he needed to see that sitting down and watching someone get kicked or accepting the kick yourself wasn't the best way to live. Sometimes you have to be the first voice to stand in protest, and even if it ends badly for you, it's still the right thing to do.

So, she told him about Connor Sutton's speech . . . repeated it as close to word for word as she could. Then she explained how his words had stayed with her and made it impossible for her to watch Mr. Svete belittle Mrs. Tellier.

"She didn't stand up for you?" he asked with surprised outrage. "She just let you get fired?"

"I didn't want her to. She's almost seventy, Whitney. And she has people who rely on her. I can find another job. Where would she go?"

"I like Mrs. Tellier."

"I do too."

Eyes too solemn for someone his age, Whitney met Angelina's gaze. "We could find her a new job."

You mean after I find one for myself? How did I luck out and get such a good kid? "We could sure try." She straightened off the railing. "I don't know about you, but I'm starving. What do you say we go out to lunch?"

He perked up. "To celebrate our freedom."

"Our freedom," she echoed his words. Was that what Mr. Svete had given her? It felt scarier than that.

Her son didn't look afraid, though. He looked happy. Happier than he'd looked in a while. She smiled and ruffled his hair. *He was right—everything was going to be okay.*

First, lunch.

Then a hot bath, early pajamas, and some mind-numbing movie binging—hopefully with a huge bowl of popcorn and this kid at my side.

Tomorrow is a whole new day.

I'll shine then.

Chapter Five

ARLY THE NEXT day Connor was in his office in New York City, kicking his own ass in a game of darts. Having an office had never been a goal for him, but everyone in his family now had one. Claire said having it lent him a level of credibility. No one needed to know the filing cabinets were empty or that his secretary spent her time writing romance novels rather than doing any actual work. Like everything else in his life, she was a prop he tolerated.

And thankfully, she was happily married. It kept things easy between them.

He was feeling restless. He'd spent the night thinking about a woman he told himself he'd be better off forgetting. He couldn't shake the look that had entered Angelina's eyes when he'd asked her if things were really that bad where she worked.

I should have done more.

But what?

He headed out to his secretary's desk. "Kimmie."

She looked up in surprise. "Yes, Mr. Sutton?"

"I need your honest opinion of my badass impression."

She smiled and closed her laptop. "Sure. Is this for a new role?"

"You could say that. Promise not to laugh, though. I can't break character."

With a wave of her hand over her face, she erased her smile. "No laughing, okay. I'm ready."

Connor turned away, did a few facial exercises, then shot for the same expression he'd held to the day before. He channeled his inner Bradford and stared down the petite brunette with purple-rimmed glasses. "How long have you worked here, Kimmie?" He shook his head. A real badass wouldn't use her first name. "Mrs.—Mrs.—what's your last name again?"

"Sanchez. My name is Kim Sanchez. Same as the day you hired me. And it has been almost a year." She didn't even crack a smile. Damn she was good.

"Do you think you're funny?" he demanded.

Her eyes twinkled with humor. "No, sir."

He motioned toward his office. "Hold my calls. My morning is back-to-back meetings. Unless it's the president himself, take a message."

"You have meetings? Did I miss something?" she asked.

"Of course not." He chuckled, then narrowed his eyes at her. "Focus. If you didn't know me and I looked at you like this would you think I'm an asshole or dangerous and mysterious?"

She tapped a finger on her chin. "When I first met my husband he used to do this thing with his hand." She stood up and pushed her jacket aside to rest her hand on the belt of her slacks. "I thought it was sexy in a dangerous way."

Connor mirrored her stance. "Like this?"

"Slower. Like you're reaching for a gun you haven't decided if you need to use yet."

He shook his arm out, then brought his hand to his hip again, slower.

"That's it," she exclaimed. "Want my honest opinion?"

He threw both hands up in the air. "Why wouldn't I?"

"I love that about you." She smiled. "If you're really trying to look dangerous you shouldn't bound into a room. When I picture a badass, I imagine someone with tense, abrupt movements. Your expression works for me, but your body still says relaxed and happy."

Connor flexed his shoulders then walked to the door of his office again. "Okay, take two." He spun on his heel, narrowed his eyes, and walked toward Kimmie's desk in a deliberate, slow fashion. When he came to a stop, he brought his hand to his hip and stared her down.

"Oh, that's good," she exclaimed. "You've got it."

The outer door of her office opened and Bradford walked in. Slow and tense. Coiled like a snake about to strike. Connor nodded rather than offering his more enthusiastic greeting.

"We need to talk," Bradford said in a terse tone.

Kimmie clapped. "Is he helping with your character study? Good choice! Yes, copy those mannerisms and you'll nail badass."

"Don't encourage him," Bradford said with no humor. "Am I interrupting?"

"No, no," Connor assured him. "Bradford this is my secretary, Kimmie. Kimmie, this is Bradford—Do you have a last name?"

"I do," he replied but didn't offer it up.

Connor thumbed at Bradford. "Coolest guy I know."

"We need to talk," Bradford said without acknowledging Connor's compliment.

"See, I have meetings. Hold my calls," Connor said to Kimmie with a wink and a smile before attempting a stern, serious expression.

"Will do, Mr. Sutton," she said in a respectful tone as she opened her laptop to likely write another chapter of her novel.

After leading the way into his office, Connor closed the door. "What's up?"

Bradford walked around the room to study the photos on the wall as well as the shelves full of an eclectic collection of books—classics, nonfiction, biographies, thrillers. "What do you need an office for?" he asked.

Another man might have been insulted, but it was a valid question. Connor went to sit behind his impressive oak desk, then laced his hands behind his head, leaned back in his chair, and propped his feet up on it. "Claire thought it fit my image. Mostly I nap—or read. It was a good place to memorize my lines."

He scanned the photos without commenting on any. "Your instincts about the headmaster at Reemsly were spot-on. On the surface his record and reputation are spotless. When I dug deeper, things got murkier. Since he joined the school, the administration has undergone several major turnovers. Anyone who questions him is instantly let go. Everyone in the finance department is fresh from college. I can't imagine they know how much money has come in or gone out since he took over."

Connor dropped his feet to the floor and leaned forward. "You think he's embezzling from the school?"

"I don't have proof yet, but he's dirty. I'd bet my life on it. How involved do you want to get in this?"

After surging to his feet, he groaned and pocketed his hands. "What are my options?"

"Do you think shit like this comes with a menu? All I need to know is if you want to keep your hands clean."

He didn't want to admit it, but he had to. "You'd have to tell me what that means."

"Never mind." Bradford sighed and pinched the bridge of his nose. "Should I bother to tell you what else I learned?"

"You don't have many friends, do you, Bradford?"

Bradford's head snapped back, but he said nothing.

"You've got to learn how to talk nicer to people. Your little digs don't bother me, but when you use them on Dylan they actually hurt his feelings. Is that what you want—to hurt people all the time? Wouldn't it be more fun to sit around, shoot the shit, and laugh? That's what I miss doing the most . . . hanging out with my buddies, sharing a case of beer, and doing nothing."

"Sounds like a complete waste of time."

"Or a little piece of heaven. Don't knock it until you've tried it. Life is about balance, Bradford. According to

Aristotle that's the secret to being a happy person."

"You read Aristotle?"

Connor nodded toward the bookshelves. "I started reading more only recently. He has some interesting ideas. *Moderation.* A coward sees a building on fire and runs from it. A reckless fool rushes in and dies. A firefighter goes into the building in a balanced, prepared way with the tools needed to actually make a difference. Courage is intelligent action in the face of adversity."

Bradford walked over to the bookshelf. "That actually sounds like a good read."

Connor cleared his throat and dug the graphic novel version of Aristotle's teachings out from beneath a pile of scripts and slapped it down on his desk. "It's even better with pictures. The Greeks definitely knew how to party too. Nothing we do today would have shocked anyone back then."

Rather than walking over to check on Connor's suggestion, Bradford continued to study the books on the shelf. "*The Billionaire Wins the Game.* You have an interesting selection of books."

"Kimmie introduced me to the author. I thought romance novels were just for women, but I binge read that whole series. Joseph Anderson has three single sons and he wants grandchildren . . ."

Bradford turned around and cocked an eyebrow.

Flashing a sheepish smile, Connor shrugged. "Hey, it's helpful to know what women find sexy and Melody Anne writes a good story."

"I'll take your word for it," Bradford said, turning his back on the bookshelf. "So, anyway, your girlfriend got canned."

Connor froze, all humor leaving him. "Angelina?"

As if he hadn't just dropped a bombshell, Bradford made his way over to Connor's desk and picked up the comic version of Aristotle and flipped through it. "From what I could gather she took what you said to the soccer team to heart. She overheard Svete laying into his secretary and intervened. He tossed your girlfriend and her kid to the curb."

Fists clenching, Connor fought a desire to hunt down Svete and unleash on him all the fury building inside him. "How did you hear about it?"

"Mrs. Tellier, the secretary. I bumped into her at the grocery store next to her house, and she had no problem telling me exactly how it all went down."

Connor paced the room. "This is my fault."

"It's not and she's probably better off. Now when his ship sinks she won't go down with him."

With a growl of frustration, Connor said, "People watch everything I do now. I can't just go over there and punch him in the face. I need a plan." He stopped. "What would you do?"

"You're not me, Connor."

Rubbing a hand over his face, Connor conceded that fact to himself as well. He wasn't some badass international spy. He wasn't even that smart of a person. Neither had ever stopped him before. Yes, he needed to be careful now that his name was linked to the Barringtons . . .

The Barringtons.

That's it.

"Sophie would know how to handle this." He dug his phone out of his jacket breast pocket.

"You're serious."

The disbelief in his tone gave Connor a moment of pause. "I would call my sister, but she and the rest of the Barrington ladies are helping Claire gear up for the wedding. I don't want to lay any of this at their door."

"What do you expect Sophie to do?"

"She'll probably call a family meeting."

"Hang on. You honestly believe all you have to do is make a phone call and the Barringtons will drop everything they're doing and rush to meet with you?"

"Yes. That's what family does." *God, how was Bradford raised?*

"This I have to see."

With that, Connor called the matriarch of one of the country's most powerful families.

She picked up immediately just as he knew she would. "Connor, Dale and I were just talking about you. Will we see you Sunday for game night?"

"Actually, I'm hoping you have time to see me before then."

"Of course." Her voice filled with concern. "Is something wrong?"

"Yes, very wrong. Could you gather everyone? At least the men? I'm in need of advice."

"Do you want us to come to you?"

"No, I can fly up."

"Then get in the air. If you're quick about it, we'll have your favorite dinner waiting for you."

"Carbonara," Connor said with a good amount of yearning. He could almost taste pancetta and pasta dripping with a creamy parmigiano reggaino cheese sauce and a generous amount of pepper and garlic. *Oh, yes. No, this isn't about food.* He shook his head to clear it. "You don't have to do that, Sophie, but please don't tell Viviana about this call. Or Claire. I don't want them to worry."

"Are you in some kind of trouble?"

"No, but I'm open to suggestions on how to keep it that way while addressing a certain situation." Connor started pacing the room again. He was a spontaneous man by nature. Thinking things through had never been his strong suit, but there was no returning to the innocent time in his life where he could have run buck naked across a football field as a prank and shocked next to no one.

His blinders were off now.

His family needed him to think first, leap later—and keep his clothes on while he did both. He'd heard that talk more than once over the past year.

No more heavy drinking.

No more bar fights.

Sex only with women he knew the names of.

Being rich was not nearly as freeing as people made it sound. "A friend of mine has recently been unfairly terminated from her position. Bradford has been helping me with a project and thinks the situation might be complicated."

"Ian's Bradford?"

"The one and only."

"Sounds serious."

"It is. If this were all going down in my hometown I'd know how to handle it, but I understand that my actions reflect on the whole family. I don't want to do this wrong."

"I'll have all the boys here at seven. Would that work for you?"

"Perfect. Hey, do you think we should ask Clay? He hates to miss anything."

"As long as you take his advice with a grain of salt."

"I will. I would like to hear his opinion. He doesn't pull any punches." Connor looked across the room. "Bradford will probably—" He stopped when Bradford shook his head vehemently. "It'll just be me. See you at seven. Thank you, Sophie."

"Hang on, Dale wants to say something."

Connor swallowed hard. His own father had a booming voice when he was angry, but a look of disappointment from Dale cut deeper. He commanded respect quietly. Men stood straighter around him, swore less. "Hi, Dale."

"A family meeting? Must be something serious. May I ask the name of this friend you're concerned about?"

"Her name is Angelina Kroll."

"Have you mentioned her before?"

"No, sir."

"Describe her to me."

Connor closed his eyes as Angelina's image came back to

him so vividly his heart started racing. He couldn't easily reduce someone as dynamic as she was down like that. He almost said beautiful, but she was more than that. Gorgeous. Stunning. Impossible to forget. He considered describing her as intelligent, witty, fantastically sarcastic. As memories from their time together filled his head, a funny warmth swept through him and he sighed. Not just smart, not just beautiful, but brave too. Someone who couldn't stand by and watch someone suffer without stepping in. "Strong. Brave. Intelligent. Beautiful. And probably doubting herself even though she did the right thing. She makes me wish I were a smarter man."

Dale made a sound in his throat. "Come on home, son. We'll help you figure this out. Should we call your father as well? How about Dylan?"

"Dad, yes. Dylan, no. He's filming on location in Iceland. This is a big opportunity for him. I don't want to distract him."

"See you at seven, then. We'll fly your father in as well."

"Thanks, Dale."

Connor ended the call there. After pocketing the phone, he looked up to find Bradford watching him.

"I don't get it," Bradford said.

With a nod, Connor clapped a hand on his friend's shoulder. "I know. But one day you will. You're sure you don't want to come with me?"

"Positive."

"What will you do?"

"Once I get the scent of a dirtbag I can't walk away until

I know everything."

"And then?"

"Then I handle the situation."

"Do you want me to stay?" Suddenly it didn't feel right to leave.

"No, I want you to go have some Carbonara then get your girlfriend and her son as far from this situation as you can."

"That doesn't sound good."

"There is always a price to be paid for getting involved. If you're not willing to pay it, you don't belong in the game."

"I don't understand you sometimes."

"There's not much more dangerous than the desperate. When I take this guy down, and I will, he's going to try to pin his sins on anyone he can. You don't want your woman anywhere around him."

Connor nodded. He looked at the Aristotle book on his desk. Screw moderation. "This is a pretty busy office. I could use a second secretary. If you see Mrs. Tellier again, tell her I'll match her salary as long as she promises to proofread Kimmie's novels. She's been looking for another editor."

"I'll do that. Is this the kind of position that comes with a signing bonus and a month off before she starts?"

"It's exactly that kind of position."

Bradford frowned. "I don't like very many people, but I like you. Don't put yourself down. You're good just the way you are."

Connor smiled. "Thanks, Bradford." He glanced down at his phone. "I need to get going. I can't be late for dinner.

Sophie's cook makes biscuits fresh every day." His stomach growled in anticipation.

Bradford laughed. "I'll contact you if there's anything you need to know."

Back at Kimmie's desk, Connor said, "Kimmie, I'm going out of town. Get the helicopter prepped. Have my housekeeper pack my bags and send them over. Oh, and order a second desk for this office. I just found you an editor."

SHE'D BEEN IN worse places. Angelina sat on the couch in the house her aunt had left her and sipped on a steaming cup of chai.

Day one of what Whitney called their *freedom* was going as well as it could. He looked over the websites of countless schools with her and had agreed to visit some the following week. He hadn't even balked when she'd given him a list of interview questions and essay topics the schools had requested.

She'd spent a good amount of time after that making sure they'd still have health insurance and securing digital copies of Whitney's school portfolio as well as her annual job performance reviews. Thank God she had friends in the main office as well as the human resource department. Most likely Mr. Svete wouldn't have a reason to mess with either file, but she was of the opinion that it was always better to be safe than sorry.

Around lunchtime, she updated her résumé and sent it out to several private schools as well as colleges. She was good at what she did, but she had no idea what kind of reference Mr. Svete would give her. By law, he wasn't supposed to say more than how long she was employed, but he was a nasty enough man to break that law simply out of spite. He'd know prosecuting him for it wasn't worth emptying her financial nest egg. And unless he did it in writing, things like that were difficult to prove.

I refuse to worry about something that hasn't happened yet.

When her phone chirped with a text, she gladly reached for the distraction of it.

It was Mrs. Tellier. **How are you today?**

***Angelina responded:* We're good. Did you get to the doctor?**

I did. He just wanted to warn me that my cholesterol was up again. Said I could either change my diet or start medicine for it. I asked him if having more sex would help. He didn't laugh.

Angelina did. *What was she like at my age?* Relief flooded through her at news that Mrs. Tellier's health condition wasn't more serious. **How is the office today?**

***Mrs. Tellier:* I wouldn't know. I took the day off to go shopping for healthier food for my fridge. I get nauseous just thinking about going back to the office and looking at Mr. Svete after the way he treated you.**

That was heartbreaking to hear. **We're okay. How it happened was a bit of a shock, but sometimes change is good. Don't let him win again by saying anything to him about it. You need that job.**

***Mrs. Tellier:* I should have spoken my mind yesterday. I regret that I didn't. Everyone told me to tell you they'll miss you.**

Thank you.

Mrs. Tellier: **So, have you heard from Connor Sutton?**

Angelina read the question twice before answering. **No. Why do you ask?**

Mrs. Tellier: **I told his bodyguard all about how you stood up for me and what Mr. Svete did.**

Angelina: **What?!? When?**

Mrs. Tellier: **While he was helping me load my groceries into my car. What a nice man Bradford is. So, sad, though. You can see it in his eyes.**

Wait, Bradford shops where Mrs. Tellier does? No.

But if it wasn't a coincidence . . . that means Bradford was there with the intention of what? Talking to Mrs. Tellier? Why?

What did Connor Sutton want?

She went back over their time together. Yes, there had been a spark of attraction, but then she'd offended him.

She remembered him asking if things really were that bad at the school.

And her answer.

Had she left him with the impression that the school was dangerous? She hoped not.

If that were the case, had Connor sent his bodyguard to watch over them?

She put her phone down on her lap for a second as she mulled over how she'd feel about it if he had. Aunt Rudi had always said that the only happy woman was an independent one. Most of the time Angelina agreed with that philosophy, but every once in a while she wished she had someone to tell her things would be okay.

Does that make me weak?

Aunt Rudi, didn't you ever want someone who'd wrap his arms around you and just hold you?

I'm a strong, modern woman. I know I don't need anyone.

But sometimes, I wish . . .

After taking a fortifying deep breath, Angelina picked up her phone and wrote: **I'm applying to a slew of local schools. I know your work history. Would you like me to put in your name as well as mine? I hate the idea of you in the same office as that man.**

Mrs. Tellier: I hate the idea of me there too. I'm going to give my two weeks and maybe use up my sick days. I should have done it a long time ago. You don't have to worry about me, though. When one door closes another one opens. I believe that. It'll be the same for you. You'll see.

Angelina: Every adventure begins by taking a step forward.

Mrs. Tellier: Adventure. I need that. I've spent the last fifty years working hard and what did it get me? I'm quitting from the same desk I started at. Who knows? At my next job, I might just sleep my way to the top.

It was impossible not to smile at that. **Just don't write that on your résumé.**

Her response was quick and hilarious. **Or maybe that's all my résumé will say—in bold letters.**

Angelina was laughing out loud as she typed: **I'll check in on you tomorrow.**

Mrs. Tellier: TTFN

Whitney walked into the living room. "What are you laughing about?"

Waving her phone at her son, Angelina said, "Mrs. Tellier."

He sat on the arm of the couch. "Is she okay?"

"Yes, looks like she'll be leaving the school as well."

"I'm glad."

"Me too."

He slid down the arm onto the cushions. "I wrote two essays. They're pretty good. Want to read them later?"

"Absolutely."

"I finished the book I was reading, I'm not in the mood to start another. Want to watch a movie together?"

"Sure." After her busy morning, Angelina could use a destressor. She flipped on the television and went to the movie section. Of course, *Danger Doubled*, came up as a suggestion.

Whitney leaned forward. "What was he like?"

Still pointing the remote at the television, Angelina stalled. "Connor Sutton?"

"Yes. All the girls at school talk about him. Their moms do too. Was he nice?"

She took a moment to answer then decided on something safe. "He was a good public speaker. We didn't actually have that much time to get to know each other."

What would he be like away from the school? On a date? In bed? Her body warmed as she imagined the possibilities.

Whitney gave her a long look. "Why is your face red?"

Time to choose a movie. She used voice control to ask for the sci-fi selections. The scarier, the better. Whitney liked them, and she needed to knock Connor out of her thoughts.

They settled on one about a space station being taken over by a carnivorous alien, but it wasn't enough to stop Angelina from remembering Connor's smile. Big-screen

Connor, bare chested and romantic, melded with the more restrained reality of him. Which was the real him?

Did he look at every woman the way he'd looked at her?

Did they all want him to carry them off to his bed the way she had?

Fantasies were healthy, right?

She picked up her chai and hid her face in the cup, pretending to be interested in the movie while she imagined how Connor would kiss. He'd seemed too uptight at first, so distant . . . but she'd glimpsed another side, a deeper one. A side that had been there while he'd spoken to the soccer team, then again just before he'd left.

He might have sent Bradford to make sure they were okay.

If so, why hadn't he called her?

And if he did call—didn't she have too much going on right now to indulge in any of the things she'd just imagined doing with him?

She glanced over at her son who was too lost in the movie to notice she wasn't. He was her priority—all that mattered.

Instead of trying to find meaning in something that was likely a coincidence, she'd be better off focusing on enrolling her son in a school and landing a new job. Although it was nice to imagine having someone beside her at night, she'd learned it wasn't a requirement for happiness.

Thank you, Connor Sutton, for reminding me that I'm not dead from the waist down.

When the dust settles from this, I might actually have one of my friends set me up with the guys they keep telling me would be right for me.

While Mrs. Tellier sleeps her way to being CEO of some company.

She coughed on a laugh and some of her drink went down her windpipe.

Whitney looked over. "You okay?"

She nodded, but inwardly conceded that the jury was still out on that.

Chapter Six

THAT EVENING CONNOR bounded up the front stairs of
Sophie and Dale Barrington's home. It was large but not
flashy, which he'd initially found surprising. However, after
getting to know them he realized that, although they were
wealthy, they preferred to live a simple life.

Well, their version of simple. They didn't fly commercial
and he doubted Sophie had ever cleaned her own bathroom,
but he didn't hold that against them. What mattered most
was the warmth with which they'd welcomed his family into
theirs when his sister had married their son.

When Sophie threw open the door, Connor practically
wiggled with joy like a tail-wagging Labrador seeing its
person at the end of the day. She was the closest to having a
mother he had, and just a smile from her somehow made
even the most challenging day easier to bear. He swung her
up into his arms. Everything a person needed to know about
her was right there in the way she laughed and hugged him
back. She was one hundred percent love.

Her husband, Dale, joined them, less open with his af-
fection but his handshake was warm and his smile

welcoming. When Viviana had first said she was marrying into the Barrington family, Connor had been afraid they'd lose her. He'd never imagined she'd take him, as well as his father and Dylan, along for the ride. He now had a herd of rich relatives and couldn't imagine his life without them.

"You look well," Dale said, closing the door after Connor walked through it.

"Thank you. I'm trying to work out more and drink less. So far, so good."

"I have the same goal," his father said as he joined them. Close to his height, Sean Sutton had also undergone a transformation since meeting the Barringtons. He looked relaxed in his tailored Italian suit, but Connor wondered if he also longed for simpler days.

"Dad, thanks for coming."

"Always. You know that. I'm glad you didn't ask Dylan to come. He would have, but he's deep in filming. I spoke to him yesterday and he sounded happy, but stressed."

"I spoke to him before he left. I'll have to call him. This week has been nuts."

Sophie linked an arm with Connor and guided him farther into the house. "All my boys are here except Andrew. He's still down in Florida because Helene has an exam. He said we could call him if we need him to chime in."

"No, don't bother him."

"Okay. Then I thought we'd talk before we eat."

"Sounds good," Connor said despite the audible rumble in his stomach. At nearly seven feet, his body required regular fueling.

Sophie chuckled. "We'll make it quick."

As they entered the living room, conversations stopped and all eyes turned toward them. Grant was the first to walk over with a sleeping Sean bundled tightly against him in a baby carrier. He gave Connor a warm back-thumping hug for a greeting. *I taught him that . . . well, without the baby between us.* When they stepped back he studied Connor's face for a moment before saying, "I'm always here for you, Connor. Whatever's going on, I should have been your first call."

Connor took a moment to appreciate the perfection of his nephew's sleeping face, then shrugged. "I would have called you, but it's about a woman."

Asher, the eldest Barrington son and the one everyone called "the hammer" joined them with a huge smile on his face. "That was some serious shade. Granted, deserved, but must still sting." He shook Connor's hand. "This is about a woman? It sounded more complicated when Mom described it."

"It is complicated. Or I wouldn't be here. I've never had problems knowing what to do with women," Connor said.

Lance, the most easygoing of the Barrington boys, laughed as he joined the group. "No one can accuse you of having low self-esteem, Connor. Good to see you."

Connor shook his hand and asked about his twin daughters. "How are Wendy and Laney?"

"Not much different than the last time you saw them," Lance said with a huge smile. "I don't know why we thought we should teach them to speak. All they do is talk now. And want to play dolls. Save me."

Connor chuckled and felt his pants leg being tugged. Asher's son, Joe, was nearly three and so damn adorable he'd be a heartbreaker for sure. Connor crouched down to greet him. "Hey Big Man, are you here to help me decide what to do?"

Joe threw himself into Connor's arms and gave him a tight hug. "I go to preschool, Uncle Connor. I know everything."

"I'm sure you do, Big Man." After hugging him back, Connor pointed toward his shoulders. "Get on up there."

Sitting on Connor's shoulders was something Joe often asked to do. He was so light it was an easy request to grant. When Connor rose back to his full height, Joe clung to his head.

Child on board, Connor greeted Ian, Kade, Dax, and Clay.

Smiling in approval, Asher nodded toward his son. "If the topic isn't appropriate for his ears he can have a snack with the cook, but he wanted to see you."

"Did you, Big Man?" Connor asked the boy on his shoulders.

Joe ruffled his hair. "I missed you, Uncle Connor. Can we go fishing?"

"Next time I come up, how's that?"

Joe stuck out his bottom lip. "Take me right now."

Dale reprimanded him in that quiet tone of his. "Joseph Dale Barrington." With Dale, a lecture wasn't required and even at his young age Joe had already learned that.

"Sorry, Uncle Connor."

"It's okay, Big Man. If I could take you tonight, I would. First, I have to get some good advice, then I need to eat. When I get hungry I become a bear." He hunched down a bit and made a growl. "And you don't want that. I might accidentally eat you."

"Noooooo." Joe giggled and hung on tighter.

Asher stepped closer. "I have a feeling we're not going to get much done with him in the conversation." He held out his arms for his son. "Come on, Joe. The cook made you those little dinosaur sandwiches you like."

It was enough to get Joe sliding off Connor and into his father's arms. "I love dinosaurs."

"We know," Asher said lightly. To the room in general he said, "I'll be right back."

Sophie patted Connor's arm. "Why don't we all sit down? Are you thirsty? Can I get you anything?"

"I'm all set, thanks Sophie." He settled on a couch and sat forward, hands between his knees as he planned what he'd say. Speaking had been a whole lot simpler when no one had paid much attention to what he was saying, and lately he'd gotten used to Claire dictating most things he said.

Asher returned before Connor had figured out what to say. He stood off to the side and looked Connor over. "I'm sorry, I have to say this. Do you ever look in the mirror and not recognize yourself?"

Connor straightened and flexed his shoulders. Then sighed. "All the time."

"I almost miss the plaid shirts."

"Me too. Every day." Connor hadn't meant to reveal as much, but the catch in his voice changed the expressions on the faces around him. Suddenly they looked concerned. He forced a smile. "I'm fine. That's not what I'm here for."

Clay pulled a chair closer. He was an interesting man. Difficult to like at first. Insanely rich. Rumor was he could buy and sell even the Barringtons without making a dent in his fortune. None of it he'd worked for. Dax, his best friend, said he became bored easily and warned Connor to not confuse any favors from him as proof that he cared. Outside of his wife and the Landon Veteran Foundation he's established, there wasn't much that moved Clay.

Connor had a different impression of him. He felt that Clay was a man without a family of his own, seeking connections, while fearing rejection. His indifference was too practiced. Under all that bravado and posturing, Connor was pretty sure there was a man whose feelings were hurt more often than people realized.

And he did care. Sure, he'd tossed money at Connor to "spit shine" him, but he'd also made trips to upper New York with his wife, Lexi. More than anyone else in the room, outside of Grant, Clay knew what Connor had left behind to join the Barrington family. He was the only one who understood that life before them hadn't been bad at all. "Start at the beginning and tell us everything. And don't leave out any part of what Ian's friend Bradford has been doing for you. If it was big enough to bring him back from Bulgaria, consider me fascinated."

"Me as well," Ian said in a terse tone from beside Asher.

Asher frowned at his brother. "Ease up, Ian. There's enough of Bradford to go around."

Ian let out an audible breath, seemed to strive for patience, then said, "You wouldn't be as calm if you knew Bradford's area of expertise."

"Which is?" Dale asked.

"Not my place to say," Ian answered evasively. "But to be clear, Connor, you don't bring a machine gun to a spitball fight."

Connor raised both hands in protest. "Hey, I hear an insult in there and it's not helpful."

Grant stepped closer and gave Ian a stern look. "It's not. Connor why don't you do as Clay requested and just start at the beginning?"

The show of support from Grant brought the smile back to Connor's face. Not all of the Barringtons were easy to get along with, but they were loyal. It had been impossible to stay annoyed with any of them once Connor had realized that. It was the reason he felt equally protective of them. Not just for Viviana, but because he valued his relationship with them.

With that, Connor settled back and began. "It all started when I went up to Reemsly Preparatory School to speak to the drama department. Claire usually writes my speeches and accompanies me to the venues. This time she couldn't, and I didn't want to go alone."

"So you called Bradford," Clay joked.

"I did," Connor admitted with a shrug. "I knew he wouldn't judge me, and like I said, I didn't want to go alone.

I'm not the person the public thinks I am. All I have to do is open my mouth and people know it."

"Hang on," Ian said, leaning in. "You asked Bradford to hold your hand because you were afraid to speak without Claire? I don't believe it. And I don't believe he'd fly back for that. So why don't you tell us what really happened?"

Asher jabbed Ian in the ribs. "I used to be the asshole of the family so I feel qualified to say you sound like one right now. I've seen Bradford and Connor together. They crack each other up." His voice turned more sarcastic. "Don't worry, Ian, Bradford can have more than one friend."

"Shut the—" Ian didn't finish because Dale cleared his throat. He started over. "Thank you, Asher, for that insight." He turned to Connor. "Please, go on."

Sophie stood and moved to sit next to Connor on the couch. "Ignore the sarcasm and focus on how they all came when they heard you needed them. Ian always sounds like this when he's worried. He'll feel better once he knows all the facts."

Connor nodded in agreement. She was right. Ian was actually a lot of fun to be with since he'd met Claire, but when he was concerned about something he still sounded like he had a stick up his ass . . . or a silver spoon . . . Connor smiled, remembering a conversation he'd once had with his brother on the topic. It was impossible to be intimidated by Ian while wondering how much silverware he had stuck up his anus. "Okay, so back to Reemsly. After meeting with Bradford, I decided the best way to handle the school visit was take on Bradford's badass personality so no one would ask me anything I couldn't answer." He schooled his expression to one similar to Bradford's. Cold. Emotionless. Jaded.

Sophie clapped her hands together. "Those acting classes have really paid off. Wow. I wouldn't mess with you."

"Right?" Connor joked, giving in to a smile. "Anyway, you need to know that part because that's who I was when I met Angelina Kroll." He sighed at the simple pleasure of her name rolling off his tongue. After that, the entire story of their time together flowed. From his attraction to her, her insult, what he'd learned about her son, his realization that she was being nice to him only to gain access to the Barringtons, then how she'd been fired from a job that hadn't been a healthy environment anyway. He also summarized what Bradford had said about Svete as well as his suggestion that Connor keep Angelina away from the situation. "I want to work with Bradford to nail Svete, but I don't want to do anything that endangers this family. I want to call Angelina and tell her the man she met doesn't even exist, but Claire has put so much work into making me into this man." He hung his head. "I used to embarrass Viviana almost daily. I don't want to go back to that. I like this woman, but I don't need this to be about that. I just want to help her."

Sophie took one of his hands in hers and gave it a squeeze. "Oh, Connor. You've never embarrassed any one of us."

Asher interjected, "We can't help him, Mom, if we're not honest with him. There was the time he threw up all over the bathroom at Annie's parents' house. Then he lost Clay on a mountain. Am I the only one who remembers when he had sex with that princess in a hall closet at your Christmas fundraising ball without knowing who she was and almost had to marry her? I could go on, but—"

"We get it," Ian cut in. "That's not you now, Connor. We know that."

Connor rubbed a hand over his face. "It is, though. Beneath this suit there's a man who just wants a good beer and a bonfire. I still get stupid ideas all the time. The only difference is I don't act on them anymore."

Clay arched an eyebrow. "I believe that's what's called growing up, something I've been told many times to do myself. Don't change who you are on the inside, Connor, but you were embarrassing your sister. I admire your desire not to. Do you want me to buy Reemsly and fire whoever this Svete guy is?"

For the first time, Dax interjected himself into the conversation. "Clay, you're not buying a school Bradford thinks is being embezzled from. I don't care how bored you are, being investigated by the IRS as well as the FBI won't be entertaining."

"I'm not bored," Clay protested, turning to face his long-time friend. "Why do you always assume everything I do is due to that?"

"Because it usually is." Dax folded his arms across his chest. Kenzi Barrington couldn't have chosen better. Not many men could hold their own in a room of Barringtons, but Dax was a powerhouse in his own right. He loved his wife and her family, but he certainly wasn't a pushover.

How he and Clay had become friends and remained

close for so long was a mystery to Connor. They had very little in common. Dax was a self-made hardened business-man. Clay had been born with a trust fund the size of a small country's economy.

They often bickered like an old married couple, but somehow it worked. Connor almost smiled as he imagined Dax's expression if he'd shared that thought aloud.

Clay mirrored Dax's stance in mockery. "Was. That's not who I am anymore, either. Connor and I have that in common. We've both enjoyed prolonged bouts of immaturity and strive on a daily basis to leave that part of us behind."

"Tell me more about this woman," Sophie asked, bringing Connor's attention back to her.

"She's incredible. Very intelligent, but earnest too. I wasn't upset when I realized why she was being so nice to me, because she really cares about that school. I didn't see her son, but my guess is he's a tiny thing . . . and shy. You'd really like Angelina, Sophie."

Sophie smiled and gripped his hand again. "I'm sure I will. Now let's see if we can unravel this. First, Bradford and whatever he's doing at Reemsly. Ian, I want you to find out exactly what's going on there and keep a lid on it. If this man, Svete, is really stealing money from the school I have no problem with exposing him so the law can deal with him, but don't let Bradford get hurt in the process. I like that boy."

"I can do that," Ian said.

Sophie continued, "Clay, look me in the eye. Do you honestly want what's best for Connor?"

"I do." He looked intrigued.

"Great," she said. "Then you are now officially Connor's fairy godfather. Make sure he has everything he needs to make this happen." *I like the sound of that. Hope it includes my own jet.*

No, I'm not into money, but come on, that would be cool.

"I don't want to brag, but it's a role I excel in." Clay said with a smirk.

What? Really?

Sophie was just getting started. "Asher and Kade." The two men stepped closer. "You are very different men, but each in wonderful ways. Asher, when you want something, you don't let anyone's opinion stand in your way of getting it. Connor could use a little of that mojo. Kade, you're grounded and Asher needs that to balance him out. I don't want to hear that Connor left her stranded in Paris."

"One time, Mom," Asher said in defense. When he saw the surprised expression on Connor's face, he said, "It wasn't as bad as it sounds."

"Kade, you've been where Connor is—straddling two worlds. More than any of us, you could guide him through this. None of us wants to lose the old Connor. And Grant, you and I need to talk to Viviana. Her family is now our family, and they could no more embarrass me than any of my children could."

Sean Sutton said, "You mean that." There was wonder in his voice.

Sophie smiled across at him. "Of course I do. Sure your sons are rambunctious, but you've met mine, they've all had their moments."

From beside the fireplace mantel, Lance protested, "Hey, let's not clump all of us together."

With an amused shake of her head, Sophie conceded, "Except Lance. He's my sweet one."

Grant stepped closer to his father-in-law and looked him over, then shook his head as if just realizing. "Sean, my mother's a very wise woman. Let's go get a beer tonight and talk."

"I'd like that," Sean said.

Connor rubbed the back of his neck and replayed everything Sophie had said. Fairy Godfather Clay. Idea Asher with Kade to rein him in. It still wasn't clear to Connor what Sophie was suggesting. "So, what do you want me to do?"

Ian clapped a hand on his shoulder. "Leave Svete to me."

Asher waved a fist in the air. "I'll mentor you in the fine art of being a badass who actually gets the woman."

Kade rolled his eyes. "What did I agree to?"

Smiling, Clay said, "This actually sounds fun. With my money and your looks there's no woman who will be able to resist you, Connor."

"I don't have a problem with—" Connor started to say but stopped when little Joe ran back into the room and tackled his leg. Professional linebackers couldn't knock Connor from his feet, but he made a big show of toppling to the ground for Joe. The young child took a flying leap to tackle him. Connor caught him easily, but rolled with him, pretending the boy was besting him in a wrestling match.

At the noise, little Sean woke and was swept up into his

grandmother's embrace. Sophie soothed him, then smiled as he immediately fell back asleep in her arms.

Above the ongoing tussle, Connor heard Dax say, "You might want to work on that first."

He would have stopped there, but without hesitation Asher said, "Are you kidding? This is part of what I love most about Connor. Get him, Joe."

When Connor finally called truce, he was sitting up with Joe hanging off the back of his neck. They were both laughing. "I give up, Big Man. You win."

Joe hugged him tightly then he ran over to his father. "Dad, did you see that? I won. I am the strongest man in the world."

Asher picked up his son, propped him on his hip, and gave the side of his head a kiss. "You sure are." With his free hand, he helped Connor back to his feet. "*Angelina Sutton.* It has a nice ring to it."

Connor swallowed hard. "I didn't say I wanted to marry her. I like her, but—"

Asher laughed. "Don't worry, we've got this."

It wasn't the wrestling match that had Connor suddenly feeling unsteady on his feet. He'd come because he'd wanted to make sure he proceeded in a way that was best for his whole family. He felt like he'd stepped into some kind of romantic comedy that ends with the hero getting married.

I just want to help Angelina and her son.
And possibly get laid afterward.
What have I set into motion?

Chapter Seven

THE FOLLOWING SATURDAY morning Angelina stood in the kitchen of one of her closest friends, Joanna, and sipped on coffee that their mutual friend Aly had handed her. Busy lives meant they got together only a few times a month, but when they did Angelina always left smiling. They were the kind of girlfriends who were the first to cheer each other on when one of them scored a win and the last to leave when things got rocky.

Since Angelina didn't see her family often, Whitney considered these women his aunts as well. They'd attended all of his major life events and loved him as if he were their own. Which was why it was time to get their opinion on what was continuing to be an unnerving week. Angelina glanced out the window to where her son was setting up an obstacle course for Joanna's mini horse, Betty. "Thank you for encouraging Whitney to play with her today. It's been a long week and there's so much I want to tell you that I don't necessarily want him to hear."

Joanna moved to look out the window as well. "Betty loves him and he's so good for her. She passed her test to become a therapy horse, but the more positive experiences she has with children, the better she'll respond to them. Children can be unpredictable. Hell, adults can be as well. Some woman tried to look in her mouth to check the length of her teeth. No warning. Didn't ask permission to. Just went up to her like she was going to pet her then started prying her mouth open and commenting on how young she was. Betty took it well. I nearly chewed the woman's head off. At least now I know what Betty would do if a child grabbed her lip. All she did was pull her head away and look at me like, 'Mom, did you see that?'"

"Put that in your book about her," Aly suggested.

"I'll add it to my notes," Joanna said with enthusiasm. Soon after saving Betty from a kill pen, Joanna had started journaling about the experience and Betty's journey from being terrified of people to not only trusting them, but becoming a source of comfort for many. It was such a touching story Aly and Angelina had convinced her it had to be shared. She'd sent off a proposal to a publisher and wham!—she landed a contract and a New York editor to create a children's series based on Betty.

Who says you can't live in New Jersey and make it big in the city? Aly checked her watch. "Start talking, Angelina. I don't have a ton of time today. My first patient is scheduled at one." Aly was the area's most highly sought-after gynecologist. Word of mouth had spread about use of her prototype camera that allowed her to look inside a woman with digital video accuracy without the need for the 150-year-old speculum, which was designed for a physician to view the cervix from outside the body.

Who didn't want to go to a doctor who utilized cutting edge technology to increase a woman's comfort during an exam no woman enjoyed? Her waitlist for new patients was extensive. Healthcare tools for women, by women. She was a pioneer in the industry and her life story was worthy of a book of its own.

Although not a children's book.

Joanna and Aly were two of the most intelligent, grounded woman Angelina knew and that was why she was anxious to hear their opinion of her week. Angelina put her coffee cup down on the counter and said, "Okay, I'll just jump in. Do you remember I told you Connor Sutton was coming to speak to the drama department at Reemsly?"

Joanna perked up. "How could we forget? Is he as good-looking in person as he was in the movie? Even if he isn't, just lie to me. Leave me with my fantasy."

"He's even better in person," Angelina said, her cheeks warming at the memory of just how good it had felt to be near him. A simple memory shouldn't have the power to set her heart racing, but it did.

Aly laughed. "Wow, you liked him. I don't know if I've ever seen you get flustered over a man."

Trying to downplay her reaction, Joanna said, "I don't meet many movie stars."

Aly's eyes narrowed with skepticism. "All of a sudden you're impressed by celebrity status?"

Angelina hopped up on the counter and looked skyward as she admitted, "He was hot, okay? I'm talking about the kind of hot that is dangerous. I have too much I'm responsible for to have sex with a guy who is probably with a different woman every week."

"Whoa," Joanna said in amusement. "You turned down sex with Connor Sutton? Aly, you need to check if her bits and pieces are faulty. If he'd asked me it would have been a yes, wrapped in a yes, with a side of hell yes."

Shaking her head, Angelina said, "I'm serious."

"So am I," Joanna insisted. "I have watched his movie five . . . maybe twelve times. Oh my God, that scene of him in just a towel. I would have pulled it off with my teeth."

Angelina turned to Aly. "What do you think she needs? Therapy? More batteries?"

Aly shrugged, but a smile stretched her lips. "Did you really turn down Connor Sutton? I don't know that I could have. I believe in carefully choosing sexual partners, but an opportunity like that? Oh, sweetie, did you at least get his number?"

I should have started this conversation with how I'm currently unemployed. This is ridiculous.

"I just mentioned him because meeting him kicked off what is turning out to be one crazy week."

"Crazier than turning down that beefcake?" Joanna asked.

"It doesn't get crazier than that," Aly added.

Angelina clapped her hands to get their attention. "Focus. I need my two clearheaded friends to help me decide what to do."

"I thought we were being clear," Aly joked.

"Crystal," Joanna said with a laugh as she high-fived Aly.

"I was fired from Reemsly," Angelina said in a frustrated tone.

"Oh," Aly and Joanna said in unison as all humor left their faces.

"How? Why?" Joanna asked.

There was no way to explain it without walking them through the whole week. She started with meeting Connor, thinking there might be a spark, offending him, then how moving his speech to the soccer team had been. She quickly shared what she'd overheard Mr. Svete saying to Mrs. Tellier and how she'd been unable to turn a blind eye to it. Her subsequent termination. Whitney's expulsion. Mr. Svete's threats.

"He can't do that," Joanna said in outrage.

Aly made a pained face. "He shouldn't be able to, but I'm glad you removed Whitney from that situation."

"Poor Mrs. Tellier," Joanna said with a shake of her head. "I hope she quits. She's too old to put up with that ass."

"She gave her notice." Angelina jumped off the counter. "This is where things start getting strange. I spoke to her two days ago and she said she's accepted a job offer from Connor Sutton. An offer that was delivered by his bodyguard. She starts at his office in New York in a few weeks, but her signing bonus was enough to pay off her granddaughter's college loans in full. In full. Who does that?"

"A man you definitely should have fucked," Joanna said wistfully.

"He didn't technically ask me out." It wasn't easy to admit that.

"Ah, now this all makes sense." Aly exchanged a look with Joanna.

"I would have said no even if he had."

Joanna hid her face in her coffee.

Aly gave Angelina's arm a pat. "You don't have to explain. He didn't ask either of us out, either. You've got nothing to prove. Lucky Mrs. Tellier. She definitely landed a job with a view."

"You don't think it's strange that he offered her a job? Weird that he knew she'd quit hers in the first place? Mrs. Tellier said she'd told his bodyguard everything when she ran into him while shopping. Shopping. Doesn't that sound unlikely?"

They both seemed to ponder the question. Joanna answered first. "You said you left him with the impression that the school wasn't a great place to work. I bet he was just checking if you were okay."

"Maybe."

Aly cocked an eyebrow. "What nefarious reason could he have for offering employment to a senior citizen? Sounds like a simple good deed to me."

Angelina wasn't paranoid by nature, but things were happening that she couldn't explain. She went to her oversized purse and pulled out seven manila envelopes. She withdrew a few from the bunch and laid them on the table. "These are acceptance packets from the three schools Whitney applied to this week."

"That's fantastic," Joanna cheered.

"These are acceptance packets from four elite private schools we didn't apply to." Angelina laid those on the table as well. "They're willing to take Whitney immediately and on full scholarship. No records requested. No references needed. He's just in."

After looking the packets over, Aly said, "Perhaps word got out about what happened? Your aunt was in good standing with high society. Could her name still have pull?"

"Not this kind of pull."

"At least it's not college acceptances," Joanna joked. "I'd hate to see you in the news."

Angelina's hand went to her throat. "Oh my God, I didn't even think of that. Would it be illegal for me to say yes?"

"Did you forge test scores?" Joanna asked.

"Of course not."

Aly didn't look concerned at all, which did a lot to calm Angelina's nerves. "You're fine, then. Are these the same schools you applied to work at?"

Angelina scanned the packets and practically smacked herself in the forehead. How could she not have thought of that? "They are."

"There you go," Joanna said. "I bet the next contact you get from those schools is to set up a time to interview you for the position you applied for. It's a small world. They probably heard you're awesome at what you do and are vying to snap you up."

"I guess that's possible." It made more sense than anything she'd been tossing around. It had started to feel orchestrated. *This is why it's best to talk things out with friends. I'm worrying about nothing. Simply because two events happened during the same time span doesn't mean they were related.*

Connor Sutton, get out of my head.

Just then, her phone beeped with an incoming text. **Connor Sutton here.**

She read the text twice, nearly dropping her phone when she turned it to show her friends who had just sent her a message. "What do you think he wants?"

Aly and Joanna exchanged a knowing look.

Looking down at her phone again, she read the second message. **You made quite an impression on me.**

Angelina read his message out loud. "What does that even mean?"

Joanna put a hand over her eyes and shook her head.

Aly smiled. "It means he likes you. Answer him."

Short of breath, Angelina typed: **Thank you?**

Joanna groaned. "What's with the question mark? Do I need to teach you how to flirt?"

"Let her figure this out, Joanna. I've seen your moves. You could use a little guidance as well," Aly quipped.

Joanna's eyes rounded in mock outrage. "At least I date."

A third message arrived. **Get someone to watch your son and be ready by nine tomorrow morning. I'm sending a car for you. Do you have a passport? Bring it. How does dinner in Venice sound?"**

"Who does this guy think he is? And who would say yes?"

Joanna and Aly waved their hands in the air, but Angelina had already given up on them being rational when it came to Connor Sutton. She hated the part of herself that was tempted to impulsively say yes. What had being impulsive gotten her? Pregnant at sixteen and ditched. Not that she regretted Whitney. He was her life. But she wasn't starry-eyed and needy anymore. With that in mind, she typed: **No, thank you.**

Aly read her response and asked, "Did your fingers just slip? Because it looks like you just turned down a chance to see Venice with *Connor Sutton.*"

"I did," Angelina ground out. "Stop saying his name like he's the holy grail of men. I'm sure he's a nice enough person, but I'm not looking for a fling with an actor. He doesn't know me but he wants to fly me halfway around the world? I'm not some rich man's sex toy."

Joanna laughed. "First, if you were a sex toy you'd be a dusty one, because you might be the only person I know getting less action than Aly."

"Ouch," Aly said, then added, "but true."

"I'm not celibate. I have sex. Plenty of sex. And not just in my mind."

Both Aly and Joanna's expressions changed and they nodded toward the kitchen door. *Whitney.* Angelina turned and briefly met the eyes of her son.

He quickly looked away. "Joanna, do you have carrots? I wanted to teach Betty to bow."

"Sure, hon, hang on." Looking like she was doing all she could to not burst into laughter, she retrieved a bag of them from beside her refrigerator and handed them to him. "Here you go."

"Thanks," he mumbled and practically sprinted out of the kitchen.

Angelina groaned. "That, ladies, is why there is no room in my life for a man like Connor Sutton. I don't care what most people think about me, but I want to be a mother Whitney can be proud of."

"You already are," Aly said with conviction. "Sex is natural. Consider this a conversation starter to many more the two of you will have on the subject."

"Awkward conversations," Joanna joked.

"Only if you make them so," Aly countered. "I talk to a lot of mothers and answer countless questions about both daughters and sons. They usually ask me because their child asked them and they weren't sure how much information to give them. Sexuality isn't like Santa Claus. I don't believe in lying to anyone about it. Teach them the real words and be upfront about both the good and bad. You know how many teenagers come to me and ask questions about STDs? Too many. Sex is more than penetration. It's a complicated subject that we owe it to the young to have an open dialogue about."

"Can I pretend he didn't actually hear me?" Angelina asked.

"Sure, I would," Joanna added. "When I do have children, if I ever do, Aly's going to give them 'the talk.'"

Aly shook her head. "That's my point. It's not a one-time deal, said and done. It should be—"

Why fight it? You know you want to see me again.

Heat swept through Angelina as she read the message that binged her phone. A voice in her head whispered: *Would it be so bad? One day of fun? When was the last time I did something wild?*

I don't need wild.

I'm a mother now.

She had to end this before she did something stupid like agree to go. She began typing her defense. **I appreciate the offer, but I'm not currently in a place where flying to Venice for dinner fits into my plans. I suggest you ask someone who has less responsibility as well as self-respect than I do. Goodbye.**

"You seriously just typed that," Joanna said, "to *Connor Sutton.*" As if realizing how she'd said it, she raised a hand and laughed, "Sorry. But—wow. You don't play."

Aly read the message and whistled. "It'll be interesting to see what his next move is."

"Next move? I just said no."

"Exactly." Aly nodded. "I'm sure he doesn't hear that often. His next move will show us precisely how interested he is in you. If this is just about sex, he'll move on to an easier choice. I don't believe it is, though. I thought you were reading into things at first, but he wants you. I bet he did send his bodyguard to make sure you were okay. If he has feelings for you, it's not implausible to guess he hired Mrs. Tellier because he knew she was someone you care about." She waved at the manila envelopes. "Following that train of thought, acceptance letters to schools your son didn't apply to does seem linked to him. The question now is how far will Connor Sutton go for something he wants?"

Angelina buried her phone in the back pocket of her jeans and hugged her arms around her, returning to the window to watch her son with Betty. He was standing beside her, tapping her side while offering her a carrot between her two front legs. She had no doubt he wouldn't give up until he succeeded.

She didn't know Connor Sutton well enough to say that about him.

Worse, even as she claimed he wasn't the right man for her, she had to admit it was thrilling to imagine a man like him lusting after her.

The best thing for me and my family is if we never hear from him again.

So why is it so exciting to imagine that he wouldn't give up that easily?

Maybe because I really am the only one having less sex than Aly?

BEHIND HIS DESK in his New York office, Connor dialed the number few people had. As soon as Asher answered, Connor said, "I did exactly what you told me to and she said no."

"Hang on, I'm in a meeting." In a gruff tone Asher asked whoever else was in the room to take a ten-minute break. After the sound of a door closing, he said, "What do you mean she said no?"

"Want me to read it to you?"

"Yes."

Connor read his texts to Angelina as well as her responses. This whole thing was ridiculous. He'd never had problems getting women to agree to go out with him and he'd never been to Venice. "I should have asked her to meet for pizza."

"Is that what you usually do?"

"Yeah, women love carbs. I love carbs. Add a few beers and it's practically foreplay."

Asher groaned. "Oh my God. Don't ever say that again."

"Carbs?"

"No. Forget it. Her refusal is actually a good thing."

"Really?"

"It means she's probably not after your money."

"I don't have that much money." Not compared to the Barringtons.

"You will. And trust me you don't want a woman who is with you for it. I like this woman. She has standards."

"Yeah. She said no."

"Where's that overly healthy ego of yours? You're letting one *no* scare you off?"

"Women *like* me. I like women who like me. That's how I tend to choose my dates . . . the ones who say yes. I don't know what rules you play by, but no means no. Right?"

Asher sighed. "Always. With sex. There's a gray area when it comes to asking a woman out. If every man gave up the first time a woman shot him down, there'd be a lot fewer married people in the world. Do you think Emily liked me at first? Hell, she thought I'd burned her museum down. And look at us now. Do you want this woman or not?"

I think I do.

This is all going a little fast for me.

There was also a lot to unravel in what Asher had shared. "You burned her museum down?"

"No, but she thought I had. My whole family did. Honestly, for a while there, I thought it might have been the work of one of my guys but luckily it was an electrical fire."

"Don't take this the wrong way, Asher, but your advice won't work for me."

"Evidently. You're definitely not a hammer."

Nor do I want to be. "On that we can agree. Thanks, Asher. I mean it. It was nice of you to get this involved."

Asher was quiet a moment, then said, "I'd like to see this work out for you. You're a good guy."

That did put a smile on Connor's face. "So are you, Asher. Say hi to Big Man for me and Emily too."

"Will do. On that note, I should get back to my meeting. You know how antsy prime ministers can be."

"Oh, yes," Connor said, although he really had no idea.

After the call ended he called Clay. "Looks like I won't need your jet. She said no to Venice."

"Really? I like her even more now."

"Asher said the same thing. I don't know if I want to be rich. It makes everything so complicated."

"This isn't complicated at all. Where you went wrong was by starting with Asher's plan and not trusting your fairy godfather, Clay."

That he could describe himself that way in a serious tone was amusing as hell. "I did accept your offer of the jet."

"Yes, but if this woman is as wonderful as you say she is . . . she deserves better than Asher's smash and grab technique."

"There was no mention of smashing or grabbing."

"It's an expression. I don't even have to ask you what he told you to say. I can guess. Something Neanderthalish. That never works with the intelligent ones. They need to be wooed. If you really want this woman to want you, you have to make her think you're a challenge."

"Play hard to get? Isn't that advice women get?"

"Do you want to land this one or not?"

"That's the thing, Clay. I like her, but—" He was about to say he had no idea if he wanted to *land her*, not if that meant marriage.

"Didn't you say women get bored with you and move on because you're too nice?"

"I didn't say it like that."

"But that's the essence of it, isn't it? You can pull them in with your looks and personality, but then you make it too easy for them and they move on. When it comes to women, you're a puppy, Connor. Women don't want that. Sure they might use you as a mood lifter after they break up with another guy, but unless you challenge them, you'll never be the one they choose to stay with."

Put like that, he could see a few areas where he could do better when it came to women. Sex was great, but if one more woman started a breakup conversation with, "You're a nice guy, Connor, but—" he'd throw up in his mouth.

Was he destined to marry Angelina? Who the hell knew? But suddenly she was his Mount Rushmore. She was everything he liked in a woman. Could he get her not only into his bed but to want to stay there?

Could I be a challenge?

"What do you suggest?"

"You have to spend time with her without fawning all over her. I have an idea. Yep, it would work. They didn't give me this fairy godfather wand for nothing. You, Connor, are about to be the head of my Gold Star initiative. I'll start moving it over to your building today."

"Your what?"

"It's a branch of my Landon Foundation. It provides support services for families of fallen soldiers."

"Sounds amazing, but I don't know anything about running something like that."

"You don't have to. It practically runs itself. You'll just be the token famous face of it."

"I don't know." It sounded like a lie and his life was already overflowing with those.

"Hey, when you have money, it's important to give back. This is a project that's dear to my heart."

If it was important to Clay, it was important to Connor. He didn't know how yet, but he'd make sure he was more than just a token face of Clay's charity. Supporting veteran families. *That's something real I can stand for.* "What do you want me to do?"

"First, sit back and watch the magic happen. I'll need to clear out your floor. There's no time for me to buy the building, although I'll test the waters on that. Either way, by the end of the week your floor will officially be the New York headquarters for my Gold Star initiative. All you'll have to do is convince your woman to work for you."

"Won't that sound odd? I hired Mrs. Tellier. Now her?"

"Then you'd better make the job sound like a dream one."

Connor was direct by nature. All this plotting was foreign to him. Still, if it solved an employment issue for Angelina while helping people, how could that be a bad thing? "She does know how to fundraise. That would help the program."

"Absolutely. The more it becomes self-funded, the more I can expand it."

"Okay. I'm in."

"Connor."

"Yes?"

"Keep the jet for now. An opportunity to take her somewhere might come up, and it's a nice touch."

"Thanks, Clay."

After ending the call, Connor headed out to talk to his secretary. She closed her laptop when he pulled a chair up to her desk. "Kimmie, we need to talk."

Her eyes filled with concern. "You're not firing me, are you?"

He shook his head. "Never. Listen, things are about to change around here. They're going to get crazy."

"In what way?"

Connor propped his feet up on the corner of her desk and flexed his hands in front of him. "It's a long story."

She propped her chin on one hand. "I love stories."

"Before you get excited about this one, it might be more

of a slapstick comedy than a romance."

"I enjoy both. Tell me everything."

So, he did. Right down to feeling rushed when all he was looking for was a date with Angelina. When he finished, Kimmie was chewing her lip and seemed deep in thought.

"I should probably stop writing at the office."

Connor dropped his feet to the floor. "No way, I just got you an editor. Besides, I love this book as much as your first two, and I need to know what happens."

Without missing a beat, she said, "They end up together. It's kind of a thing in the genre."

Connor threw his head back and laughed. "You know what I mean."

With a look of wonder on her face, Kimmie said, "Whoever this Angelina Kroll is, she's one lucky woman. Outside of my husband, you are the sweetest man I know."

"Sweet," Connor wrinkled his nose. "Did you not hear what I said about how I'm trying to change my image? Women don't want nice."

"Then you've been banging the wrong women."

Connor shrugged. That had recently occurred to him. *Maybe I should try the women who say no.* "Kimmie, I love that you weren't surprised by any of this. Isn't it batshit crazy?"

She smiled. "Yes and no. I'm definitely taking notes. Not sure anyone would believe a plot like this, but I'm hanging on the edge of my seat dying to know how it turns out, and that's a good sign for any story."

"This is real life, Kimmie."

"Not after I change your names and set this in a foreign country." She snapped her fingers. "I'll make you a nice prince, forced to choose a bride, reluctantly alpha."

"Whatever," Connor said, rising to his feet. "Now I have to figure out how to ask Angelina to work for me without sounding like a total creeper."

"Leave that to me, Mr. Sutton," Kimmie said with confidence. "You just work on finding the right balance between badass and sweetheart."

Connor nodded but stopped just before re-entering his office. "I do like her, Kimmie."

"I know. That's why I have no problem with any of this."

"Whatever she decides, we need to make sure she leaves happier than we found her."

"She won't leave, Mr. Sutton. You've got this."

Chapter Eight

A FEW DAYS later Angelina woke from a nightmare to the sun streaming into her bedroom. She lay there, coming down from a burst of adrenaline, telling herself that dreams were not premonitions.

And sleeping late one day doesn't mean I've lost my drive. Stress takes a toll on a person.

She pulled a pillow over her face, trying to wipe the fears of her subconscious out of her mind. Whitney was not dropping out of school. He was temporarily enrolled in a homeschool program. Okay, so he hadn't liked the first two schools they had visited. That didn't mean he wouldn't love the next. Just because he wasn't interested in talking to any of the children he'd known at Reemsly didn't mean he hadn't had friends there. Why were bad dreams so much easier to remember than good ones? In reality, the "talk" she'd had with him after leaving Joanna's house had been less painful than she'd feared it would be. He knew what sex was. They'd had that talk. And, at her age, he said he figured she was having some.

He just didn't want to know about it.

Fair enough.

Whitney was mature beyond his years. So, why . . . why had her subconscious mind tortured her with images of her child never enrolling in school again, never having friends, only wanting to stay home and watch porn all day?

Because dreams are stupid.

And, as my friends say, I tend to see things worse than they are.

Angelina tossed her pillow across the room. She wished the residual feeling of unease was that simple to discard.

She hadn't heard from any of the schools she'd applied to work at, but she had followed up with phone calls. So far nothing had been decided. Which didn't mean, as her dream had implied, she would never find a job and would slowly go through all her savings until she lost her house.

She threw back her blanket and sat up. She remembered that feeling. Back when she'd first moved in with her aunt, pregnant and scared, she'd feared she'd ruined her life. She hadn't. All she'd done was start a new chapter.

That's what this was—a chance to start fresh.

From her nightstand, her phone rang. She didn't recognize the number, but since she was anticipating employers contacting her she answered. "Hello?"

"Good morning, Miss Kroll. My name is Mrs. Sanchez. I hope I didn't wake you."

Angelina cleared her throat. Great, that's exactly the impression I want to give—that I normally sleep in. "Not at all. May I ask what this call is regarding?"

"Yes. Of course. It's regarding a job I feel you'd be perfect for."

Yes. Yes. Thank you, Lord. Yes. "I'm sorry, I missed which school you're calling from."

"It's not a position at a school. I'm recruiting for a fundraising position with Landon Foundation. The salary is quite generous, and you'd be compensated for your travel time getting into the city."

The Landon Foundation? It was run by . . . the name eluded her for a moment. "I've heard of that program. It's a nationwide support network for the families of veterans, isn't it?"

"That's it. We're looking for someone like you to help in our New York office. When can I schedule you for an interview?"

"Oh. Um. Let me check my calendar on my phone." *Holy shit. An interview. In New York. I could commute. Depending on the salary, I should be able to afford tuition for Whitney. Traveling into New York though will mean I'm not around if Whitney needs me.* A fun thought brought a smile to her face. *On the other hand, Mrs. Tellier and I could commute to New York now that she's working for Connor Sutton . . .* She gasped as she remembered something. *Clay Landon, known friend of the Barringtons. Connor Sutton—brother-in-law of the Barringtons. New York City.* One had nothing to do with the other, right? "Can I ask who I would be working under?"

Silence.

That can't be good.

"Mr. Sutton," the woman said slowly.

"*Connor Sutton?*" Angelina's hand gripped the phone

tighter.

"Oh, dammit, I did this wrong, didn't I? Forget I said his name and come on in for the interview. It's really a great office. Mrs. Tellier and I have already had lunch and talked about how perfect you are for . . . for the job."

"I thought Mrs. Tellier didn't start there for a month."

"She technically doesn't, but she came in to meet us and she said she wants to start right away."

"Wow. Okay. I need a moment to wrap my head around this. Did she suggest me for the position?"

Mrs. Sanchez made a frustrated sound. "I am a horrible liar, so I'm going to stick to the truth—no, but as I said she does believe you'd be perfect for it."

"So, Mr. Sutton was the one who requested you call me."

"Sort of. I'm his secretary, and I can attest that Mr. Sutton is an incredible man. Think of this as an adventure. You seem like a woman who isn't afraid of one. Take a leap of faith, come in, see the office. I guarantee you won't regret it."

And this is his next move? I guess I should be flattered that he's willing to go this far to get into my pants. But, no. "Adventure? You apparently don't know me. I'm the opposite of adventurous. Tell Mr. Sutton I appreciate the job offer, but I'm hoping to find employment closer to where my son attends school."

"There are good schools in the city."

Is she trying so hard out of loyalty to Connor or because he's holding her job over her head like Mr. Svete did with me? "I'm sorry, but it doesn't sound like the position for me. Tell Mr.

Sutton I said thank you, but no thank you." With that, she followed her gut instinct and hung up.

Telling herself she'd made the only sensible choice, Angelina showered and changed into slacks and a blouse. She made herself a coffee then went to check on Whitney. He was still sleeping soundly. She stood in his doorway, sipping coffee and reassuring herself that she had the situation under control.

She couldn't have said yes to Connor Sutton.

Dinner in Venice? I have too many responsibilities to run off like that.

Work in his office? I'm not naïve. He didn't offer me a position because of my fundraising skills.

Saying yes would only have led to hot sex on his office desk.

Lots and lots of really yummy, name-screaming, sweaty, orgasmic pounding.

I don't need that.

Oh, my God, especially not with Mrs. Tellier in the next room.

No, no, no.

I don't need a man in my life. Sex would just complicate everything.

I need all the clarity I can get right now.

Impulsive? Irresponsible? Been there, done that.

Whitney needs to find a school. I need to find a job—a real one.

She closed the door to Whitney's room then grabbed her laptop and sat on the couch without opening it. Images of Connor kept muddling her thoughts, frustrating her, exciting her. Was Connor really out there somewhere wishing he could see her again?

Imagining the two of them together?

Involving his secretary in his plans out of desperation?

How could she concentrate after imagining that?

Saying no was the right choice.

It didn't feel right.

It felt disappointing.

Empty.

Like her sex life.

She opened her laptop and forced herself to sift through emails. Each time her thoughts wandered back to Connor, she gave herself a firm inner shake. She'd read her share of romances. Sure, she had fantasies of being swept off her feet by some rich alpha hero. She enjoyed escaping into those stories, but that didn't mean she wanted that man in her life.

In reality, that man was a controlling asshole.

He swept in, had his fun, and moved on.

In books those men were fantastic in bed. In Angelina's experience, the bigger the man's ego, the less effort he put into his partner's pleasure. He considered showing up enough of a gift.

No man had ever gone as far as offering her a job, though, in an effort to see her again. *What would that have led to had I said yes? Chasing me around his office? Banging by the water cooler? On the copy machine?* Angelina sighed. *Probably quickly followed by me either being fired or watching him chase the next skirt.*

Fantasy vs. reality.

Her phone rang with another number she didn't recognize. She almost didn't answer it, but ended up giving into curiosity. "Hello?"

"Good morning, Miss Kroll, my name is Sophie Barrington."

Angelina stood up in surprise, catching her laptop just before it hit the floor. She looked around the room quickly, regretting the slight disorder of the room, despite the fact that the woman on the phone couldn't see it. "Good morning," she said in a strangled voice.

Aunt Rudi had admired the matriarch of the Barrington family. Stories of her charity work had inspired Angelina to go into fundraising. Angelina normally didn't fangirl the rich and famous, but Sophie was an icon. Classic. Refined. Known for championing many causes, but also elusive and protected. No one Angelina knew had ever spoken to her in person.

"I hope it's okay that I'm calling out of the blue. I remember your aunt and she was a remarkable woman. When your name came up in a conversation the other day I didn't make the connection at first, but once I did I knew you would be the perfect person for . . . the position at the Landon Foundation."

On shaky legs, Angelina sank back down onto the couch. "You knew my aunt?"

"When we were younger we attended many of the same social events. She was always pleasant and positive. I understood why she withdrew from our circle, but I've thought of her often over the years. I wish I'd done more to remain in contact."

Hold on, Aunt Rudi had known Sophie Barrington? No. She would have told me that.

Wouldn't she?

As Angelina thought about it, she realized there were chunks of her aunt's life they'd never discussed. Sure, Angelina knew her aunt had once been part of New York's high society, but—*wow.*

"Why did she withdraw?" Angelina voiced the question that took hold of her.

Sophie didn't answer immediately, quiet long enough that Angelina regretted asking. She couldn't imagine her aunt doing anything illegal or immoral, but if she had, perhaps that was an indiscretion best laid to rest with her. When Sophie did speak, her voice was gentle. "I wasn't privy to her reasoning, but it followed her divorce. These things happen. She pulled away. No one thought she wouldn't return."

"She was married?" Angelina had gone through her aunt's papers after her death. There'd been no mention of a marriage in any of them. "She never told me."

"Oh, dear. I'm sure she had her reasons. I'm sorry. I shouldn't have mentioned it."

There was such concern in Sophie's voice, Angelina felt compelled to reassure her. "No, it's okay. My aunt was one of the finest human beings I've ever known. I still miss her every single day. I guess I'm like a child realizing my parents had a life before me, that's all. Was it an ugly divorce?"

"Very. Despite their breakup being clearly his fault, he

didn't handle her departure well, and because of that, unlike her, he became a persona non grata."

"That must have been so difficult for her." Aunt Rudi was the epitome of a soft-spoken, well-educated woman. For her to withdraw from her friends and essentially hide in New Jersey, it really must have been an ugly situation. Not much had ever seemed to intimidate Aunt Rudi. This explained so much, though. Aunt Rudi's compassion for Angelina's broken heart. Her insistence that Angelina didn't need a man.

Sophie sighed. "I should have done more for your aunt. We weren't close, but I could have reached out to her. It happened a long time ago and during a period of my life when I was struggling with my own demons. That's not an excuse—just a fact. I'm sorry I didn't attend her funeral. So much time had passed—"

There was a pause in their conversation. The few times Angelina had imagined what it would be like to meet the powerful woman, she'd never imagined the conversation would be as heartfelt and personal. "My aunt always spoke highly of you. Not every friendship is meant to last a life-time, but she had only good to say about you and your family."

Sophie sniffed before saying, "I'm sorry. This was not the reason I called at all." She cleared her throat. "I wanted to talk to you about Connor Sutton."

That snapped Angelina back to sitting up straight. "Okay."

"I heard you declined a job offer from him."

The whole call felt surreal. Sophie Barrington wanted to talk to her about Connor Sutton? What in the world was going on? "I did. It was nothing personal. I'm looking for something closer to where my son will attend school."

"You have to do what's best for your family, of course. I probably shouldn't get involved, but I adore Connor. He is truly the sweetest soul."

Sweet? That wasn't the first word Angelina would have used to describe him. "I'm sorry. I'm confused. Is this about the job?"

"Yes and no. I couldn't stand back silently and simply hope this works out. The days of me doing that are over. If it's not too much, I have one request. I understand you don't know me or owe me anything, but I would forever be grateful if you made me one promise."

Angelina took a moment before answering. "If it's one I'm comfortable with—sure."

"Whatever happens between you and Connor—be kind to him. He'll act like nothing bothers him, but he is all heart. If you're looking for a good man who will do just about anything to make sure you have what you need . . . that's Connor. He'll make you laugh and be your biggest cheerleader. You can be yourself with a man like him. He needs someone who will love him—all the wonderful sides of him."

Wow, that was a lot to take in. "Mrs. Barrington—"

"Sophie, please."

"Sophie, I'm afraid you may have confused me with someone else. I've only met Connor one time, and it was to give him a tour of a school. He did offer me a job, but we're not—we've never . . ."

"Then take the position with the Landon Foundation. See where it goes. If nothing else, you'll have a good addition to your résumé if you decide not to stay. A recommendation from Clay Landon will open many doors for you."

It would. Still, the whole thing felt disingenuous. "I'm not clear on the expectations of this employment opportunity. Is it reliant on me agreeing to 'see' Connor? I feel uncomfortable with the whole idea. I believe I should stay with my initial instinct and respectfully decline the opportunity."

"Oh, dear. Have I made things worse?"

Angelina didn't like to lie. "A little."

"He's such a sweetheart. I do hope you change your mind. He really likes you. I probably shouldn't have said that, either. I'm hanging up now. Good luck. And now that you have my number, regardless of how things turn out with Connor, don't hesitate to call if you ever need anything."

"Thank you," Angelina said and continued to feel a bit dazed by the conversation after Sophie hung up. She sat there, phone on lap, going over everything Sophie had said . . . then every interaction she'd had with Connor.

He likes me.

I kinda got that from his offer to take me to dinner in Venice.

I can't work for him.

She called Aly, who thankfully picked up right away, then added Joanna to the call. This story was too incredible to tell twice. After she brought them both up to speed, she asked them for their advice.

"You have to take the job. How can you even think about not?" Joanna exclaimed.

"I'm in agreement. This is next level romantic," Aly said.

"Is it? He offered me a job because he hopes I'll sleep with him. There are laws against that, aren't there?"

Joanna said, "Hear that sound? That's me slapping myself in the forehead because I can't believe you are considering turning down an opportunity I would kill for. Sophie Barrington told you what this is about. He likes you. You turned down his dinner offer. You have a gorgeous, rich man, trying to figure out how to spend more time with you and you're putting a bad spin on it? Please, give him my number."

Am I putting a negative spin on it?

Aunt Rudi wouldn't have approved of any part of this, because it's wrong. Or because some man hurt her so badly she never gave another man a chance to?

I know what it's like to be used and tossed aside.

Is that the only lens I see men through now?

The only way I'll ever be able to?

Aly piped in. "The situation is unusual, I agree, but sometimes life tosses us life-changing opportunities. Most people aren't brave enough to take the leap of faith and go for it. Evaluate this as I would. Best case. Worst case. Is the possibility of the first worth the potential of the second?"

"Best case? You mean with the job? Or with Connor?"

"Both," Aly said. "Either."

"I guess the best case would be I love the job . . . and marry a movie star? Does this even sound realistic?"

Ignoring the question, Aly asked, "Worst case?"

That was a harder one to answer. "The job doesn't work out and I discover Connor Sutton is a pervert with connections."

"Wow, you really are a pessimist," Joanna said.

"Aly asked for worst case," Angelina defended.

Aly added, "I don't think Sophie Barrington would call to convince you to take a job for a pervert. Is that really the impression you have of Connor Sutton? It didn't sound that way when you described him to us the other day."

"No," Angelina conceded. "No, he didn't come across that way at all. I can't picture him doing anything inappropriate."

"Then I'd take the job," Aly said with conviction.

"Seriously?" Angelina asked, and her heart started to pound at the possibility. "Mrs. Tellier started working there already because she wanted to. How bad could it be?"

"That's my almost optimistic friend," Joanna joked. "Good for you. Don't forget to call me daily with updates. I'm going to live vicariously through you on this one."

"Me too," Aly said with a laugh.

Angelina twirled a hand through her loose curls. "If I say yes to this job, what would I do with Whitney during the day?"

"What job?" Whitney asked as he hopped over the back of the couch and took a seat beside her.

"Talk to you two later," Angelina said, ending her call

with her two friends who both wished her luck. She turned to her son. "I was offered a position at an office for the Landon Foundation in New York City. Interestingly enough, Mrs. Tellier was hired there first."

"Hey, she got you a job. That's great. See, things work out."

"Yeah. I guess. Anyway, if I take the job, I'd be commuting into the city. That would be too long of a day for you to be here alone."

"So, we'd have to move to the city?"

It was difficult to tell if he liked the idea or not. "Probably."

"I'm okay with that."

"We'd have to get you into a school there."

"Okay."

Just like that? "It would be a big move for both of us. Are you sure?"

"I've been looking at schools affiliated with Columbia University. Some of them are in New York and two of them have awesome soccer teams."

It was the first time Whitney had seemed excited about choosing a potential school to enroll in. "If you're onboard, I'll tell them I'll take the job contingent on finding an apartment and a school you like."

"You can do that?"

Angelina's face warmed as she remembered the way Connor had looked at her before she'd offended him. "I think so. They seem to really want me."

By "they" I mean Connor.

And I'm either bravely taking a leap of faith because this is a life-changing opportunity I'd be crazy to pass up.

Or . . . nope, I'm not going to put a bad spin on this.

Connor Sutton . . . please be the man Sophie Barrington thinks you are.

Chapter Nine

TWO WEEKS LATER, Connor paced back and forth in front of Kimmie's desk. Mrs. Tellier called out from her desk across the room. "You'll wear the rug out if you keep that up."

Connor paused and adjusted the sleeves of his jacket. "Are you sure today is the day she's scheduled to start? It's nine fifteen."

Kimmie didn't turn to check her calendar. "I told her it was okay to be here by ten. Her son started at his new school today as well. She'll be here."

"Her office is all set?" he asked.

"Everything is ready for her," Mrs. Tellier assured him.

"I actually have a few phone meetings scheduled this morning. We're looking into buying an apartment building in downtown Brooklyn. I'm coordinating with some local urban renewal experts to rejuvenate not just the building, but also the area surrounding it. If we do this right, the families of veterans will have an affordable community option. Clay has the job-assistance program in place. The medical support. I'm adding a community center and a park."

Kimmie's smile was bright. "And you weren't sure you could do this."

He looked at her with a confident smile. "It's a big endeavor, but these families have no money, and I completely know what that's like. They don't want a handout—they want opportunities."

Mrs. Tellier sighed. "If Angelina doesn't marry you, I'll marry you myself."

Connor's hands went cold and he cleared his throat. "I never said I wanted to marry her. Let's take this whole thing down a notch. She needed a job. I wanted to see her again. She may not want to date me."

Kimmie chuckled. "You're adorable when you're nervous."

"I'm not nervous. Women throw themselves at me all the time. That's all Angelina is—just another woman. You both need to relax."

"*We* need to relax?" Mrs. Tellier joked.

Connor stopped when he realized he'd begun pacing again. He'd had two weeks to think about this day and plan how he would act. If he didn't calm down he was going to blow it. "Don't you two have a book to work on?"

"Yes, sir," Kimmie said with a salute.

"Connor," Mrs. Tellier said in a more serious tone.

Connor had already started walking toward his office. He stopped and turned. "Yes?"

"Just be yourself and you'll do fine," she said.

He nodded then walked through his office door and closed it behind him. *Myself? I don't even know who that is anymore.*

He moved to stand at the large window behind his desk and looked out over the city. His brother Dylan wanted to know when he intended to start his next movie. His agent was asking the same thing.

Connor had a pile of scripts to read through.

He hadn't started any of them yet.

It wasn't that he didn't enjoy acting. Hell, he still couldn't believe how much people got paid to pretend to be someone else. The problem was he felt like acting didn't stop when he stepped off the set. Part of him wanted to walk away from all of it, but he couldn't.

He loved his family and this was now who they were.

Working for Clay's foundation was surprisingly more rewarding than intimidating . . . as long as he remembered to be the Connor Sutton his fans thought he was. Was it worth it? Hell, yes. The more families he met through the program, the more he realized the enormity of the impact he could have on their lives. It was humbling. Such power belonged in the hands of a better educated man, someone more deserving.

All I can do is my best to make things happen for them and try not to fuck up.

His first business call rang through. He did his impression of Bradford and negotiated the cost of the building down significantly, then put them on hold for no reason other than to make them wait. Working off the advice he'd received at his last meeting with his team, he returned with a non-negotiable list of things that would need to be fixed on the building. When the seller agreed to them, Connor nearly let out a whoop, but kept his cool.

He couldn't break character. Not while so many were relying on him.

Claire called him next to remind him of a photo shoot the next day he'd agreed to months earlier. It was for an online subscription calendar, the proceeds of which went to support local animal rescues. Who could say no to helping puppies and kittens?

"What should I wear?" he'd asked.

She'd laughed. "They provide the outfits, but the theme is you on the beach throughout the seasons. Apparently women want to see that chest of yours twelve months of the year."

Great. Thankfully, he wasn't self-conscious. There was a difference between being on a beach, though, and prancing around in trunks in a studio while someone called out for him to smile more, or less, or differently.

It took acting to a whole new level.

After hanging up, he pocketed his hands and let out a long sigh. Any moment, Angelina would walk in. In his fantasy, he swept her into his office, popped open two ice-cold beers, and laid the whole messed up story out for her. They laughed, she proclaimed the real him was so much sexier than his public persona, they fucked on his desk and lived happily ever after.

Sometimes his fantasy involved that leading to them fucking on his couch.

A few times against the wall.

Once in front of the window.

More than once on the plush rug.

He'd had enough time to think about this that he'd imagined some creative things they could do with the other furniture in the room as well.

It was a dangerously addictive fantasy to indulge in. The reality of their relationship was that so far she'd said no, followed by no with a side of hell no.

And now she works for me.

Why did I think this was a good idea?

There was a chance seeing her again wouldn't live up to the hype. Two weeks of thinking about her might have built her up to be more than she was. Sure, she was pretty, but was she really the best-looking woman he'd ever met? In male time, two weeks was practically an eternity. When he finally did see her again whatever zing had been might be gone.

It wasn't as if he'd pined for her for fourteen days. He'd gone to dinner with a couple of women. Both had asked him out. He'd had no reason to refuse.

He hadn't fucked either of them, though. Which was— unsettling.

They'd both been beautiful.

They'd both been funny.

Smart too.

Somehow, though, his dick had stayed in his pants . . . on strike. Connor would have been concerned, would have rushed to the nearest doctor, if it weren't for the fact that every time he thought about seeing Angelina again he got an instant boner.

He glanced down at the tented front of his pants. *Dude, since when are you so picky?*

He'd tried to talk to Dylan about his dilemma. After Dylan had stopped laughing . . . something that had taken a good amount of time . . . he'd assured Connor there was a cure. Sex with Angelina, even one time, would solve the issue. Men only obsessed about what they couldn't have.

That was Dylan's theory, anyway.

Connor wasn't convinced it was that simple. There were plenty of women in the world who wouldn't sleep with him, but that had never stopped his dick from working before.

Still, the idea of sex with Angelina was enough to have his heart pounding and his face flushing. *I would definitely fuck her.*

If she asked me to.

I'm her boss now, I can't ask her.

Wait a minute. Why did I agree to this? Clay got lost in Australia looking for a bathroom in the Outback and I'm taking advice from him?

I'll probably never have sex again.

Shit.

Connor froze when he heard Kimmie's voice rise in welcome. Angelina had arrived.

His chest constricted.

His stomach fluttered.

He flexed his hands at his sides.

Any moment Kimmie would announce Angelina's arrival. He'd have to open the door to his office and choose which version of him to be. The Barringtons practically had

Angelina and him walking down the aisle together.

He just wanted to see her again. Work their way around his office, see where that led them. The possibilities were endless . . . boats, private jets . . . he'd heard helicopters held potential . . . although he did wonder what the pilot thought of that going on behind him. It probably required one of the larger aircrafts. Yeah. Definitely not one of the four seaters.

There was a knock on his door. "Mr. Sutton, Miss Kroll is here." Kimmie stuck her head in the door she had opened just enough to peek around. "Would you like to see her now or should I settle her into her office first?"

He rolled his shoulders and took several deep breaths. Mrs. Tellier had told him to simply be himself. He would have considered that wise advice if he didn't know his own track record with women. If all he wanted with Angelina was sex . . . then sure he could be whoever he wanted to be with her.

But she was different.

No other woman had left him tongue-tied and unsure.

None had ever felt important enough to make him worried they'd like him.

That had to mean something.

Could it be that Angelina really was . . . *the one*?

He swayed on his feet at the thought and his hands clenched. *If so, everything I say is important. This is a day we'll tell our kids about.*

Kids.

He swayed again. *I want kids. Me. Holy shit. When did that happen?*

Kimmie gave him an odd look and said loudly, "Oh, I'm sorry. I didn't realize you were on the phone. I'll take her to her office first."

He nodded because that's all he was capable of in that moment.

She closed the door.

He went to his desk, sat down behind it, and laid his hands flat on its surface. Angelina was a refined woman. Intelligent. Responsible. She wouldn't be impressed by his greasy jean-wearing, off-road driving, water-tower-climbing old self. That wasn't the Connor she'd met. It wasn't the one she'd agreed to work for.

My family doesn't even want that Connor anymore.

His phone rang again with a call from New York's mayor. He wanted to discuss the park Connor was proposing and what the city could and couldn't do. The old Connor would have been excited by the call and shown it. That wasn't how to win in the city, though. Connor played it cool, let the mayor talk himself out, gave him enough time to second-guess his proposal . . . and won more concessions from him without even asking for them. Bradford was right about intelligent people. In response to sustained silence they often talked themselves right out of sounding smart.

When the call ended, he sent a message out to his team so they could act on the mayor's concessions before he changed his mind. He also called the legal department to get everything sewn up for the purchase of the building. Clay's signature was the one required, but the legwork was done, and if the team's enthusiastic response was any indication—

Connor had negotiated good deals.

He leaned back in his chair, folding his hands behind his head. New Connor wasn't a bad thing. He was hard-working, socially responsible, and effective. Rocking forward again, Connor flipped through the top script on his desk. His agent said his name was gold right now. He could name his price if he accepted any of these roles. Grant promised to take whatever amount Connor made and grow it into a fortune.

All he had to do was not be himself.

Old Connor would have already been at Angelina's desk, sitting on the corner of it, making her laugh with stories of ridiculous situations he'd found himself in over the years. He wouldn't have felt the need to conceal how he felt. Women liked him.

Or they used to.

Back when I liked myself.

Despite how much he'd anticipated Angelina's reappearance in his life, he chose to stay in his office rather than seek her out. New Connor couldn't bound into rooms. Even if he wanted to, he didn't have the luxury of time to flirt inappropriately with his newest employee. There were too many emails to answer, too many people counting on him, a pile of scripts to read.

Angelina would just have to wait.

LATE IN THE afternoon, Angelina gathered her purse from the side drawer in her desk, stood, and hesitated. Overall, it had been a great first day. It had consisted of introductions to the various departments and her support role for each. She felt welcomed and needed. Her office was one door down from Mrs. Tellier and Kimmie's and their perma-smiles. Mrs. Tellier repeatedly gushed over how much she was enjoying her new job and she wasn't alone. Almost everyone Angelina met that day was a walking commercial for Connor Sutton. He was amazing to work for, an invigorating asset to the program's growth, and someone who got along as easily with wounded veterans as he did politicians and the press.

Kimmie said he was the kind of person people would walk through fire for.

Angelina hadn't expected Connor to be so well liked.

It made her question if she'd allowed the stress of her old job to taint her impression of him. There had definitely been an attraction there, but she was having difficulty reconciling the arrogant, closed-off man she'd met with the one everyone else seemed to know. Although, as she thought back, she had glimpsed another side of him . . . when he'd spoken to the soccer team. Was that the real him? The side everyone else saw in him?

It felt wrong to leave the office without even thanking him for the job.

That's not the only reason I'm having trouble leaving.

Angelina had spent so much time worrying about how she'd handle any advances from him that she hadn't considered how disappointed she would be if he didn't seek her out. She checked the clock. She had a little time before she picked Whitney up from his after-school enrichment program. *I should just stop by Connor's office, thank him, and go.*

"Miss Kroll."

Angelina spun around at the sound of Connor's voice. There he was, filling the doorway of her office, and so damn good-looking her jaw dropped a little. He didn't smile so she held her own back. "Mr. Sutton." It was all she said because it was all that came to mind. She'd convinced herself that she'd imagined how good it felt just to be near him. Her body hummed for him like it was already his for the taking. She swallowed hard and gripped her purse at her side.

"How was your first day?" It was an innocent question, yet the way his gaze raked over her was anything but. Her skin warmed as if in response to his caress.

"It was wonderful." Even to herself her voice sounded husky and strangled. *What is wrong with me? This is a good job. Whitney seemed happy enough with his school choice. I have my life back on track. Having sex with him would put all of that at risk again.*

And why am I imagining sex with a man who isn't even flirting with me?

I've worked way too hard to make a good life for Whitney and me to start making irresponsible decisions again just because he has the kind of lips a woman wants to feel run over every inch of her body.

He's so big. So strong.

What would it be like to be taken by a man who could lift me with ease?

"Good," he said abruptly. "Have a good night."

Just as he was turning away, Angelina said, "Wait."

He stopped and turned back.

"Thank you for this opportunity." God, she sounded lame.

He nodded. "I heard your son started at a new school today as well."

"He did."

"Which one?"

"Binston Preparatory. It's affiliated with Columbia University."

"Impressive. You must be proud of him."

"I am. He's brilliant."

His expression softened. "That's not surprising."

She blushed. Of all the things she could have responded with, she had no idea why she said, "Every parent worries if they're doing the best for their child. Sometimes I feel like I am. Sometimes I'm not so sure. He signed up for computer coding after school, but he chose the Binston because of their soccer team." Connor didn't say anything, just looked back at her as if waiting for more. She added, "I'm afraid he's choosing what he thinks I want him to do rather than what will make him happy."

Connor studied her face then stepped closer. "He's lucky to have a mother like you."

"That's nice of you to say." Angelina licked her bottom lip. *Sorry, Whitney, you're the last thing I'm thinking about right now.*

He came to a stop just a foot before her. The air sizzled between them. He opened his mouth as if about to say something. Or possibly kiss her.

Angelina leaned closer, ready for either.

Kimmie's voice had them both jumping back a little. "Mr. Sutton, I wanted to remind you about the thing you have scheduled for tomorrow. Claire said she has a conflicting appointment so she can't make it. Have you considered taking Miss Kroll? Might be a good way for her to get out there and start making connections."

"When I want suggestions from you, Mrs. Sanchez, I'll ask for them," Connor said, his expression closing off. Without saying more, he spun on his heel, strode past his secretary, and disappeared down the hall.

"Well that was clear enough," Angelina said. And a bit of a kick in the pants.

Kimmie didn't look put off. In fact, she was smiling, which absolutely made no sense. She stepped into Angelina's office and lowered her voice. "He's so sensitive when it comes to you. At least he came by to say hello."

Sensitive? Connor Sutton? *Am I missing something?* "He was just checking on how my first day went." A thought came to her and she had to ask, "What kind of 'thing' does he have tomorrow?"

Kimmie rolled her eyes in a full circle before answering. "Now I'm not so sure I should say. My problem is I spend so much time creating situations for my characters to fall in love that I can't help but want to nudge the two of you together. Now that I think about it, though, I can see why tomorrow might not work in reality. Even for a romance it might be a little over the top." She tapped her chin. "Or really hot. I just changed my mind. I'm definitely writing that scene into my next book."

"You're an author?"

"Sure am. I almost gave up on the dream, but then I met Mr. Sutton, and he convinced me that dreams are worth following. I'm writing a three-book series. When I finish the last one I'm going to put them up for sale and dedicate them to my husband and Connor Sutton. Without both of them I wouldn't have finished the first and I'm halfway done with the last one. They're going to kick off a whole new career for me, I just know it. Mrs. Tellier is spicing up the sex scenes. Wow, that woman knows her stuff."

Following her instincts, Angelina excused herself and headed over to Connor's office. His door was closed. Some might have taken that as a no, but Angelina's curiosity outweighed everything else in that moment. "Mr. Sutton?"

"Come in."

She pushed the door open and stepped through it. He didn't turn to greet her, instead simply continued to look out the window beside his desk. It wasn't until she was standing in his office that she realized she didn't have anything to say. All she knew was that she didn't want her first day to end with him walking away. "I just wanted to say thank you again. This is the perfect job for me, and I'm grateful to have it."

He folded his arms across his chest and turned toward her. "It's a photo shoot tomorrow."

"Oh."

"A calendar for local animal rescues. Me in swim trunks, themed to each season. Hopefully without having to explain why I won't wear a speedo. Probably hours of me holding puppies and kittens while pretending I'm actually on a beach or anywhere they think I'd be in a bathing suit with a cat. I figured I'd spare you that."

The images that rocked through Angelina made it near impossible to breathe. "It doesn't sound like something I'd mind."

His brows come together briefly, and she could have sworn there was a spark of humor in his eyes. She decided she must have imagined it, though, when he frowned. "It's for a good cause. I'll have to pretend I'm enjoying myself."

And I'll have to pretend I'm not.

It was difficult to think clearly while his attention was focused so intently on her. She swallowed hard and clasped her hands in front of her. Connor Sutton was a complicated man. If he was the sensitive, caring man his employees said he was . . . the one she thought she'd glimpsed during his visit to the school . . . then why did he also seem defensive and closed off? As soon as she thought of a possibility, she blurted it out. "Are you worried what I'll think of you?"

Her question hung in the air between them.

He didn't deny it nor did he give any indication that her guess was correct. He just continued to look at her with those incredible eyes of his until she nearly forgot she'd asked a question at all.

Once the silence dragged on to an uncomfortable length, she cleared her throat and began to backpedal. "I'm sorry. I don't know why I said that. Of course you don't care what I'd think. You hardly know me."

His frown deepened. "What are you looking for, Angelina Kroll?"

In that moment? With the job? In her bed? She wasn't sure, but she answered as honestly as she could. "I thought I knew, but I'm not so sure I do anymore."

He dropped his arms and stepped closer. In a tone close to a growl, he said, "I'm not the man you think I am."

Her lips parted and her breathing quickened. "That would be a relief because my first impression of you wasn't that good."

There it was, that light of humor in his eyes again. He stepped even closer. "I'm who I need to be, not who I want to be."

Lord, he smelled as good as he looked. He was so tall that she had to crane her neck back to look at him, and broad chested enough that she would have just as happily closed her eyes and wrapped herself around his middle. Even in a suit, the definition of his pecks made her want to run her hands up his flat stomach and over them. She was too levelheaded, though, to let herself do it. "Are any of us who we wish we were? In my mind I'm a hell of lot more exciting than I'd ever allow myself to actually be."

A smile curled one side of his mouth and desire shone in his eyes. "I'd test your resolve, but that would be irresponsible and I'm not that anymore."

There was a sexual sincerity in his words that struck a chord in her. Just above a whisper, she said, "I'm not either."

He traced the line of her cheek gently. "Things were a lot easier when I didn't think about how my actions would affect anyone else."

"Yes." She understood that feeling so well. "My son is and has to remain my first priority. I need this job more than I need . . ." She didn't finish her sentence, sure he'd understand.

"Your job here is secure. You shouldn't come to the photo shoot, but if you want to, be here by nine."

Before she had a chance to respond, her phone beeped to remind her it was time to get Whitney. "I should go. I can't be late for pickup on the first day."

His smile widened. "Then go."

Damn, it was hard to when he looked at her with promise in his eyes. Ever since Whitney's biological father had signed off on his rights to him, relieved to not be part of the journey, Angelina had found it easy to say no to men. She couldn't explain why it was different with Connor.

It simply was.

She forced herself to turn and start walking away. At the door, she stopped and looked back at him. She opened her mouth to wish him luck on his photo shoot. He was right—she shouldn't go to the photo shoot. The responsible thing to do would be to hide in her office and kick ass at her job.

I shouldn't go, but I really want to.

She left without saying what she'd decided, because she really didn't know what she'd do.

Chapter Ten

"LOOK THIS WAY," the woman behind the camera said. "Try to relax. We'll get a few shots of you alone then we'll bring out a puppy."

Connor turned his head toward the photographer and tried to take her advice, but she wasn't the reason he was tense. Thoughts of Angelina were distracting him. The way she sought him out the day before, leaned in, licked her lips. She wanted him.

So, where was she?

Why wasn't he exchanging secret smiles with her between poses?

What was he doing wrong?

"Strong eyes are powerful, but the mood of the calendar is more playful. You're a gentle giant. Confident. Imagine you're at your girlfriend's house, she has the most adorable kitten, you pick it up, cuddle it, then she walks in. Make me believe I'm the most beautiful woman in the world. Look at the camera and see the woman you want more than you've ever wanted anyone."

Great, she wants me to think about Angelina more? How

will that put me in a better mood?

"I like your posture. And you look amazing. Try shaking out your arms. See if you can release some of that tension."

He did as he was asked but only grew more irritated. *I used to have a swagger women found irresistible. All I had to do was nod toward the bedroom and their clothing started to fly. I can't even get Angelina to watch me take off mine.*

So, yeah, I'm tense.

I haven't had sex since I met her. Can a man die from prolonged abstinence? I don't know, I've never experienced a dry spell before. For all I know my dick will shrivel up and drop off. God knows, it hasn't worked right since Angelina gave me a tour that was so long and so boring I had time to imagine a life with her.

I could have my pick of women right now. What is my problem?

"Why don't we take a break?" the photographer suggested, excusing herself from the room.

A few minutes later Connor's phone rang from the dressing room and was surprisingly fetched quickly by one of the photographer's assistants. As soon as he saw the caller, he understood. "Hi, Claire."

"Connor. What's going on?"

"I'm mostly naked and apparently not living up to your famous photographer's expectations."

"She said you look angry. Did something happen?"

"I'm not angry. Confused. Not angry."

"Okay, what in particular are you confused about today? Give me something to work with." When Connor didn't immediately volunteer something, Claire lowered her voice. "Is it about that woman you like? The one Bradford was looking into? Is she involved in the embezzlement somehow?"

Connor waved a hand dismissively through the air. "No. Of course not. She's as strait-laced as they come."

"But this is about her?"

"I don't want to talk about Angelina. If you really want me smiling for this photo shoot, you'd be better off telling me a joke."

"Knock, knock."

"Who's there?"

"Someone who wants to know what's going on in your head. I can't help you if you don't talk to me."

Connor shot a glare at the people still in the room. They hastily retreated. Honestly, there were perks to being a badass. Once he was alone, Connor said, "I'm not used to this feeling."

"What feeling?"

"Liking a woman who may not like me back."

Claire laughed, seemed to realize he wasn't joking, and sobered. "I'm sorry. I did not mean to laugh. So, why do you think she doesn't like you?"

"She's not here, is she?"

"All right. I'm getting a clearer picture of what's going on. You invited Angelina to your shoot and she said no."

"I didn't invite her. I told her she shouldn't come. But she looked like she wanted to come. I used to understand women. I don't get Angelina."

"This might take me a moment to unravel. You told her not to come and now you're upset she's not there?"

He ran a hand through his hair. "When you say it that way it sounds bad."

She chuckled. "Any way you'd say it would sound the same."

He rolled his eyes, but conceded to himself that she had a point. "What happened to being the person who says nice things to make me feel better?"

"I'm a life coach, not your mother. I say what you need to hear not what you want to. You're disappointed. I get it. You only have one decision to make. Do you want to do the calendar or not? If not, I want you to go into the other room, meet some of those homeless puppies and kittens and ask yourself that question again. Then, once you decide the calendar is worth doing, put on your big boy acting pants and smile."

"They won't give me pants, something about needing to see my incredible thighs," he joked.

"There's the Connor I know. Is this about more than Angelina? You can tell me."

Claire had an uncanny ability to cut right through bull-shit to a problem. He looked down at his light blue swim trunks and kicked at a pile of fake snow. He wasn't from a family who talked about their emotions, especially not after his mother died, but Claire was good at her job. She could dig past a person's defenses, like a doctor asking a person to drop their drawers, and somehow leave someone feeling better rather than worse for having been honest. "Lately I feel like I'm losing myself, Claire. I'm not a model. I don't belong in movies. I like running the Landon Foundation because I get to meet regular people—people like me. They don't see me, though. All they see is my suit and the Connor Sutton you created. I don't recognize the man I see in the mirror. All I know is that he doesn't like much about me, either."

There was a pause. When Claire began speaking again, her voice was softer. "That man in the mirror—he's wrong. The old you, the Connor who welcomed me into the family . . . he was amazing. I miss him."

"Sure."

"Hey, he's the reason I'm at a cake tasting today. Ian and I wouldn't be together if you and Dylan hadn't kidnapped him and brought him to my hotel room."

Connor smiled as he remembered how surprisingly easy it had been to duct tape Ian Barrington and stuff him into a laundry cart. "He was so pissed."

"But he needed a shake-up and you gave him one because you cared about him—and me. Part of your charm has always been how little you worry about what others think of you. If I took that away from you—I didn't mean to. My goal was to help you, not make you into someone you don't recognize."

"It doesn't matter. The old me doesn't fit"—he waved his hand in the air—"this."

"Then make *this* fit him. Take the rules I taught you and make them your own. They're not meant to confine you . . . they're meant to free you. Like learning a second language or culture. You can master something new without turning your back on who you are in your heart. This new Connor doesn't have to be you. You can put him on and take him off along with your suit."

"Wouldn't that make me a fraud?"

"No, it would mean you're smart enough to know that some situations call for certain behaviors while others don't. I don't swear in front of Sophie and Dale, but I still swear like a sailor when I'm angry and not with them. Ian and Bradford have done a lot of things they could never share at the dinner table, but that doesn't mean they shouldn't have done them. I don't know if you want my opinion when it comes to Angelina, but I have a feeling if she met the real you and saw the reason you have more than one side . . . she'd love you as much as the rest of us do."

"Thanks, Claire. That helps." He caught his reflection in a mirror across the room and cracked himself up by flexing like a bodybuilder. "And don't worry, I'll rock this photo shoot. I'm in the best shape I've ever been in. I mean, look at that six-pack. That shit belongs in a calendar."

Claire laughed. "Yes, it does. Especially since the calendar will raise money for a good cause. Let yourself have fun today. This doesn't have to be painful. You love animals. Forget about everything else and just cuddle with a few of them. Let the photographer worry about getting the shots she needs."

"I will." The photographer chose that moment to poke her head back in the room. He smiled and waved for her to enter.

He didn't yet know how he would fit his old self into his new life, but for the first time he didn't feel bad about wanting to. It didn't have to be all or nothing. People spoke more than one language, some lived in the city during the week then retreated to the countryside for the weekends.

He remembered his last trip home and groaned when he realized where he'd gone wrong with it. He'd driven his flashy car instead of his old truck. He'd worn his suit instead of his favorite plaid shirt and stained jeans. No wonder his friends hadn't known how to connect with him . . .

I won't make that mistake again.

I'm going to make room for the old me.

Balance.

Aristotle, you really had this life shit down pat. No wonder we're still talking about you.

ACROSS TOWN, ANGELINA was in her new office reading the same email over and over again and cursing Connor Sutton for being the reason she couldn't concentrate. On paper, her life was back on track. Whitney had a good first day at school. He even said he enjoyed the after-school program.

She was gainfully employed in an office full of smiling people.

All she had to do was work hard, keep her head down, and prove she was a valuable asset to the Landon Foundation. She had already identified fresh opportunities for fundraising. If she held the course, losing her job at Reemsly would actually turn out to be a good thing.

As long as I don't have sex with my boss.

She cringed.

Seriously? Is that all I can think about? He's not that amazing. First, he barely speaks. How fun would that be on a date? Second, he's broody. That wouldn't be a good role model for Whitney.

Not that he'll ever meet Whitney, because we're going to keep our relationship purely professional.

When she realized she was staring off into space again, she slapped both of her cheeks lightly then started the email over from the beginning.

"You're right, she's in here," Mrs. Tellier said from the door of her office.

"I told you I saw her come in after Connor left," Kimmie said from beside her.

Without waiting for an invitation, Mrs. Tellier pulled a chair close to Angelina's desk and sat down. "Close up your computer. I didn't want to have to do this, but there doesn't seem to be any other way. Let's go. I'm taking you to Connor's photo shoot."

Kimmie laughed as she pulled up a chair beside her. "I call bullshit. Linda is looking for any excuse to spend a few hours ogling a bare-chested Connor. I'll take you."

Mrs. Tellier turned toward Kimmie and crossed her arms across her chest. "You're married. I should do it."

Kimmie cocked an eyebrow and rolled her eyes. "I'm only thinking of you. At your age, your heart is fragile." She raised a finger as inspiration seemed to hit her. "Plus, a photo shoot would count as research for a future book."

"Research? Really?" Mrs. Tellier scoffed. "That's a

stretch. Fine. You want to call me old . . . I'll throw down my old lady card." She turned to Angelina and gave her sad eyes. "Angelina, I turn seventy in a few months. I'm on a limited budget. My life keeps getting smaller and smaller. I struggle to find reasons to get out of bed each morning. Please, let me be the one to take you to the photo shoot. Give this little old woman one more wonderful memory to make all my lonely nights easier to bear. But hurry, because I don't want to miss a single month of that calendar."

Kimmie's mouth dropped open in mock outrage. "You are the least lonely woman I know." She thumbed at Mrs. Tellier while leaning toward Angelina. "You should hear what she says to her boyfriends on the phone. The woman could be a sex hotline."

Chuckling, Angelina covered her eyes briefly before saying, "Sorry to disappoint both of you, but I'm not going to the shoot."

"You're going," both women said in unison.

Angelina shook her head. "I'm not. I have a ton of emails to read through already. Why don't the two of you go?"

Kimmie looked at Mrs. Tellier and asked, "Was she always this little fun?"

Mrs. Tellier nodded. "Since the day I met her. She acts like she's the only woman who ever got knocked up as a teenager and therefore must spend the rest of her life doing some kind of penance. Her son is an incredible kid. One day I hope she starts celebrating the miracle of him rather than seeing him as a mistake."

Instantly defensive, Angelina rose to her feet and

growled, "I have never considered Whitney a mistake."

Mrs. Tellier didn't even blink at the show of aggression. She shrugged. "Then stop acting like your virginity is something that'll come back if you keep your legs closed long enough. You can have sex without getting pregnant. There's this amazing invention called condoms."

Never. Ever had Angelina heard her speak this way. "Mrs. Tellier, have you been drinking?"

"Oh, Lord. First, my name is Linda. You've known me for over a decade, you can use my first name. Second, I couldn't say anything at Reemsly in case there was a child around. You see any children here? Trust me, Kimmie doesn't care if I say the word condom. Condom. Condom. See? It's fine."

Kimmie leaned over and hugged Mrs. Tel—Linda. "I love this woman."

Slowly, Angelina sank back onto her chair. "I do too. Sorry, Linda. You know how I get when people talk about Whitney."

Linda's expression softened. "I've watched you grow up, Angelina. You're a smart woman, a good mother, and a friend I am thankful to have. To be happy, though, you'll have to forgive the young woman you were before you went to live with your aunt. I didn't know you back then, but I have feeling the young you was pretty wonderful as well. I bet she would have gone to the photo shoot."

"She absolutely would have." Angelina's hands shook slightly as she clasped them on her desk. "But she didn't have the responsibilities I do. This is a good job. Whitney is back in school. I'm not looking for exciting anymore. It's not worth the risk."

Neither Kimmie nor Linda spoke for several moments. *Because they know I'm right. Motherhood and movie stars don't mix.*

Finally, Kimmie pursed her lips and stood. "The one I feel bad for is Connor. I bet the shoot isn't going well."

"Why do you say that?" Angelina asked.

Kimmie wrinkled her nose. "He puts on a good act, but usually Claire goes to things like that with him. With her wedding coming up so fast, he has been flying solo and that hasn't been easy for him."

Linda sighed. "He's such a sweet boy and he tries so hard." She looked Angelina over. "Maybe I'm wrong about the two of you being right for each other. He needs a woman who will love him just the way he is. A woman like that would have to be comfortable enough with herself to help him find the same confidence."

"Hang on, are we talking about the same Connor Sutton?"

Kimmie shook her head. "She doesn't know the real him because he's afraid to show her."

Linda stood. "It's sad, but life is too short to waste it trying to talk sense into these people. They're either going to figure it out, or they won't. When you write Connor as a reluctantly alpha prince, you'll need to add more sex scenes. Readers won't want an overly sensitive hero or an indecisive heroine. When I picture Connor wanting me, he picks me up and fucks my brains out against a wall."

"Me too," Angelina thought, then went beet red when she realized she'd said the words out loud.

Kimmie leaned across the desk. "Then what are you still doing here?"

Suddenly it was difficult to breathe. "This is a bad idea." Her body warmed as she remembered the desire in his eyes when he'd looked at her the night before. "I can't believe I'm even considering going."

"Go." Linda chuckled. "Some of my favorite memories started with me turning off that judgmental voice in my head. What about you, Kimmie?"

Kimmie blushed. "Javier and I are pretty tame, but we do like to role play. We get funny looks when we buy so many costumes at the Halloween store, but that's even part of the fun. Sex is supposed to be fun. Sex with Javier in a gladiator outfit is hilarious and surprisingly erotic."

After glancing over at Angelina's face, Kimmie burst out laughing. "Hey, don't knock it until you've tried it."

"Kimmie Sanchez," Linda said with humor. "You've been holding out on me. I need to hear more about this side of you."

Linking arms with Linda, Kimmie started walking away while saying, "I will as long as you don't tell anyone. Javier would be mortified."

"It'll be our little secret," Linda assured her. "We'll keep it between me, you, and all your readers."

Angelina was smiling as they walked out of earshot. Those two were quite a pair. She could only imagine what Kimmie's books would be like. Probably best sellers. The way nothing seemed impossible lately, they'd be made into movies.

Smile fading, hugging her arms around herself, Angelina went over the last few minutes in her head. She'd never considered Whitney a mistake, and her aunt had never called him one, but Angelina could clearly remember what some of the people in her hometown had said when they'd heard she was pregnant.

Slut.

Whore.

Easy.

The terms were so outdated and sexist, Angelina had told herself they didn't matter. If they didn't, though, why did they still ring so clearly in her head? Were they why she'd never taken Whitney back home? Was that the real wedge between her and her family?

I'm not ashamed of Whitney, but of who I used to be.

She blinked back tears. *It was all so long ago. It shouldn't matter anymore.*

But it does.

I worked so hard to prove that I'm not that person, to prove that I'd never be that person again.

An image of her son filled her thoughts. *But if I'd never been her, I wouldn't have him and I can't imagine a life without him in it. He's a better version of me.*

So, how could it have been a mistake to create him?

When will I stop making myself pay for something I don't regret doing?

Snippets of so many of the long talks she'd had with her

aunt circled in her thoughts. "You don't need a man." "You're better off on your own." "You've come too far to throw away your dreams for a man."

How did I not see that her voice had become the one in my head?

I'm sorry, Aunt Rudi, I don't believe I have to be alone to be successful.

I'm so grateful for the support you gave me. I'm not you, though. I don't want to be alone.

Yes, this is risky, but maybe, Aunt Rudi . . . maybe sometimes taking a risk turns out to be worth it. I have to believe that.

And I refuse to live in the past. I've given those idiots back home too much space in my head. That ends now.

She grabbed her purse and rushed from her office to Kimmie and Linda's. "Where is Connor's photo shoot?"

"There's a car waiting for you downstairs," Kimmie said with a huge grin that was mirrored on Linda's face.

"Don't forget to pick Whitney up from school," Linda said.

"I'm sure this won't take—It's not like we're not going to—I'll remember, thanks," Angelina said with a smile as she turned on her heel and rushed down the hallway. She didn't want to miss any of the months, either.

Chapter Eleven

DRESSED CONSERVATIVELY IN a navy sheath dress with matching jacket, Angelina felt out of place as soon as she was greeted by a young receptionist in oversized pants, a white T-shirt with a black vest. There was probably no more than a five-year age difference, but looking at the other woman made Angelina wish she'd worn her hair in a less severe style. She caught a reflection of herself in the glass of a large window. *I look like a tax collector.*

Or a building inspector.

What am I doing?

"You must be Miss Kroll," the receptionist said with a smile.

"I am."

"Mr. Sutton told me to bring you right in. Isn't he the best? When I heard he was making a calendar to raise money for local animal shelters, I considered asking him to marry me right then, but then he told us to watch for you. I'm sure there are other gorgeous, successful, socially conscious men out there." Her eyes narrowed. "I don't know you, but I hate you a little bit. Follow me."

They walked through a door into a large open loft that was divided into monthly sets. One had sand and a beach chair. Another had a tree with bright yellow and orange leaves.

"Looks like he's still in the winter area. I'll tell him you're here," the woman said.

Giving into a burst of uncertainty, Angelina said, "No. I don't want to interrupt. Would it be okay for me to watch for a few minutes, and I'll just announce my presence when he takes a break?"

"Whatever. He's going to be so happy to see you. I hope they catch that moment on film."

Angelina's stomach quivered at that. Everyone seemed to think Connor had feelings for her. They saw a softer side than he'd shown her. Which was the real him?

Following instructions from the receptionist Angelina headed to January and froze when she saw Connor. He was in bright gold bathing trunks beside a fake snowman. The photographer asked him to pick up a snowball and throw it. Her heart thudded wildly in her chest and he seemed to move in slow motion, muscles bunching as he did. His smile was natural and Angelina knew which calendar every women would be buying for Christmas. God, the man was perfection.

"Okay, release the puppy," the photographer said. "Let's see if we can get a shot of him catching that snowball."

The hundred pound or so Saint Bernard that bounded toward Connor from off set didn't look much like a puppy. Connor called to it then tossed what looked like a white tennis ball into the air. The dog ignored the ball and launched himself up as if expecting Connor to be able to catch him.

Angelina held her breath.

Connor's eyes widened and he shifted his weight. The sound of the large dog slamming into his chest was followed by exclamations from onlookers. "Easy boy," Connor said with a laugh that boomed through the room.

A handler came rushing in. "I'm so sorry. We've been working on his jumping. It's why he was returned to the shelter. Jumping puppies are cute when they're little. He doesn't have a lick of aggression in him, but he scared his first family because they couldn't control him."

Connor held the massive puppy away from his face to evade its enthusiastic tongue. "What's his name?"

"Button. He was the smallest in his litter. His family thought that meant he wouldn't get that big, but he's nowhere near done growing."

"Hi, Button. Who's a big scary dog?" The puppy whined and squirmed, trying to lap at Connor's face. "Not you. Are you going to be good if I put you down?"

The wild whoosh of the puppy's tail made no promises.

"I can use this as well," the photographer called out. "Get out of the shot, Martin."

The handler stepped off set.

Gently, Connor lowered the puppy onto its feet. "Sit." The pup's behind approached, but didn't touch the floor. Tongue hanging out, it seemed to be smiling up at Connor. Surprisingly, Connor was smiling right back.

Connor crouched with his hands on his thighs. "Who wants to catch a tennis ball? Do you want to catch a tennis ball?"

When the puppy launched upward, Connor laughed and stepped back. "Not me. A ball." He picked another fake snowball off the ground and waved it in front of the dog. "See, this is a ball."

The puppy continued bouncing in place. When Connor tossed the ball up in the air, the pup launched itself forward and used Connor's chest as a springboard to jump higher. Taken unaware, Connor stumbled backward and landed on his back in a pile of snow. Tennis ball in mouth, the puppy pounced him.

There was a real joy to Connor's laughter that made it impossible to not laugh along. The dog was utterly ridiculous and Connor was loving it. If Angelina had thought Connor was attractive before, he was now jaw-dropping off-the-charts her type.

"Good boy," Connor said as he sat up and took the dog by the face. "You caught it. Good dog."

The puppy whined again and gave a full body wiggle.

"No more," Connor said firmly as he pushed the pup off his lap. "Sit."

Unbelievably, ball in mouth, the puppy did as Connor asked.

Connor stood, brushed the fake snowflakes off him and smiled at the puppy. "I'm the alpha in this relationship. I know, I know, it's not fair, but I have opposable thumbs and you probably still shit on the rug. I stopped doing that years ago, which puts me at an advantage here."

"He likes you," Martin said as he stepped onto the set again.

So do I.

"I grew up with a Newfoundland. I still miss her. What is a dog like Button doing in the city?"

Martin shrugged. "People don't think decisions through sometimes. I bet he was cute at eight weeks old."

Connor gave the pup a pat on the head. "He's cute now, just big." He bent again to pet the pup. Button rolled onto his back and Connor gave it a hearty rub. When he stood, Button leapt to his feet, but before he jumped Connor told him to sit again then praised him when he did. "Tell me if he doesn't find a good home. I know people who would love him."

Angelina looked around the room. The men were smiling. The women were practically swooning. He could probably go home with any of them, regardless of their sex. *And he wants me?*

The one who can't even remember what cutting loose and having fun feels like?

What would I be to him? An indulgence in curiosity?

A meaningless fling?

Would that be enough for me?

And then what? Could we adult and continue to work together?

"Did you get the shot you needed?" he asked the photographer.

"Sure did. Go change into the trunks with hearts on

them and meet me in February."

He nodded then looked in Angelina's direction. She dropped her purse then scrambled to pick it up as he walked toward her. By the time she straightened he was right in front of her.

"You're here," he said, those blue eyes of his giving none of his feelings away.

She cleared her throat. "I am."

Despite the others in the room, it was just the two of them . . . nothing and no one else mattered in that moment. A smile spread across his face. "You do like me."

Her face warmed, but she smiled back. "I guess I do."

"I'm glad." He lifted her by her waist and swung her around. It was exhilarating. She laughed in surprised delight. When he came to a stop, he lowered her slowly, letting her slide down his bare chest and come to a rest against the evidence of his excitement. "I like you too."

Apparently and with impressive size.

Wow.

She steadied herself by holding on to his muscular, bare arms. She had to remind herself that they weren't alone. "Don't let me interrupt your photo shoot."

"What photo shoot?" he asked playfully.

She ran a hand up his chest and breathed in the clean, masculine scent of him. "I can't be the reason animal shelters don't get funded. Get your ass into that heart bathing suit."

His eyes lit with challenge. "I will on one condition."

Oh, Lord, is it wrong that my answer is already yes?
"Which is?"

He bent and whispered into her ear, "Lose the jacket."

When he raised his head, their eyes met, and she knew one yes would lead to more. Without breaking eye contact, she stepped back and placed her purse on a nearby chair then slid her jacket off and dropped it on top of her purse. The way his gaze roved over her one would have thought her modest, sleeveless dress was a whole lot more revealing.

"Beautiful," he said in a guttural tone.

After licking her bottom lip, she said, "You're not so bad yourself."

A smile returned to his eyes. "Wait until you see my best part."

Her eyes rounded at his innuendo.

Then he winked. "I have an adorable tattoo on my left butt cheek. What did you think I was referring to?"

Laughing, she shook her head. No way was she going to say.

His grin said she didn't have to—he knew.

"A tattoo, I didn't see one—"

It was his turn to look surprised.

She finished quickly. "In the movie. The one time I watched it." She flushed all over as his grin widened.

"Concealer," he said with laughter in his eyes. "It's just a tiny thing. My tattoo, that is."

She swallowed hard. "I knew what you were referring to. An ass tattoo, sounds like a drunken mistake."

"Worse. It's a small yellow rose in memory of my mother. Any mention of her used to make my father sad, so I remember thinking my ass cheek sounded like the perfect place to conceal it. Over the years, though, explaining to women why I chose to honor my deceased mother with a flower on my ass has been—entertaining to say the least."

A laugh bubbled out of Angelina. "I can see how it would be. That's sweet, though. I'm sure your mother understands."

"I like to think she does. Hey, life is tough. You can either laugh or cry your way through it. I choose to laugh."

Angelina searched his face. "You're not at all the way I thought you were. You're so—"

He interrupted. "Don't say nice. Women fuck nice men once . . . three times tops. Say I'm mysterious. Intimidating. I'd rather you call me an asshole."

She cocked her head to one side and trusted her instincts. "Who have you been with? I don't think there's anything sexier than a kind man."

His face transformed with pleasure that sent warmth shooting through her. "I do have to finish the calendar. Can you wait for me?"

It would be a real chore, but . . . "I have to pick Whitney up at five, but I have until then."

"Good." He erased the question from her mind by cupping her face between his hands and giving her a sweetest kiss that had her toes curling in her high heels. When he raised his head, he was breathing as heavily as she was. "This may take a while."

"That's okay," she whispered.

Only when he stepped away did she realize all eyes had been on the two of them. She smiled awkwardly and gave everyone a quick wave.

The receptionist appeared at her side again with a steaming cup of coffee. "I'm having a chair brought out for you. And I thought you might want this. You two look good together, but I still don't like you. He was supposed to be mine."

Angelina accepted the coffee and waited for the younger woman to give some sign that she was joking. When she didn't, Angelina thanked her for the drink but ditched it as soon as she'd left the room. *I'm not taking any chances.*

The chair, though, was high backed and comfortable. According to the man who brought it to her, it was also light enough to move around the studio as Connor switched to other sets.

Connor was back almost before she'd settled into the chair. He scanned the room, then headed over to her as soon as he spotted her. Barefoot, bare-chested, in the tackiest Valentine's Day swimming trunks Angelina had ever seen . . . he was still mouth wateringly gorgeous. "Don't you dare laugh," he growled near her ear.

Laugh? Or squirm my way to an orgasm just watching you? "It's not that bad."

"I have a problem."

"You do?"

"Before I start, I need one more taste . . ." His mouth closed over hers again. This time, his tongue slipped between her lips and his hand cupped the back of her head. She opened her mouth wider for him, swirling her tongue around his, meeting his passion with her own. He raised his head. "Now I have a second problem, but I'm hoping the photographer doesn't notice."

Her eyes fell to his tented bathing suit and then rose to meet his gaze again. "I can't help you with that."

"Not here anyway," he said, his sexy grin returning. He gave her a quick kiss then shook his head. "No more. I need to focus."

The way he looked at her made her feel ten years younger and free. "Or just one last one."

His nostrils flared and he bent in for another kiss, murmuring, "I like the way you think."

At the photographer's prompting Connor straightened and trotted away. Angelina raised a shaking hand to her lips, let out a sigh, and smiled. *Holy shit.*

Connor Sutton wasn't the man she'd thought he was—he was a million, trillion times more irresistible. The man who turned while posing with a kitten to smile at her—well, that man might just break her heart—or renew her faith in men.

Did she really want to give any man that power over her?

"That's it," the photographer said. "That's the look I was asking you for earlier. If you looked at me that way, I'd have sex with you, and I don't even like men."

Connor's smile twitched with humor, but he kept his attention on Angelina. There was a possessive need in his gaze so intense Angelina was finding it difficult to think of much else beyond getting him alone.

She told herself his expression was the result of his skill as an actor, but he still looked pretty damn excited for a man who was acting. *He likes me.*

Really likes me.

This could go somewhere.

She blinked back tears as hope and fear warred within her.

Slow down.

I barely know him.

There's no reason to think what I'm feeling now is anything more than lust . . . or that it will last.

But it sure feels real.

TEN PHOTO SHOOT months later, Connor shimmied out of candy cane patterned swim trunks and reached for his own clothing. As he stepped into his boxers he read the quote on the front of them and smiled. Since his brother Dylan had left for Iceland, he'd started sending gifts back to Connor. Dylan's latest one had been a set of boxers with motivational quotes on them.

He'd probably intended them as a joke, but wearing them had actually lifted Connor's spirits over the past week. To give him confidence running his first meeting with Landon Foundation he'd worn the ones that said: **Want hard. Work hard.**

When negotiating the cost of the new building they were acquiring, he'd worn: **No matter how you start, finish unforgettable.**

The day he'd met families the Landon Foundation was helping he wore: **Do it with passion or don't do it at all.**

Today's boxers were meant to keep him motivated

through what had sounded like a long day: **I don't quit before I'm done.**

Standing there looking in the mirror, he imagined what Angelina would think of them. Wait, she was standing right outside the door of the changing room. He didn't have to imagine. He opened the door and called her over.

Eyes wide she approached his changing room. "Yes?"

"Read my boxers. My brother sent me a bunch like this. I thought they were motivational messages, but now I think he's ragging on me because I always joke I have more sex than he does."

Angelina's mouth rounded but no sound came out. Her eyebrows came together and her cheeks flushed as her gaze dropped.

Beneath her attention, his cock sprang to attention, tenting his boxers. Connor looked down, then met her eyes and smiled. "Sorry. I can't control that around you."

Still she didn't say anything, she just nodded.

The air was thick with a sexual tension that he didn't feel right about acting on there. His body was hyperaware of every inch of hers—the catch in her breath, the way she bit her bottom lip as her gaze roamed over him. She was as excited as he was. He would have kissed her, but she wasn't someone he wanted to fuck in a changing room and their attraction was like a racehorse rearing and ready. Exciting, but he wanted what happened between them to matter. He'd slept with a fair share of women he hadn't expected to see again. Angelina was different. He didn't understand why . . . she simply was. "I hope I didn't embarrass you. I didn't want you to see them later and think . . ." An image of her gloriously naked and riding him, those amazing breasts of hers jiggling against his chest temporarily distracted him.

Didn't I just tell myself that's not where this is going today?

"They're fine," she said in a husky voice.

He decided to ease the tension with a joke. "I should have caught the sexual connotations when I wore the pair that said. 'I'm not here to be average.' I thought they were meant to bolster my confidence. Oh, I will find the perfect gift for payback."

Her lips curved in a smile. "I'd love to help you choose something. I used to enjoy tormenting my brothers." Her smile faded almost as soon as she mentioned her family.

If Connor wasn't sporting an awkwardly impressive boner, he would have pulled her in for a hug. She was strong and independent, but she was also a little broken. He'd realized that the day they'd met at Reemsly. Now he saw her pain ran deeper than her job.

"I should get dressed." His dick was apparently unable to pick up on mood changes and it was impossible to pretend it wasn't dancing in the air between them, begging for her to notice it. He checked the time on his watch. "It's only two o'clock. Are you hungry?"

She nodded.

All the signs were there that she was as eager to be with him as he was to be with her. Normally, they'd be halfway back to his place. If a cookie was placed on his plate, he'd never been the type to eat his vegetables first. Life was too short to not choose pleasure first.

But not this time.

As much as he wanted her in his bed, he wanted to make sure she was okay even more. He needed to know what was behind the sadness he'd sensed in her. It wasn't something he bragged about, but he'd always been able to feel the pain in others. *An eighth sense.* Nothing formal. Nothing flashy. He simply felt an ache around certain people. Usually he helped them by playing the clown. Laughter was a great healer.

There'd been long, sad days after his mother had died. He remembered the comfort every member of his family had found in the antics of their Newfoundland, Piper. Her wagging tail and enthusiasm had brought smiles back to their faces when nothing else had.

Connor had taken that lesson to heart. Most people, regardless of how hurt or hardened they were, wanted to be loved. They yearned to be welcomed with dog-level enthusiasm. He'd changed many things about himself to fit in with the Barringtons, but he hadn't changed that. He didn't care how many times they threatened him, that family needed hugs more than most.

Allowing himself the briefest of kisses, Connor teased his lips over Angelina's then closed the door between them before he changed his mind. In a flash he was dressed in his charcoal suit and fancy leather shoes.

"Ready?" he asked as he exited the changing room. "How does pizza sound?"

Chapter Twelve

A NGELINA'S HEAD WAS still spinning as Connor parked his Mercedes behind a small family restaurant in Queens. When he'd whisked her out of the photographer's studio, she'd half expected him to drive straight to his place or ask for her address.

Instead it looked as if they were actually going to have pizza.

Her hands were clasped on her lap. They hadn't kissed again since they'd been alone. She didn't know what to think. Her heart was beating about a thousand times a minute, though. She couldn't remember being so excited to be on a date with a man—ever.

After parking, he released his seat belt and turned to her. "Before we go any further, there's something you need to know."

Oh, shit.

I knew there was something. Is he dying? Secretly married? Contagious?

She'd once gone on a date with a man who'd chosen just such a moment to tell her he had an unusual fetish—nylons.

As in, he couldn't orgasm unless he was wearing them. It had been a deal breaker for her.

Please don't let it be anything I can't handle.

She also released her seat belt and turned in her seat. Honesty deserved to be treated respectfully, even if it changed things.

He reached for one of her hands. Their fingers laced and her body revved wildly even from that innocent touch. *I could overlook a fetish or two to keep feeling this way.* "Yes?"

Caressing the back of her hand with a thumb, he took a moment before saying, "Remember I said I wasn't the man you think I am?"

He used to be a woman?

No, look at him. Medicine may have come a long way, but he's more muscled up than most born a male.

And he has an Adam's apple.

Shit, he's a criminal.

Please don't be a criminal.

"I remember."

"You were dead right when you said I'm not the character I played in *Danger Doubled.* I never went to college. Until this past year, pretty much the only thing I read were comic books. Now I have a Kindle and if I die the thing should be buried with me because I've one clicked some weird shit."

Some of Angelina's inner panic began to subside. Was his secret simply bad taste in literature? "I'm not sure what you're trying to tell me."

He turned her hand over and traced the lines on her palm, distracting and exciting her at the same time. How was it possible to be clothes-shedding ready from barely touching? "I was nervous the day I went to Reemsly to speak. Bradford isn't my bodyguard. I brought him for moral support. Really intelligent people intimidate me because I'm not considered the brightest guy in any room. The man you met that day doesn't exist. I was acting."

Her heart broke for him as she realized he meant every word. She wanted to slap whoever had made this man feel like he was anything short of incredible. Despite the emotion misting her eyes, she forced a smile. "That's a relief, because I thought you were an asshole." A memory came back to her from his speech and she amended, "Except when you spoke to the students. Was any of that real?"

"I work with a life coach who wrote the first speech for me. The soccer team talk was all me."

Yes!

"Even the part about your sister taking down the bully?"

He shot her a boyish smile. "That story doesn't fit my image so I don't normally share it, but Viviana is a real firecracker. She can still beat most men at arm wrestling. You'll love her."

He wants me to meet his family? Breathing became difficult again. "I'm sure I will."

Connor raised their linked hands between them. "When my sister married Grant Barrington we all sort of did too. The only time I wore a suit before we met him was at my mother's funeral and I was a kid. This watch—a gift. This car—another gift. My movie deals? I wouldn't have them if it weren't for Clay Landon's connection to a producer. I have to act like I belong in this world because it means a lot to my sister. The truth is, I'm a regular guy living an extraordinary life, but most of the time all I really want is a loaded pizza and a cold beer. I don't want to act with you. I want to be myself. That's why I brought you here. Ada and Joel see *me*. I want you to, too."

Could a woman fall in love with a man in a moment? Was he the key to finding a way to reclaim the part of herself she'd closed off? "I was born and raised on a farm in Oklahoma. I only moved to New Jersey when I got pregnant with Whitney and then I had to learn how to fit into this world as well. Nobody noodles around here. They don't even know what it means."

"Noodles?"

The door she'd closed between who she was and who'd she'd once been opened just a crack . . . enough for her to pull out a memory that brought a smile to her face. "Fishing with your hand. Essentially, you put your bare hand near a catfish nest, hope it latches on, and wrestle it to the surface while it tries to drown you. They make good eating. It's an adrenaline rush, but dangerous." She touched the back of her hand. "That scar is from a snake I thought was a catfish. You only make that mistake once."

His grip tightened on her hand. "Hold on. Wait one damn minute. You stuck you hand in a catfish nest? This little hand?"

With anyone else she might have felt embarrassed, but he sounded genuinely impressed. "Bet your ass I did. There is a pond near the house I grew up in that the locals filled with cars in the 1980s. Just the outside shell of old vehicles. Catfish love them and the pond is shallow enough to dive down without a tank. Trunks are the best place to find catfish, but you'd better have a strong spotter—that's the person who makes sure you get back to the surface—because those catfish can be fifty to eighty pounds. It's not a sport for the meek . . . or really for anyone after they realize they're not immortal."

A huge smile spread across his face. "I need to see this."

She blushed. "Oh, I haven't done it in over a decade. I doubt even my brothers do it anymore."

"Don't you know?"

She looked away. "We don't talk much anymore."

"How about your parents?"

Eyes still averted, she said, "We had a falling out." Her face tightened and she blinked a few times quickly. And there it was . . . the source of her sadness. Family.

He cupped her chin and brought her face around until her eyes met his again. "This is where I'm supposed to say you don't have to tell me what happened, but any woman who can stick her hand in an underwater car trunk as bait isn't one who's afraid of much."

Tears filled her eyes. "That's where you're wrong. I tell myself I'm strong, but it's a lie. I stopped going home because I couldn't face the people in my town who'd judged me when I got pregnant. I lied to my parents about why I refused to visit because I was ashamed. I stopped talking to my brothers because I felt bad about myself every time they pushed me to come home and I refused. Eventually, they just stopped calling and I told myself we were all better off for it. So, I guess I'm not who you thought I was, either."

He hugged her then, pulled her to him and enveloped her in muscle and comfort. "Nope. You're a million times better. I'm not perfect. I don't want perfect. I'm looking for someone I can be myself with."

"Me too." She leaned back and met his gaze. "I've never told anyone about my family before. My friends know I don't see them, but not why."

He combed a hand through her hair. "There's something else you should know."

Her breath caught in her throat. Whatever it was, she was willing to work with it. "What?"

"I've had a lot of sex. A lot. More than I probably should have, although some might argue that too much is never enough—"

She put a finger over his lips. "I get the idea."

He kissed her finger then lowered her hand. "No, I don't think you do. If I'd wanted to, we would have already fucked."

She frowned and opened her mouth in protest.

He kissed her lips lightly and her argument died before it was voiced. *Okay, we probably would have.* His kiss was so sweet, so tender that she wrapped her arms around his neck and gave herself over to it.

When he raised his head, they were both flushed and breathing heavily. "Damn, it's hard to think around you."

"I could say the same thing." For someone who'd spent the last thirteen years cautiously making plans and sticking to them, she felt wildly spontaneous. No possible outcome outweighed how good he made her feel. At least none she could think of while her body was humming for his.

He set her back from him, turned away, and gripped the steering wheel with both hands. "This would be so much easier if I didn't like you so much. I know I'm saying this all wrong. Let me start over. I want to date you, meet your son, go home with you to meet your parents, and learn how to noodle from your brothers. I want to take you to game night with Sophie and Dale and all those crazy Barringtons. I want to make you happy first, then make you mine. If that means I'm too nice—the kind of guy you'll fuck three times and walk away from—I guess there's not much I can do about that. I'm done feeling bad about who I am."

It was so different from how any man had ever treated her, she didn't believe it at first. Men said whatever they thought would get them sex. So why was he turning it down?

Because he wants to see me happy first?

Who does that?

In a society where everyone was accustomed to instant gratification and tended to put their own needs above those of others . . . could a man like this actually exist?

And if he did, a woman would be a fool to walk away from him. "Are you horrible in bed?" she asked then gasped. "I'm sorry. I'm trying to figure out what kind of woman wouldn't want what you just described."

A look of sheer horror entered his eyes. He pulled a phone out of his jacket pocket and swiped through numbers then held up a hand in a request for silence. "Hold on."

Who in the world was he calling?

"Gracie, do you have a minute? I have a quick question. You know the multiple orgasms I gave you on that ski trip to Tahoe? Did you fake those? Are you sure? She says no. Gracie, don't be nice about it. Give me the truth here because I think I met *the one* and if there's room for improvement I need to know. Okay, so everything was good, but the ice was cold on your back. I should have thought of that. Yep. Yep. I can understand that . . . Oh, that's not good . . . Thanks, but I'm pretty sure I'll be off the market soon. You too . . ."

He was smiling after ending the call. "I was with Gracie a few months ago. I might be able to find someone more recent." He swiped through more of his contacts.

Angelina grabbed his phone. "No need. I believe you." As what he'd done sunk in, she asked, "What was she saying?"

He grinned and glanced at his crotch. "She misses the big guy, but she has an unhealthy attraction to men who treat her like shit. We weren't together long. The guy she left me for only wanted to be with her because he lost his job and was looking for a free place to crash. She said she's open to giving us a second shot if things don't work out with you."

"Yeah, you can delete her number now," Angelina said forcefully, a reaction that surprised her.

With mock fear, Connor retrieved his phone from Angelina and made a show of deleting Gracie's contact information. He was all smiles when he dropped his phone back into his coat and said, "You get jealous. I like it."

"I don't—" Angelina stopped as she realized there was no reason to lie to Connor. "Not *normally*, but I don't like the idea of you with anyone else."

His smile widened. "We have so much in common. I don't like the idea of me with anyone else, either."

The kiss he swooped down to give her was interrupted by the arrival of a solemn looking man at his car door window. "Connor. Behind you. Do you know him?"

Connor looked over his shoulder then turned more toward his door. "With those bushy eyebrows? I bet I do." Connor opened his door, slid out and offered the much smaller man a handshake in welcome. Angelina got out as well but remained on the other side of the car. "Am I finally meeting Joel and Ada's son?" Connor asked.

The young man seemed nervous, but he shook Connor's hand. "Yes. My name's Jacob. My father told me what you did for me and that it was finally safe for me to come back for a visit. I wanted to say thank you. It'll take me a while to save up the money, but I will repay every penny."

Had Connor lent him money? Paid for his school? What did Jacob mean it was finally safe to come back?

Connor clapped a hand on the boy's shoulder. "The best way to repay kindness is to pass kindness along. You've got two amazing parents. Take care of them. Not just today, but when they're older and not so fun to be around. That would be the best way to repay me."

The young man's face beamed with gratitude. "I will. I see how lucky I am now. Maybe you can help me convince them to move to Rhode Island. We have family up there and when I graduate it's where I'd like to remain."

"I'll miss them, but my guess is they'll love anywhere you all are." Connor turned and waved for Angelina to join them. "Jacob, this is Angelina."

Angelina slid beneath Connor's arm and it felt natural—right. She shook Jacob's hand. "Nice to meet you, Jacob."

"You too." After releasing her hand, Jacob said, "Perfect timing. The lunch rush just ended. Come on in. Mom and Dad will be excited to see you."

As they followed Jacob through the parking lot, Connor bent to near Angelina's ear and said, "I didn't do anything. It was all Bradford, but he doesn't like his name attached to anything. Something about having to kill us if we ever found out what he does."

Angelina laughed.

Connor didn't.

She didn't have time to ask him if he'd been serious. The moment they entered the restaurant she was welcomed and not so subtly cross-examined. Not that she minded one bit. As Connor laughed and bantered with Joel and Ada, Angelina understood what he'd wanted her to see. They didn't care about his fancy watch or that he was famous. As the five of them sat around a table, sharing a pizza and toasting with mugs of beer, there was a real sense of friendship.

These kinds of connections wouldn't have been possible for the alpha she'd once thought he was. This was a humble man, hilariously self-deprecating at times, but with a sense of integrity and rightness that few had. Angelina could have sat there all night in a chair next to Connor, his arm around the back of hers, listening to him swap stories with the Fetters.

Her phone dinged with a reminder to pick up Whitney from school. *No.* She wasn't ready for the day to end. "I have to go. My son," she explained.

"I'll call you a car," Joel said. "You too, Connor. I know you can hold your liquor, but some things are not worth the risk."

Connor agreed.

Not all risks were bad. At least that's how it felt in the moment.

Before getting into the car that came to take her to her son's school, she impulsively jumped up, trusting that Connor would catch her. He did, holding her against him, her feet dangling above the ground. Laughing, he shifted her higher so they were face-to-face. "Thank you for today," she said, and kissed him boldly.

It was a deep and passionate exchange that ended too soon. He lowered her to her feet. "You're welcome. See you tomorrow."

She cocked her head to the side in confusion. Had he asked her out and she'd missed it?

"At work," he added.

"Yes. Of course. See you there."

Feeling dazed, Angelina slid into the back seat of the car. Just as she was about to close the door, he asked, "Are you free on Saturday?"

"I can be." *Oh, yes.*

"Great. Now, be honest, do you want to spend tonight wondering how I feel or should I call and gush about how much fun I had today?"

Angelina smiled as her heart thudded wildly. "Call."

He leaned in, gave her a quick kiss, then closed the door and waved.

As they drove away, the driver said, "Holy shit, was that *Connor Sutton*? I should have asked for his autograph."

Angelina settled back and gazed out the window as they sped along the busy streets. "It was and he would have been okay with it because he's a really nice man."

I have no idea how any woman could think that's a bad thing, but I'm so glad they did.

LATER THAT NIGHT, Connor nursed a beer on his penthouse balcony. It still didn't feel like his. Claire had found the apartment for him. The building had the tight security celebrities required and a helipad. Never in his life had he imagined either would be a criteria for choosing a place he'd live, but since Kade Barrington had married a woman with her own air transportation company, calling for a helicopter was often quicker than having his car brought out of valet and fighting traffic.

One thing he'd learned about the rich—they didn't like to be kept waiting. That was a downside to privilege. When a person's needs were anticipated and seamlessly fulfilled, it skewed the way they looked at life. Connor hadn't updated his family about Angelina because he doubted the Barring-tons would understand his desire to take things slowly. His father once told him, "Patience is like fertilizer. You can grow something without it, but it won't be nearly as impressive."

There was no one Connor admired more than his dad. He could have moved to Boston, but instead had kept his house in Upstate New York and encouraged Viviana and Grant to raise their children there.

Missing his father, Connor pulled out his phone. "Hey, Dad."

"Connor? It's late. Anything wrong?"

"Nope. Finally right. I have a date with Angelina on Saturday."

"That's fantastic. Everything I've heard about her has been positive."

"She's amazing. You'll really like her."

"I look forward to meeting her." There was a pause in their conversation that was eventually broken by his father asking, "Why does it feel like you have a question you're holding back?"

Connor downed a good portion of his beer. "I do have something I want to ask you."

"Anything."

"Were you happier before we met the Barringtons?" He rushed to add, "I'm not saying I don't like them, I've just been thinking about all the changes we've made. Is my closet back home still full of my old clothes?"

"I haven't thrown a thing of yours out. You looking for anything in particular?"

Not sure how to articulate how he was feeling, Connor didn't attempt it. "But you're happy, right, Dad?" That mattered more to him.

"Happy? I don't know if I've been truly happy since I lost your mother. That doesn't mean I'm unhappy. I have a good life—a good family, good friends. I can't complain." It didn't surprise Connor that his father hadn't mentioned the recent success of his construction company. Money had never mattered much to him.

"You really loved Mom."

"I still do." His father's voice was thick with emotion.

"Dad, if you don't want to talk about this, it's okay."

"No. Your mother would have loved the people her babies became. The more years that pass, the more I regret not talking about her. It hurts to remember, but I'm becoming more afraid she'll be forgotten because I didn't say her name."

"No one will forget her, Dad." Connor settled himself into a chair on his balcony and propped his feet up on the railing. "Tell me something about her. Did you know right away that she was the one for you?"

There was a smile in his father's voice when he said, "You'll think I'm crazy, but I did. She had a boyfriend, some guy with a flashy car and perfect teeth. You know those teeth that are so white they don't look real? That's what I remember most about him. Anyway, I was working at a gas station to pay for college and they pulled up—asked for full service, and I fell in love the first time she smiled at me. Her boyfriend went inside for cigarettes so I gave her my number. I told her to call me if she was looking for a good man who could imagine forever with her."

"Whoa. What did she say?"

"Nothing. But she pocketed my number before he returned. I didn't know her name or where she was from, so there wasn't much I could do after they drove off. I told my friends about her. I said I'd met the woman I was meant to marry. They couldn't believe I'd let her go, but I knew I'd see her again. We felt destined to be. Six months later, she called. We met for lunch, then dinner, then spent every day together after that. I've dated some amazing women since your mom passed away, but none have touched my heart the way she did."

Hearing his father talk about his mother with love warmed Connor's heart. He'd always hoped there'd been happiness before her illness. "Do you have any regrets?"

"Every argument we ever had where I let my pride stop me from apologizing when I was wrong. Also, we got married quick, started having kids right away. Things happened so fast my focus was on work and providing for my family more than it was on you kids. That changed when she got sick. I realized then that none of this is forever. It changed how I looked at everything. At the end of the day, the people you love and the ones who love you are all that matter."

"Are you missing us, Dad? Because you're starting to sound like a Hallmark card."

He chuckled, but when he spoke his tone was serious. "I *am* missing you. When are you coming up to see me?"

"How about tonight? I have a pilot on call and a need to kick your ass at darts. You pick the bar, I'll pick the beer."

"Your own pilot on call? Fancy."

Connor swung his feet to the floor and joked, "Not all the changes in my life have been bad. Did you know they make helicopters with passenger sections so quiet you can make a business call from it? After you've ridden in one there is no going back."

"Oh, Lord. Yes, I know about the soundproof ones. I get flown around too, you know. I don't want to brag, but as Viviana's father, I bet I get better door to door service than you do."

"What? Oh, we will talk about this again. Hanging up now. I will need to fly back tonight, but I'll be at the house in about an hour and a half."

"Sounds good. Are you coming in hungry?"

"No. I already ate." His stomach rumbled. "On second thought, yeah, I can always eat again."

"Good to see some things haven't changed." His father laughed. "Connor?"

"Yeah, Dad?"

"I know you've been struggling to be the brother you think Viviana needs, but all those voices telling you that there was something wrong with you—they're just noise you need to learn to tune out. I'm not saying you can't wear a suit now and then, but there was nothing wrong with any of the children I raised. I'm damned proud of you; I always have been."

And that was why Connor wasn't intimidated by the idea of having a family of his own. He'd had the world's best role model for how to do it right. "Thanks, Dad. I'm pretty proud of you too. I mean, at your advanced age . . . to be able to figure out how to answer your new smartphone all on your own . . ."

"Oh, I see how tonight is going to go. Better bring some cash to lose to me at darts."

"Or enough to buy you a tall drink to wallow in when I win. See you in a bit." He was just about to hang up the phone when a thought occurred to him. "Dad, did you ever think about getting another dog?" He told his father about Button.

"How big?"

"Crazy big and still growing. He'll probably destroy everything in your house. He doesn't belong in the city, but I can see him running around your backyard, digging up what you call grass."

"Where is he now?"

Connor was smiling as he ended the call. His father had promised to call the rescue and meet Button. There was no chance in hell that would end with Button not leaving with his father.

Connor texted his pilot. ETA fifteen minutes. Perfect. He turned and leaned against the railing of his balcony and chose a number he'd told himself he wouldn't call until later that night—but he wanted to hear her voice.

He didn't leave a message when it went to voice mail.

He just glared down at his phone like it had betrayed him.

Why wouldn't she answer?

Was she hurt?

Busy?

No longer interested?

No, she was into him. He could have driven to his place instead of taking her out for pizza and she would have been okay with it.

Maybe she didn't like the pizza.

No. She ate three slices. It's not that.

I can text now that she didn't answer.

What the hell do men write to women who don't pick up when they call? This was a new experience for Connor.

The excitement of his phone ringing quickly diminished when he realized it wasn't Angelina returning his call. "Hey, Clay."

"You sound down for a man who had his first date with his future wife."

"It wasn't really a date, and how do you know I went out with Angelina?"

"A fairy godfather has to have his charge under constant surveillance so he'll know when to step in."

"Just what kind of surveillance are we talking about? How many fingers am I holding up?" He waved his middle finger around at the room in general.

"One and it's your middle finger, but I don't need to see you to know that. Trust me, I don't want to know what goes on in your apartment."

Connor lowered his hand. "How do you know where I am?"

"I track your phone and pay people to report in with what you're up to."

"And that's not creepy?"

"Hey, I didn't volunteer for this job. This was a special request by Sophie Barrington. I don't take those lightly."

Connor walked to his bedroom to grab his phone charger. "I'd love to talk more about this but I'm flying out to see my dad."

"When is your next date with Angelina?"

Shouldn't his intel have already given him that information? "Saturday."

"Where are you taking her?"

"I haven't decided yet."

Clay snapped his fingers. "Two days? That's plenty of time to set something up. Don't put another thought into it. I'll handle everything. All you have to do is get in the car I send for you Saturday morning."

"I'm good. I don't need your help on this one."

"Consider it my thank you for working so hard for my foundation."

"No, Clay. I want to do this my way. Clay? Clay?"

He was already gone.

Connor attempted to call him back, but he didn't answer. *Why do people have phones if no one answers them?*

He texted: Don't plan anything for Saturday.

Clay responded: Cinderella never told her fairy godmother what to do.

Connor: I'm not Cinderella.

Clay didn't respond.

Out of desperation, Connor called the man he hoped could have some influence with the situation. "Dax, you have to rein in Clay. He's out of control."

"What's he up to now?" Dax asked in an impatient tone

that might have intimidated another man.

"Planning a date for me with Angelina for this weekend. A date I'm not entirely sure she still wants to go on. I mean I'm pretty sure. If she'd answer my call I'd be positive."

"I am no one's babysitter," Dax said. "Hang on. Kenzi, it's for you. It's Connor. Clay's driving him nuts. Oh, no, this doesn't involve me. It was *your mother* who asked for Clay's help. You wouldn't dare. Fine." Dax let out an audible breath of frustration. "What would you like me to do, Connor?"

Wow, those Barrington women sure knew how to turn their men around. "How do I get him to understand I don't need his help?"

"Didn't you say Angelina wasn't answering your calls?"

"One call. One. Not in general."

"The one that would have decided if she was interested enough in you to go out with you?"

"Maybe. Yes."

"Sounds like you do need his help. If there is one thing I know about Clay it's that once he sets his mind to something it's going to happen. You can either fight it and lose or enjoy the ride."

"I don't believe that's the philosophy you use with him."

"No, I'd fucking threaten to kill him, but that only works because he knows I'd do it. You on the other hand are too nice. He's not afraid of the hug you'd withhold if he upsets you."

Ouch. That was low. "You can be a real dick, Dax."

Dax laughed. "I know. That's why Clay doesn't screw

with me."

"So the only way I could stop him would be to become an asshole?"

Dax sighed. "Listen, Clay doesn't have many friends because he can be a little over the top. He only gets involved when he cares and he likes you. I can call him off, but he won't understand why and his feelings will be hurt. He means well. Let him plan one date. Laugh your way through it. If Angelina doesn't have a sense of humor she's not the woman for you anyway."

Dax's last comment was true enough. And Clay really had been good to Connor. "Okay, I'll ride it out." Then he smiled. "I have to ask—what did Kenzi threaten to do?"

"You don't want to know."

"I do."

In the background, Kenzi said, "You can't tell him."

"He has a right to know."

"What?" Connor asked. "Just say it."

Dax said, "Kenzi threatened to tell Sophie I wasn't being nice to you. Lately Sophie has been lecturing everyone in the family that we need to be kinder to you—no nicknames, no jokes about your IQ. We're all supposed to tell you we loved you before and will love you no matter what path you choose."

There could have been a sting to Dax's words, but Connor chose to focus on the good in them. "Sophie's incredible."

He expected Dax to say something sarcastic, but he didn't. Instead he said, "She is." He cleared his throat. "I couldn't sleep the other night and watched a special on gorillas that has really stuck with me."

"Okay." *That's random.*

"The gorilla family unit is headed by one alpha male, a silverback. It's his job to intimidate attackers while his family flees. You'd think this leader is always the strongest. Not so. Female gorillas have been known to defend a favorite silverback against younger, more fit males who would challenge him. The case they highlighted was an older silverback who was good with the young and was seen often giving the females reassuring embraces. What I'm saying is, he was an alpha gorilla, but he was also kind. That's not a bad combination."

Huh? "Good talk, Dax."

"You know what I'm saying," Dax said impatiently.

He did and it was probably the nicest thing Dax had ever said to him, but that didn't mean he would let him off the hook easily. "That I remind you of a gorilla? I'm telling Sophie what you said."

"Yeah, right."

Connor couldn't help adding, "Dax, when it comes time to talk to your kids about the birds and the bees, try to rely less on animal channels for inspiration."

"Fuck you," he said then growled to his wife, "No, that's not too harsh. You should hear the shit that's coming out of his mouth. Kenzi, next time you're dealing with him."

Kenzi's laughter rang out in the background. Connor loved how she didn't take Dax seriously. Without Kenzi, Dax would have been too hard, too cold. She brought out a softer side of him.

"Dax, you know you shouldn't have told me that you have to be nice to me in front of Sophie. I may just test the boundaries of that."

"Do it. See what happens."

Connor laughed again then sobered. "I'm heading upstate to see my father tonight. Thanks for being absolutely no help with Clay."

"Anytime. Will we see you Sunday? Game night has been moved to early afternoon."

"I'll be there." As he headed out the door of his apartment and made his way to the rooftop helipad, he considered calling Angelina again. The first time they spoke shouldn't be at the mystery date Clay was arranging for them.

I'll still see her at work. To badass or not to badass—that is the question.

He checked his messages.

Nothing from Angelina yet.

He slid his phone into the breast pocket of his suit jacket.

A kind silverback gorilla would probably wait for her to answer on her terms.

He jokingly beat his chest with his hands and roared but stopped when the elevator opened and the helicopter pilot was there waiting for him, looking at him like he was acting crazy. *I'd explain it to him, but I wouldn't know where to start.*

Chapter Thirteen

"I FEEL HORRIBLE," Angelina said into the phone she was balancing between her neck and her shoulder as she dropped some broccoli into a steamer. "I was ten minutes late in a car Whitney didn't recognize when I pulled up. He was sitting on the wall of the school all by himself, looking so sad. I don't think he really likes this new school. He puts on a brave face for me, but he doesn't know anyone yet and here I am thinking about myself and a relationship that can you really imagine going somewhere? Oh, God, am I fucking everything up?"

"No, you're not. Everything is going to be just fine." Joanna's tone was soothing, the same one she used when her mini-horse was agitated.

"Whitney asked me if I'd been drinking. I must have reeked of beer even though I only had two. He's at the prime age to start drinking and I am modeling that behavior."

"Breathe. The sky isn't falling. Whitney will be fine. You're allowed to be human and parent. In fact, I think it's preferred. You've been holding yourself to an unfair standard. What did you say when he asked?"

Angelina groaned. "I lied. Me. For the past thirteen years I've been advocating honest and open communication with Whitney. Then he asked me one hard question and what do I do? I panic and lie. You should have seen the look he gave me."

Joanna chuckled. "You're too hard on yourself. If your roles were reversed, what would you want him to do?"

"Confess, I guess."

"Try that. Tell him what you just told me. That is, if you really do believe in open communication."

"I do and you're right. This isn't a big deal. I'm overreacting. Whitney is in his room. I'll lure him out with dinner and apologize for not being truthful."

"He's a good kid, Angelina. He knows you love him. You're allowed to make mistakes. Just like he is. Now, let's get back to what you said at the beginning of this call. You went out with Connor after the photo shoot? Tell me everything."

While Angelina prepared two steaks and popped them into the broiler, she shared everything, right down to how Connor wanted to go noodling with her brothers. "I literally floated out of the pizza place to the car. Just thinking about him makes me all hot and bothered. I've never felt like this about anyone before. Oh, my God, as I was leaving he asked, 'Do you want to spend tonight wondering how I feel or should I call and gush about how much fun I had tonight?' I know he's an actor, so maybe he's laying it on thick, but it felt so . . . so . . ."

"Real?"

"Yes. But also like a dream. Ever experience something so good you're afraid it can't be true?"

"I try not to second-guess good fortune. All it does is suck the joy out of otherwise good situations."

"I envy that about you."

"Don't envy it, try it. Every time that negative voice starts up in your head, just shut it down. Replace it with a positive mantra like 'It'll all work out.'"

"That negative voice fuels my drive. It keeps me focused on what's important. Without it, I probably wouldn't have gotten as far as I have."

"But at what cost? Outside of Whitney and spending time with me and Aly, what do you do that makes you happy? Something just for you."

"I—I—nothing, really. I've always worked too much to have a hobby."

"Or a relationship."

"That too."

"You've built a good life for yourself and your son. Maybe don't turn off that voice in your head, just turn it down a little? Allow yourself to believe in miracles, magic, and happy endings."

Miracles, magic, and happy endings? I could use some of that in my life. "Connor called. I was in the car with Whitney so I didn't pick up."

"Did he leave a message?"

"No."

"Let me play mind reader for a minute. He called and you didn't answer . . . so in your head that means he won't call again. You had one shot and you blew it."

She knows me too well. "He has women throwing themselves at him daily. A man like that isn't going to chase a single mother."

"How do you know he doesn't love that you have a son?"

Angelina opened and closed her mouth without voicing a word. Then said, "Men prefer women with no baggage."

"Oh, so now Whitney is *baggage.*"

Angelina's chest clenched painfully as she began to hear what Joanna was saying. "No, he's my miracle."

"Yes, he is. You've raised him to be an intelligent, thoughtful young man. Your problem isn't with him, it's with yourself. What are you holding onto that makes you think you don't deserve a happy ending?"

Tears filled Angelina's eyes and she sniffed before answering. She told Joanna about Whitney's father and how the people in her hometown had believed the lies he'd spread about her. She finally voiced the names they'd called her, feeling lighter as she said them aloud. "I told myself I never wanted to go back there. I couldn't face those people again, but I was wrong to hide from it. Whitney doesn't have a relationship with my parents or my brothers because I couldn't admit how much that time of my life hurt. I was devastated. Even considered killing myself. When I think about how Whitney wouldn't be here if I'd done that . . . I hate myself. Aunt Rudi saved me. She swept in and told me I could do better. I could change. And I did. I'm so afraid that if I slip up once . . . I'll be who they said I was . . . and I'll slide right back into who I was." She wiped tears from her cheeks. "Whitney deserves the mother Aunt Rudi knew I could be. Not the person I was before."

"You were sixteen when you had Whitney. *Sixteen.* They don't even let kids drive at that age for a reason. I know it's scary, but you have to face down what scares you. When Connor offers to go back home with you . . . take him. Walk through your old town with your head held high because no one in that town is better than you. Anyone worth talking to feels bad about how they treated you. And your family, they'll be glad to see you. Families are like that. Sure it might be awkward at first, but just ask yourself how you'd feel about seeing Whitney after not seeing him for a while. That's probably how your parents will feel."

"There's nothing Whitney could do that would make me not happy to see him no matter how much time had passed."

"Exactly."

"And Connor said he wanted to get to know me, meet Whitney, introduce me to his family, spend time with mine. That sounds like a man who will call again. So, Whitney might need to sleep at your place Saturday night."

"That's fine with me."

"This will all work out."

"You've got it now."

"If you were here, Joanna, I would give you the world's tightest hug. Thank you for talking this out with me. I feel better."

"Hey, that's what friends are for. You've talked me off my share of ledges. You are so kind to everyone else. Be just as nice to yourself."

"I'll try," Angelina promised. Just then she heard a shuffle behind her and turned to see her son standing in the doorway of the kitchen. "I have to go." She hung up without waiting for Joanna to answer. *How much did Whitney hear?* She forced a bright smile. "Hungry? Dinner's almost ready."

Whitney didn't return her smile. He walked into the room and stopped just a foot from her. "My biological father was a real ass."

Oh, God. I never wanted him to hear that. "He was sixteen, Whitney. We all had a lot of growing up to do."

"Did you really consider killing yourself?"

Fuck.

"Yes. It's not something I'm proud of. Life is always worth fighting for. I was young and scared. I wish I could go back in time and tell myself how wonderful life was going to become with you in it."

He nodded and frowned. "Connor Sutton sounds like he really likes you."

Angelina shrugged and reminded herself to breathe. She tried to think of what to say that would make any of this okay, but nothing seemed to cover all she wanted to express.

"I want to meet him before you go on a date with him—make sure he's a good guy."

My protector. "If he calls—when he calls I'll tell him that."

"You shouldn't have sex with him on your first date. I'll stay here, rent some movies, and wait up for you."

He did not just say that. "I wasn't—" She stopped before the lie left her lips. "Seems like you were in that doorway a long time."

He gave her one of his steady, serious looks. "I love you, Mom. You deserve to be happy. Make sure this guy treats you right."

It was Angelina's turn to simply nod. Her boy was becoming a man right before her eyes and it was wonderful and scary to watch.

"And I totally knew you'd lied about drinking," Whitney added in a tone so parental in nature Angelina had to fight back a smile.

"I shouldn't have. I apologize for that." The mood lightened between the two of them. "But I am allowed a beer now and then, you know. And it was just two of them. Now go set the table."

Whitney paused from placing silverware next to a plate. "What's noodling?"

Over dinner, Angelina explained it to Whitney and answered the many questions he asked about her family back in Oklahoma. He'd never seemed interested in them before, but now she saw that he'd probably always been. *But I'd slammed the door to the past so tightly he didn't feel he could ask.*

His expression reminded her of Connor's when he asked, "I can't believe you caught catfish by feeding them your hand."

"I didn't say I was a bright child. Some people drown doing it."

"Still, I have to try it."

She held out her hand and showed him the scar. "See

that? Bite from a snake I thought was a catfish."

"Correction, I need to watch someone else noodle. I don't like snakes."

Angelina laughed. "Good choice."

Later that night, she lay in bed telling herself Connor would call. When he didn't, she texted him: **Sorry I missed your call. See you at work tomorrow.**

When he didn't answer she lay there, staring at the ceiling for a long time. Every time a negative thought tried to chime in, she took Joanna's advice and said, "It'll all work out."

That night, for a change, she didn't have a single nightmare.

Chapter Fourteen

"GORILLAS AREN'T SEXY," Kimmie said from a chair in Connor's office the next morning. "Don't ever share that story again."

"I am in complete agreement on this one," Linda chimed in from a chair beside Kimmie. "I never got the whole King Kong thing. I mean, really, how were things going to work between them? Sure, bigger is better, but there's a limit."

Connor stopped pacing and ran a hand through his hair in frustration. It might have been a mistake to ask his assistants to come in early to help him prep for seeing Angelina again. So far they weren't calming him down. "I didn't say I was going to dress up as a gorilla. I'm just sharing what Dax said about how I could be an alpha without being an asshole. I think that's what he was trying to say, anyway."

"I thought the whole badass act was working for you," Kimmie said.

Linda shook her head. "The point is he doesn't want to *act* with Angelina anymore."

"Oh, then definitely don't pretend to be a gorilla."

Connor smacked himself in the forehead. "In about fifteen minutes Angelina will be here. Do I wave to her like the other day was no big deal? Call her into my office and give her a great big kiss? Casually appear at her office door and ask her to lunch? I don't want to make her feel uncomfortable at work. What do women want in this situation?"

Linda motioned toward his desk. "I'd want to be hauled in here, hear the door lock behind me, and see if you know what to do with the blessings God gave you. First, I'd like it on the desk. Then the couch. Next against the window. I've always liked sex with a view."

Connor's mouth dropped open.

Kimmie laughed behind her hand.

In response to their reactions, Linda arched an eyebrow. "I thought we were here to be honest. Kimmie, you've seen the two of them together. What do you think Angelina is hoping for?"

After taking a moment to compose herself, Kimmie said, "She does seem really into you." She paused to chew her thumbnail. "And you have a date with her tomorrow?"

"Yes. Maybe. I don't know. She originally agreed to go. And she did text me last night but I was out with my dad and missed it. I'm going with yes. We have a date tomorrow." Connor referenced his plaid shirt and jeans. "I brought these back from my dad's last night. Normally I wouldn't wear them to the office, but I wanted to show her the real me. Now I feel like an idiot."

Linda made a tsking sound. "Sweetie, if Angelina doesn't like your plaid you open that door and toss her ass right out. I could show up in a hospital johnny and my fuck buddies wouldn't blink. It's not what you're wearing that matters, it's what happens when it comes off."

Kimmie's face was bright red, but she was smiling. "And this is why Linda is rewriting all my sex scenes. So, maybe you should take her advice."

Connor ran several erotic scenarios through his head. As painfully arousing as they all were, he grimaced and said, "I'm her boss. This is a job she needs. I can't put her in a position where she might feel pressured."

"Oh, Lord," Linda said with a sigh. "The young make it so difficult. Do you want me to ask her to sign a waiver?"

"No," both Connor and Kimmie said in unison.

"Well, at least we agree on two things: Don't act like a gorilla and don't make a big deal out of something that should happen naturally. If Angelina comes in here and that door closes behind her, consider me and Kimmie gone for the day. We'll clear your schedule, close the outer door, and you two can make as much noise as you please. I can't believe I'm going to ask this, but you've had sex before, right, Connor?"

"Of course."

"Then what is your problem?" Linda asked impatiently.

Connor hunched his shoulders forward. "She's special."

Kimmie clasped her hands over her heart. "That is so beautiful."

Linda was harder to impress. "She sure is special. She's pretty, young, intelligent . . . and kindhearted. That combination doesn't come along often, but you're overthinking this. She's a woman. You're a man. There's a desk over there.

A wall if you prefer it that way. Get her in here and figure it out."

Beginning to relax, Connor laughed. "How did you ever work in a school?"

Linda tapped her temple. "I kept all my thoughts in here."

Kimmie grinned. "I'm glad she doesn't anymore. You should see my books now, Connor. H.O.T. I'll forward you a file. I read one of her scenes to Javier and he lived up to his new caveman costume."

"Caveman?" Connor asked, cocking his head to one side.

"Oh, yes. I'll give you the name of the place Javier and I find unique costumes," Kimmie said with a wink. "For when you need to spice things up later."

"Text me the info. Who knows, maybe she's into dinosaurs."

Linda burst out laughing.

Kimmie joined in.

Women are awesome. And they enjoyed sex as much as a man did. Not every man saw that, but that was their loss. Some men spent their life fumbling around like someone trying to solve a Rubik's Cube with his teeth. Prime example—the dick pic. One guy looked down at his favorite appendage and thought . . . you know who wants to see this? Random women. He told his friends what he'd done and they thought, "Well, hell, if women want to see his dick, I'm sure they want to see mine."

No one stopped to actually ask the women what they thought when they received one of those gems. Connor thought all women should start drawing little faces on those pricks, eyes, mustaches, maybe some teeth. Possibly add bunny ears . . . and send them back. If a man could receive a cartooned-up photo of his dick and not realize how ridiculous sending it had been in the first place, well then, he was beyond hope. And, at least the woman would have had a little fun with an otherwise offensive experience.

A man could save himself a lot of grief by simply asking a woman what she wanted.

Hang on.

That's genius.

"Ladies, feel free to return to your own office. I know exactly how to handle this."

AFTER HIRING A car to drop her off at her office building, Angelina clasped and unclasped her hands nervously as she waited for the elevator. A young woman who also worked for the Landon Foundation joined her and said, "Thank God it's Friday, huh?"

"Yes." Angelina's nerves were working overtime. She'd tried on and changed her attire countless times that morning. She and Connor were on kissing terms, but she didn't know how that would affect their ability to work together. She really liked her new job. But she also really liked Connor. She told herself to play it cool, but not so cool he'd think she wasn't still interested. She'd finally chosen a simple dress, but kicked her underclothing up a notch and had gone with a pink lace bra and matching thong.

"Any plans for the weekend?" the woman asked politely.

Yes, I've given myself permission to fuck my boss. Angelina bit her lip to hold back a laugh as the thought almost came out of her mouth. She cleared her throat. "Nothing worth mentioning. You?"

"No. Not yet. Hey, what's it like to work with Connor Sutton? Is he incredible? I haven't had a chance to meet him yet, but I'm looking for a way to. That man is gorgeous. Any chance you can claim to have a tech issue with your computer?"

"He's seeing someone." *Oh, my God, I really am territorial when it comes to him.*

The woman frowned. "Really? I hadn't heard that. Bummer. Is it serious? Not that I'd care. If they're not married, it means he's still fair game, right?"

Angelina looked the other woman over. "How old are you?"

"Twenty-one. Almost twenty-two."

Angelina pinned her down with a hard look. "Ever hear of the couples curse?"

"No." The woman's eyes widened.

"You know how breaking a mirror gains you seven years bad luck?"

"I guess."

"Breaking up a couple gets you seven years of shitty sex. It's a fact."

The woman wrinkled her nose. "You're joking, right?"

Angelina shrugged. "Not everyone believes in superstitions, but I do. Maybe you're the kind to walk under ladders and not think twice. Me, I like to be careful—just in case there's any truth to them."

The elevator arrived and opened. Angelina and the other woman stepped inside. The ride to their floor was quick and silent. When it opened again, they stepped out at the same time.

The young woman turned toward Angelina with narrowed eyes. "You're the one he's seeing."

She's young, but she's not stupid. Angelina winked at her. "Let's just say I won't be claiming to have a problem with my computer." As she walked away, she smiled. Amazing how simple things were when she believed a good outcome was possible. *Connor likes me. He'd never be interested in someone who probably still goes to college parties.*

That morning she'd woken early and spent a significant amount of time going over everything she knew about Connor, every word they'd exchanged, every tender kiss he'd given her. The way she felt each time he touched her was off the charts good.

So good, she had to ask herself why she was still holding back. Those same words she'd faced again and again came back to her. This time, though, she was armed with Joanna's positive energy.

I was sixteen. It was a lifetime ago.

As she'd rolled the words that had once shamed her around in her head, she'd realized they were only powerful because she'd chosen to carry them with her—to believe they somehow reflected who she really was.

I didn't sleep with half the town—or any of Greg's friends. But would it have mattered if I had? I wasn't his first. I'm sure I wasn't his last. He wanted to hurt me and he used shame as his weapon.

But what have I been ashamed of all this time?

Of wanting to be loved?

Of believing a boy who said he cared about me?

Of having sex?

Or being scared and considering the unthinkable?

Wasn't all of that natural?

And how much longer will I allow the actions of a teenage boy to affect my adult life?

I've found a man who genuinely cares about me—a man who doesn't want to take things further until he knows I'm ready.

So what if a few ignorant people called me names.

I'm not a child anymore.

And I refuse to be ashamed of what I want.

As she strode down the hall, she imagined the scene in slow motion, wind blowing through her hair, and a sensual smile spreading across her face.

Angelina stopped at the door to Kimmie and Linda's office and took a fortifying breath. Taking a leap of faith was scary, but the idea of never being brave enough to was even more frightening. *All I have to do is believe in miracles, magic, and happy endings.*

She swung the door open and stepped through it with forced confidence. "Morning ladies."

"Morning, Angelina," they echoed.

"Is—Is—Is Connor in his office?"

"He is," Kimmie said, then smiled at Linda who returned

the smile as if the two of them were in on a private joke.

Connor appeared at his door. "Angelina."

Their eyes met and the ability to think coherently dissolved. "Connor."

"Good morning."

"Morning."

"I like your shirt."

"Thanks."

In the background, Linda said, "Kimmie, when you write this scene, we'll spice up the dialogue."

"I hope I can capture this level of tension." Kimmie sighed. "I always thought the term sparks flying was so cliché, but I'm getting all flushed just standing next to them."

Linda stood. "On that note, where's the office key? Let's lock up as we go."

The sound of Kimmie's desk drawer opening and closing was followed by them making a hasty retreat and closing the office door behind them.

Angelina swallowed hard, but didn't look away from the desire in Connor's eyes. "Maybe I should be embarrassed, but I'm not."

Connor took a step closer to her. "Never be embarrassed with me."

Angelina stepped toward him. "I have a problem with something you said yesterday."

He took another step. "I said a lot of things. You'll have to be more specific."

"You said you want to make me happy first, then make

me yours. You can't make someone happy. They have to choose that for themselves."

He nodded, but kept approaching. "Okay, then I want to be with you as you choose it."

When he stopped, he towered over her, so close she could feel the heat from his body. "And I'm a little offended that you don't think I'm intelligent enough to appreciate good character in a man."

"Are you saying you like nice guys?" He traced the line of her jaw gently.

"I don't have a lot of experience with them, but I'd say that's definitely what I'm looking for." She placed her hand over his and held it to her cheek. "I'm trying to put it behind me, but I've got some baggage—mental baggage. I overthink things. I tend to fear the worst." She closed her eyes briefly, then admitted, "Especially when things seem to be going well. I want to believe they can continue to, but . . . I'm afraid to."

He leaned down until his lips were just above hers. "Oh my God. You're . . . human."

She chuckled. How did he do it? How did he reach through her pain and draw her back into the light? "You mean everyone is this messed up?"

"Absolutely."

Everything about being with Connor felt good. Her attraction to him went deeper than just sex. She could mindlessly bask in that smile of his all day. "I like you, Connor Sutton. I like you a lot."

He brought his other hand up to cup her face. "I like you

too. And there's no reason we need to rush. I'll be right here whenever you're ready."

Real panic flashed through her, but she pushed it back. This was the side of him she'd sensed during his talk to the soccer team. So kindhearted. So openly caring. He was the answer to a yearning she hadn't allowed herself to admit she had. "What if I'm ready now?"

His face flushed. "Well, okay then." The kiss she expected didn't come, instead his smile faded and he looked down at her with an expression she couldn't decipher. "We shouldn't do this here."

Embarrassment flooded in and she stepped back from him. "Of course. I'm sorry."

He reached out, taking both of her hands in his. "You don't understand and that makes sense since you don't even know me yet. Which me do you want to fuck? The one you saw in the movie? He doesn't exist. The one you met at Reemsly? He doesn't either."

Angelina attempted but failed to free her hands from his. Why was he ruining what could have been such a beautiful moment? "I want the man who spoke about bullies to the soccer team. Are you that man or is he an act too?"

"No, that's all me." Connor frowned. "Do you like working here?"

"Yes." Where was this going?

In the quiet moment that followed, all kinds of dark thoughts circled but she kept telling herself things would work out. Her fears weren't premonitions. They were simply—fears. Connor was a good man and he was trying to tell her something. She could panic or she could listen.

After giving her hands a light squeeze, he said, "The Landon Foundation makes a difference in people's lives on a daily basis. I've never been part of something like that before. What if we fuck on my desk and you feel awkward tomorrow? Will you quit? Will you think I want you to? You're good at what you do. This place needs you and it's the perfect job for you. I don't want to mess that up. Whatever we do, I need to know you won't go back to a place like Reemsly."

Nice didn't begin to describe Connor. So decent. So kind. *Probably a better person than I've ever been.* "I don't want to go back there either." By there, she meant not only to her old employment situation, but also to being someone who couldn't trust this side of Connor to be real. "I'm starting to believe in miracles, magic, and happy endings."

He smiled. "That's a lot of pressure. I don't perform miracles. I've never been good at sleight of hand tricks. However, I am particularly gifted when it comes to mutual happy endings."

"I believe you." She laughed and hugged him. What a goof, but one that made her heart lighter. "Please don't call anyone else to confirm it."

His chest rumbled with his laughter, and he hugged her closer.

She stood there for a moment, simply enjoying being enveloped by him.

He tucked her under his chin, and said, "I don't always think things through, but I'm working on it." He sighed. "I laugh too loud. If I get past three beers I'm probably finishing the case. I love to make people laugh even if it means tossing all dignity aside. That's who I am."

She absorbed his words and considered them before saying, "I've spent the last thirteen years going to bed thinking about everything I did wrong that day and waking up worried about what I'd do wrong next. That's who I am." She tipped her head back and met his gaze. "Sometime, I'd like to laugh too loud and not care what anyone thinks. What do you think about that?"

His smile returned. "Are you afraid of flying?"

"Sorry?"

"I just had an aneurism. No, an epiphany. I just figured out the best way for us to have sex."

Angelina's eyebrows rose. "You did?"

"You're going to love this."

CONNOR TOOK OUT his phone and with one arm still around Angelina called his pilot. "Will, I need you to come pick me up at my office, but I have a special request."

"Absolutely, Mr. Sutton. What do you need?"

"Remember that copter we used in Dallas? The big one?"

"Yes."

"Do you have that, but with a bed?"

"A bed?"

By his tone, it didn't sound like one was an option. "How about a couch? Something long enough for someone my height to recline on."

"Sir, you do realize due to fuel consumption and the size

of the craft you're requesting, the time in the air at most would be two hours."

"That would be more than enough time."

"Do you have a destination in mind?"

Connor met Angelina's surprised gaze and asked, "Do you have a helipad on your building?"

Angelina shook her head.

"We'll go to my apartment, then—the long way."

"The long way, sir?"

"Whatever way takes about two hours. Text me when you're here." Connor ended the call feeling pretty good about it. He snapped his fingers. "We should make a packing list. Claire says they're essential." He patted his pockets. "Condoms. I didn't bring any with me. How about you?"

Angelina's cheeks went delightfully pink, then she said, "Three."

"Fantastic." He kissed her lips briefly then stepped back and looked around. "We'll need some tape and paper from the copy machine."

Looking bemused, Angelina didn't move to gather either. "Why?"

It didn't seem like it should require explanation, but maybe it did. "We don't know how many helicopters will be up in the air while we are. Everyone has already seen my naked ass, but do you really want yours to hit the internet? Cameras are everywhere."

Still, she stood there, smiling without moving. "Are you planning to tape up the windows of a helicopter so we can have sex in it?"

He thought that over. "You think they come with shades? Of course they probably do. Rich people think of everything. Hang on, I'll text Will to make sure he chooses a craft that does." After sending that request, he also wrote: **On the way, fill the passenger cabin with white roses. Hundreds. Pick up some champagne. Something good. And bill Clay Landon.**

Chapter Fifteen

A SHORT TIME later, Angelina's hand tightened on Connor's as they watched a large helicopter land on the roof of the office building. The pilot hopped out, ducked, and ran toward them. "Mr. Sutton. Sorry about the delay. Everything is as you requested."

"Perfect," Connor yelled to be heard above the sound of the rotors. He turned to Angelina. "Do you have everything?"

If he was referring to her purse and the condoms she'd stashed in it—then yes. "All set," she said and made a thumbs-up motion.

Connor held their linked hands up, turned back to the pilot, and called out, "Roger, this is Angelina. If things work out the way I'm hoping, you'll be flying the two of us around from now on. I can imagine forever with her."

Angelina's mouth dropped open in surprise and remained that way even as she shook Roger's hand. *Forever? It was fast . . . too fast? She wasn't sure.*

"Nice to meet you, Roger." It was strange to be yelling pleasantries, but it was the only way to be heard.

Roger leaned down, and in Angelina's ear said clearly, "You break his heart, I'll drop you from the sky." He straightened and flashed her a smile.

Angelina's eyes widened.

Roger clapped a hand on Connor's back and yelled, "Best boss ever."

Connor was all smiles. "Then make it a smooth ride."

"Will do, Mr. Sutton," the pilot said then waved for them to follow him to the back of the helicopter.

With Connor's assistance, Angelina started to climb in, then stopped. The rear of the chopper was a wall-to-wall, three-seater, ivory leather couch. Every inch of the interior was covered with white rose petals. Vases of long-stemmed white roses were placed strategically around the cabin. Between two ivory captain chairs that flanked the cockpit a bottle of champagne was chilling on ice on a mahogany bar.

There was no pretending Roger didn't know what they were about to do.

The question Angelina mulled over was did she care? It wasn't as if she hadn't had sex since being with Whitney's father. She'd been with two other men, but sex hadn't added depth to either relationship. If anything, it had weakened them.

Not because they judged me for sleeping with them, but because I did. She turned and met Connor's gaze. *Is he right? Should we wait?*

She glanced at Roger. His expression was politely blank.

A helicopter full of white rose petals.

Connor wants to whisk me away into the sky and just said

he can imagine forever with me.

It's almost—magical.

"Don't let me mess this up," she said to herself.

His expression turned tender. He couldn't have heard her, but he said, "If it's too much, we can catch a movie instead. No pressure. No worries. Your choice. Roger can fill the helicopter with roses every day until you're ready. Or not. What do *you* want, Angelina?"

He was the first man to ask her that question and really want the answer.

Angelina leaned forward, wrapped her arms around his neck, and hugged him. His arms came around her, but he merely held her to him, their breathing finding a common rhythm. It was a moment of gratitude, of friendship, and that was when she first imagined what happily ever after could be like.

She wanted a man who could love her son, a man she could be herself with, someone strong enough to lean on, but kind enough to never use that strength against her.

Connor was that kind of man.

She hugged him tighter. "I want to do this."

His playful smile reassured her that she hadn't ruined the mood. "Then get the hell in."

She laughed and released him, stepping inside the cabin and sliding all the way down to one end of the couch. He joined her and secured both of their seat belts.

As soon as the door closed, the noise of the rotors fell away—replaced by a soft jazz melody. The cabin tipped as the helicopter took off and Angelina grabbed Connor's hand.

Connor dipped his head down to near hers. "I thought you said you weren't afraid of flying."

She tipped her chin higher and tried not to look out the window. "I'm not afraid, it's just my first time."

"Helicopter virgin," he joked. "If it makes you feel better, I'm still figuring out the logistics of how this could best work."

"Really? And what have you come up with?"

Desire flashed in his eyes. "Come here." He gave one of his thighs a pat.

It wasn't a command.

It was an invitation and one she was willing to accept. She released her seat belt and hiked up her skirt so she could straddle his lap on her knees which brought her nearly face-to-face with him. "Yes?" she asked playfully.

He ran his hands up the back of her thighs, beneath the back of her skirt. "I asked Roger. No one can see inside the windows."

"That's a relief," she said with a chuckle as she balanced herself by holding on to his shoulders.

His strong hands slid higher and his smile widened as they were not impeded by more than a thin strip of lace. "Angelina Kroll, were you thinking of me when you dressed this morning?"

It was impossible not to smile back and there was no reason to lie. "I was. I don't want to brag, but the bra matches."

"Nice." He ran his hands down then up her legs again, a warm, easy, erotic caress. "I didn't think you'd see mine, but I chose one with a message that is fitting anyway."

Her hands explored his upper body as they spoke. His thick, muscled neck. Those amazing arms of his. She brought her hands between them and ran them over his well-defined chest. "What does it say?" She leaned forward, kissed his neck, and breathed in the clean, intoxicating scent of him.

His breathing deepened and he cleared his throat. "Possibilities are infinite for those who believe."

For those who believe.

She froze and raised her head. "I'm starting to believe."

He cupped her ass gently. "But you're scared."

She looked deeply into his eyes. "You're not?"

He held her gaze for a long moment. "Not with you. Something clicked in me when we first met. I saw forever with you. It was crazy. I imagined our kids, a house, the whole thing. Then you nearly bored me into a coma which almost convinced me I was wrong, but I'm glad I gave you a second chance."

She sat up straighter and gasped. "Bored you?"

He did an impression of her voice if spoken by an old English librarian. "Reemsly was founded in 1912 by the Amish. This building is made entirely with bricks. Let's count them together. One. Two. Three."

Angelina flicked Connor on the shoulder. "I didn't say any of that. You weren't even listening, were you?"

He laid his head back and pretended to snore.

She tickled his side, which jolted him back up straight. "I was trying to impress you. My job depended on it."

"It doesn't anymore." He caught her hands in his and his

expression turned serious. "And stay clear of anything to do with that place, at least for the time being. Mr. Svete won't be there much longer and the more you distance yourself from that situation, the better."

"What's going to happen to him?"

"My guess? Whatever he deserves. Most likely prison. You weren't fired because you gave crappy tours. He's dirty."

"What do you mean dirty? Like guilty of something? Of what?"

Connor shrugged. "Not my place to say."

"And how do you know?"

Connor shrugged again.

Angelina guessed. "Bradford."

"Don't tell him I said anything."

Angelina ran the last few weeks over in her head. "I knew it wasn't a coincidence that he ran into Linda at the market."

"We needed to make sure you and your son were okay. When she told us what had happened, we knew she couldn't stay there either."

"So you hired her." Angelina traced his lips with her fingertips. "I've never met anyone like you." A thought occurred to her that spilled out. "What exactly is Linda's job in your office?"

Connor's smile turned sheepish. "She's Kimmie's editor." When Angelina arched an eyebrow, Connor wrinkled his nose. "Every office needs an assistant, but I didn't actually have anything for one to do. When Kimmie interviewed and said she was looking for something temporary because her goal was to becoming a published romance author, I hired her on the spot. It was perfect. She needed a quiet place to write, and I needed someone who would look busy."

"You're serious."

"She's an amazing writer. And her plan to put three out, each a month apart, is a solid strategy to get them noticed. Linda is spicing up her sex scenes—"

"Of course she is." Angelina met and held Connor's gaze. "So, you're not only paying Kimmie to work for herself, but you've also hired an employee for her." No one she knew would have done either.

"It's just money. I can make more of it. Kimmie's goal is to earn enough to stay home and have a herd of children. When you meet her husband you'll understand why they need to procreate. The world needs more of both of them. Whatever you do, though, don't tell Javier you like spicy food. I made that mistake once and there are parts of my intestines that are still charred from the experience."

Angelina chuckled. "I'll keep that in mind."

The helicopter tipped upward, causing Angelina to fall forward onto Connor's chest. As she righted herself, her face hovered near his, and she forgot what they were talking about as soon as his mouth closed over hers.

Unlike the kisses they'd shared in public, this was more forceful. His tongue parted her lips, claimed hers with tantalizing skill. His hands became rougher, his thighs more rigid between hers. This kiss was everything they'd shared, but so much more.

She gripped his shoulders.

He slid her skirt higher until it bunched around her waist.

When his hand slid between them and beneath her front slip of lace, she moaned into his mouth in anticipation. His fingers were as oversized as the rest of him—and he knew how to use them. Connor understood a woman's body. He started slowly, gently, experimenting until he got it just right.

She writhed against his hand.

Their kiss became wilder.

She was wet and ready when he slid a finger deep inside her. So big. So long. Alone it was enough to satisfy a woman. He pumped it in and out of her, deeper each time. When he found the spot no man before had, she broke off the kiss and said, "Holy fuck, that's good."

He kept pumping against it, kissing her neck and murmuring, "I've read about the female orgasm. Some say there are over ten types. It'll be fun to see which ones you like best."

He was talking, but she was barely listening. She needed more of him. More of his kiss. More of his skin. As he pumped his thick finger in and out of her, she undid the front of her shirt and tossed it aside. Her bra quickly followed. His free hand palmed her breast as he unbuttoned the front of his plaid shirt.

His mouth claimed hers again as his finger increased speed. She clung to him, rubbed her breasts against his bare chest, then shuddered as an orgasm rocked through her. He slid his finger out then lifted her to him and placed her beside him on the leather couch.

Due to his height, he couldn't stand straight up, but that didn't impede him from quickly shedding his clothing. When his cock sprang free, Angelina's mouth dropped open. It was huge and rock-hard rigid.

Her hands encircled it, her sex imagined it pounding into her, and she nearly came again from that anticipation alone. He stepped closer and she didn't need more encouragement than that to take him into her mouth.

Giving oral sex had never been something Angelina considered that enjoyable and his size was intimidating. He didn't rush her, though, or shove himself down her throat. Bent over in front of her, he braced himself with his legs slightly apart and allowed her to learn him as he'd learned her.

His moans of pleasure vibrated through his cock and excited her in a way that was new to her. His pleasure was her pleasure. Her pleasure was his pleasure. "Stop," he said in a guttural tone, withdrawing from her mouth. "I don't want to rush through this."

Still partially dressed, she sat back on her heels on the couch. He held out a hand to her. "Stand up."

She took his hand and did. Together, they made quick work of the rest of her clothing. They stood there, taking each other in for a moment.

"You're so damn beautiful," he said.

"So are you," she answered in complete honesty. She leaned to one side, retrieved a condom from her purse, and tossed it to him.

He caught it, then placed it on one of the captain chairs. "It's a little cramped in here, but I have an idea." He sat down on the rose petal-lined floor of the cabin and leaned back. She wasn't sure what he wanted at first, but he guided her to stand over him, then move closer . . . closer . . . until she was poised above his face.

She braced herself with her hands on the ceiling of the cabin while he parted her sex and demonstrated that his tongue was every bit as talented as his fingers. So wet. So hot. Deliciously demanding. She lost all respect for the women who'd left him. No wonder they changed their minds later and wanted to come back.

She flung her head back and gave herself over to his tongue fucking. Whatever he'd read about the female orgasm should be mandatory reading for all men. *Holy shit.*

His hands caressed her legs, gripped her ass, and crushed her sex to his mouth each time he thrust his tongue inside her. Lapping. Sucking. Thrusting. It was all so good she buried her hands in his hair and clung to him as waves of heat burst through her.

As she came down from that high, he kissed her inner thighs and said, "That's two kinds. Want to keep going?"

Was there a woman on earth who would have said no? "Sure," she croaked.

He sheathed himself in a condom then put a hand on either side of her hips. Hands on his shoulders, she lowered herself onto his cock . . . slowly. He was intimidatingly large, but he was also patient. She adjusted, shifted, slid him in at her own pace.

With her feet on either side of him, she rose and lowered herself, taking him deeper each time. When he was fully in, she sighed with pleasure. So good.

Then he started to move.

His thrusts started gently. In and almost out. In and almost out.

His grip on her hips became more forceful.

His thrusts deeper.

He shifted their position so he could get more leverage.

She bounced above him, reveling in a rhythm he set but she joined. His mouth adored each part of her he could reach. She hungrily ran her hands over every inch of him she could.

All tenderness fell away. They rolled together, sweaty and demanding. He pounded down into her. She stretched wider to accept him. Any discomfort from his size was far outweighed by the pleasure storming through her.

When he came it was with a shudder that rocked his whole body.

He kept moving within her, though, after his orgasm. Kept his pace until she joined him, crying out his name.

He rolled off her, removed his condom then tucked her to his side and kissed her forehead. "So, that's helicopter sex. What do you think?"

She hid a smile. "I like it."

He frowned. "Like? That's it?"

She tossed a handful of rose petals onto his chest and chuckled. "I suppose I could get used to it."

"Me too." He hugged her closer and gave her a kiss that

had her melting against him. He checked his watch. "Luckily we have an hour left."

"And two more condoms," she joked.

"Is that a challenge?" He kissed the tip of her nose. He took a deep breath. "If so, I accept." Not a man of empty words, his cock twitched and swelled back to full arousal before her eyes.

Never had sex felt as lighthearted and freeing as it did with him. "Let's ask Roger to take us to your place. Are you any good at up against the wall sex? I've always wanted to try that."

His chest puffed. "Good at it? I was made for it. For the third time I'm thinking slow, easy sex on my balcony. A nice, easy fuck from behind while we look out over the city."

Oh, yes. Angelina licked her bottom lip. "Connor?"

"Yes?"

"We're going to need more condoms."

A FEW HOURS later, naked and sated, Connor was pulled from a deep sleep by an alarm on Angelina's phone. She didn't stir. He tapped her phone, wrapped his arms around her and growled into her ear, "Angelina, your phone alarm went off."

She murmured something and snuggled her back closer to him.

He could have stayed like that forever, but considering it was early afternoon, his guess was the alarm was her reminder to pick up her son. "Angelina, wake up."

She rolled over in his arms and her eyes opened. A smile

curled her lips. "Hey, you."

"Hey, yourself." He gave her a gentle kiss. "What time do you need to pick up Whitney?"

"Whitney." She sat straight up, her bare breasts jiggling free as she ran her hands through her hair. "Oh my God. What time is it?"

"Three o'clock."

She let out a relieved breath and nodded. "That should give me enough time to get to my car and pick him up. He gets out of the technology club at five." She looked across the room and froze when she saw her reflection in a large mirror across the room. "I can't pick him up like this. I look—I look—"

"Gorgeous." He sat up and kissed her shoulder. She had that wild hair, smudged makeup, rosy, well-fucked look that no man minded.

With her fingertips she tried to wipe away the makeup below her eyes. When it didn't work, she blinked back tears. "I can't be late picking him up."

"Hey, hey. I'll make sure you get there in plenty of time."

She covered her face with both hands. "I'm sorry."

"So am I." His post-sex euphoria drained away, replaced by gut-wrenching regret that he hadn't kept to his original plan to take things slow with her.

She lowered her hands and met his gaze. "Don't be. This isn't about you."

Another man might have taken her comment as an insult. Connor didn't. "Is it about something I could help you with?" He held out a hand to her.

She laced her fingers with his. "I don't want to ruin the day by vomiting my personal problems all over it."

He nuzzled her neck. "Yeah, because fucking and friendship should never go together."

She gave him a sidelong look and sniffed. "Is that what you want to be? Friends?"

It amazed him that someone who was so competent on the outside could be so fragile and lost as soon as emotions were involved. "Isn't that the best foundation for any relationship?"

She shuddered. "It is." She closed her eyes briefly then met his gaze again. "I'm worried about Whitney. He says everything is fine. On the surface it looks like it is. He does well in school. His teachers always like him. He's struggling, though. When I picked him up yesterday—before he saw me—he looked sad. Did you like school?"

He grimaced. "I wasn't what you'd call a good student."

"I didn't ask about your GPA. Did you enjoy it?"

"Sure. I mean, as much as anyone does, I guess."

"What did you like about it?"

It wasn't something he'd put much thought into in a long time so he took a moment to think back. "My friends. Playing football. Playing football with my friends. Hanging out. Sex. All the normal stuff."

"Whitney never talks about friends. Never invites anyone over. As far as I know, he hasn't stayed in contact with anyone at Reemsly. I was hoping this school would be different, but I'm worried that it won't be."

"He just started at the school. Give him time."

"I know. I'm trying not to worry, but he has this idea that he has to be strong for me."

"How old is he?"

"Thirteen."

"That's a tough age, but he has you in his corner. He'll be okay."

She smiled. "He asked to meet you tomorrow before our date—to make sure he approves of you."

Good man. "I like him already."

"And he warned me not to have sex with you on our first date. So try to look like—like we haven't—" Her cheeks went delightfully pink.

"Gotcha." He kissed the top of her head. "We'll play it cool."

"I've dated a few men since his father, but never anyone serious. And he didn't meet them. There was never a reason for him to." She looked embarrassed again. "Not that I'm saying there's a reason for him to meet you—"

He stopped her from saying more with a kiss. She was a self-professed worrier. He hadn't been one before he'd met the Barringtons and was on a journey back to a calmer place in his head. If she was interested, there was room for two in that space. "I like you, Angelina. I'm excited to meet your son tomorrow. Now, get your ass in the shower. I'd join you, but the goal is for you to be on time to pick him up, right?"

A smile returned to her face. "I'd say you could come with me to pick him up, but—"

He kissed her briefly again, then joked, "If your ass is

late, it's on you. I've been trying to kick you out of my bed for about twenty minutes."

She ran a hand over one side of his face, gave him a long, hot look that nearly had him backpedaling and asking her to stay. "Thank you, Connor."

It was his turn to get a little flustered. The man he saw in her eyes was comfortable with himself, kind without being a joke, a much better version of himself than he'd ever been. And for the first time in a long time he didn't feel like he was acting. "Go on, get. I have shit to do. Really important things . . ."

She chuckled and crawled out of bed. The view of her bare ass was thought-erasing. When she stood and asked him if flying back to the office would be faster than driving, he just stared at her. *Flying?*

What office?

When she asked him again, he realized his smitten grin was not an adequate response. "Yes."

"Yes, I should fly back? Or should I call a car? Are you heading back to your office?"

Yes, to whatever she wanted.

Uninhibited by her state of undress, she clapped her hands. "Are you listening to me?"

No, I'm too busy falling in love. He shook his head and continued to smile shamelessly at her. "Not really. You're even more beautiful naked than you are dressed. Not everyone can make that claim."

She laughed. "Call your pilot. I'll be right back." She gave him one last cheeky smile and darted into the bathroom.

There goes my future wife.

Sigh.

Now, what was it she wanted me to do?

A HALF HOUR before she needed to be there, Angelina was in her car in the parking lot of Whitney's school waiting for him to be released from technology club. She didn't mind waiting since it gave her time to process the sharp turn her relationship with Connor had taken.

It didn't feel like they'd only had sex . . . it felt as if they'd gone from dancing around each other to choosing to be together. Scary. Wonderful. Almost too much to take in.

In the sex department, he'd certainly lived up to the hype. So did wall sex. Her cheeks warmed at the memory of how they'd barely made it into his apartment. She closed her eyes and relived being lifted up, wrapped around him and pounded into. Connor was the perfect combination of strong and gentle—forceful but thoughtful.

He was also particularly gifted with his tongue. It was a surprising talent for a man his size. Large men, especially attractive ones, didn't have to try as hard with women. They knew they were in higher demand. Connor was confident but also attentive. Damn near perfect.

And unexpectedly really funny. There was no way not to laugh when he told a story about situations he and his brother, Dylan, had gotten into together. At first she'd thought he was joking that they had kidnapped Ian Barrington and stuck him in a laundry cart, but the story was too detailed not to believe.

And Connor had been too proud of himself about how easily they'd done it.

His method of hugging the anger out of the Barringtons? Priceless. By the time he described the day Bradford had tried to scare Dylan and him into leaving Ian alone and how it had led to their friendship—she'd been able to picture everything so clearly that she'd laughed her stomach muscles sore.

The story was one of freedom and impulsiveness, two things Angelina had denied herself since she'd learned she was pregnant with Whitney.

That particular thought might have been the reason why hearing Connor describe his etiquette lessons with Claire made her a little sad. Yes, everyone had to grow up, but it sounded like the goal had been to systematically erase all the joy out of Connor.

The Barringtons had taken a naturally optimistic, loving man and chipped away at his confidence until he'd started second-guessing every word that came out of his mouth. Not a badass at all—just a man trying to please everyone and losing himself along the way.

She understood that journey far too well.

Her heart had soared once again when he'd shared what his father had said, "There's nothing wrong with the children I raised," and how that had helped him cement his goal to find a common ground between the old him and the one his sister hoped he'd become.

What a good father. No wonder Connor was kindhearted.

Angelina's thoughts were interrupted by a call. "Busy?" her friend Aly asked.

"No, parked and waiting for Whitney. What's up?"

"Did you see the news? Your old boss was arrested on campus today. He confessed to embezzling over a million dollars from Reemsly. I'm so glad you're no longer there."

"Confessed? That sounds unlikely." Then she remembered what Connor had said about Bradford investigating him. He must have threatened to expose something worse if admitting to embezzlement was a better option. "I don't feel sorry for him. He was a horrible man. I do feel bad for the school, though. Any idea who they'll find to step in?"

"Interested?"

"Oh, no. I've closed the door on that place, but I hope they choose their next headmaster with more care. The children deserve the kind of positive Reemsly experience I had."

"That actually sounds quite healthy of you."

"Thank you," Angelina said.

"What are you smiling about?"

"How do you know I am?"

"I can hear it in your voice. So, come on, cough it up. Are things heating up at your new job?"

"You could say that."

"What? Hold on. What have I missed?"

Angelina took a deep breath then blurted, "I'm falling in love with him, Aly. If you took a miracle, added some magic, and put it in a blender with a dash of I-think-this-could-be-the-one—that's how great of a day I had with him."

"Wow," Aly said. "So, the sex was good."

"Oh, yes. But this isn't about that."

"Isn't it? The endorphins released by multiple orgasms can induce an emotional response that feels like love."

Leave it to Aly to reduce how she felt to a biological response to finally getting laid. "Have you ever been in love?"

"No, nor have you."

Low. True, but low. "I've had multiple orgasms before, though, and this is different."

"Because it didn't require batteries?"

Angelina's mouth dropped open, then she laughed. Aly had a cutting humor that could be missed in the heat of the moment. "Jerk. All I'm saying is that I had the most incredible day with Connor."

"I don't doubt that. I'm just suggesting you tap the brakes. The last time we spoke you were sure he wasn't even your type. Give your blood time to recirculate to your brain."

"What happened to thinking I should be more optimistic?"

"That was Joanna. Listen, if it works out with Connor, I'm all for it. I'm team Angelina, though. Take your time. Let him prove himself. Whitney is still young enough that what you do affects him."

Angelina sighed and gripped her steering wheel. "Do you think I don't know that? I've made Whitney my life for the past thirteen years. This isn't going to change my priorities. I had a great date. Great sex. For once I'm not beating myself up with all the ways this could go wrong. Even if it does, let me have this. I need to believe good things are possible."

Aly was quiet for a moment. "I'm sorry."

"No, I am. I didn't mean to snap like that."

"You had every right to. It's easier to advise you about your love life than ask myself why mine is nonexistent. Classic transference."

"It's more than that and you know it. You also love me and don't want to see me hurt."

"That too." Aly chuckled.

The passenger door of Angelina's car opened and Whitney jumped in just in time to hear Aly ask, "So, what made the sex so good?"

"Gotta go, bye Aly," Angelina said, ending the call and groaning audibly.

An awkward silence dragged on for long enough that Angelina broke out in a sweat. She knew she should say something, but she hadn't felt this guilty since her father had caught her sneaking some of his beer out to her friends when she was a teenager.

Angelina cleared her throat and opened her mouth, then closed it. *I could say sex is perfectly natural and . . . and . . .*

Oh, shit.

"Mom?"

"Yes?" Her voice came out as a squeak.

"Do I need to start wearing a bell?"

The humor in her son's voice made it possible for her to turn and look him in the eye. With a nervous laugh, she said, "I am so sorry. I'll pay for whatever amount of therapy you need after this week."

He tossed his bookbag into the back of the car. "I'm fine. At least it was good sex."

Angelina started the car engine. "This topic is now officially closed." She backed out of the parking spot. "How was school?"

"Not as good as your day," Whitney said dryly.

Angelina barked out a laugh. "Stop. I am attempting to adult here. Erase the last few minutes from your memory because I have every intention of pretending they never happened."

His laugh helped ease the remaining tension. After another quiet moment, he said, "Seriously, Mom, I don't care as long as you're happy. It's good to see you laughing."

She gave his arm a pat. "Thanks, Whitney. I really like this guy." She glanced over to check his expression. He seemed to be taking it all in stride.

"Is he still picking you up from our apartment tomorrow?"

"Yes."

"Good, because I have a few things I want to say to him before your date."

Oh, boy. "Whitney, he's a good man."

"We'll see."

Angelina almost told Whitney not to be rude to Connor, but she thought about what Aly had said . . . if things worked out with Connor, Whitney's life would be affected as well. Her son had yet to disappoint her. If anything, he was so well-behaved it often worried her.

What was the worst that could happen? If Whitney said something that offended Connor to the point that he didn't want to be with her—then he wasn't the man she was beginning to think he was. Whitney had the right to ask questions, to voice his concerns.

During the ride home, conversation turned to mundane topics—homework, schedules, dinner. The evening passed as uneventfully. When Whitney retired to his room, Angelina texted Connor: **Are we still on for tomorrow?**

Connor: **Hell yes.**

She smiled. **What time?**

Connor: **How about eleven?**

Angelina: **Perfect. What should I wear?**

Connor: **Go casual. I have two options for the day. I'll let you choose tomorrow.**

Angelina: **Now I'm curious.**

Connor: **Good. But I'm not saying a word.**

Angelina: **If you were here I could get you to talk.**

Connor: **I don't doubt that for a second. Hey, today was incredible.**

With a huge grin, Angelina sat on the couch and hugged a pillow to her stomach. Whether the warmth spreading through her was due to a chemical reaction or a burst of love, it felt too damn good to question. **It sure was.** She didn't want to hold back when it came to him. **I wish I could sleep in your arms tonight.**

Connor: **It would have to be sleep because you wore me out.**

She laughed. **Poor baby. You'll recover.**

Connor: **Bet your ass I will. Did you get to Whitney's school on time?**

Angelina: I did.

Connor: **Good. I'm looking forward to meeting him tomorrow.**

About that. *Angelina:* **I'm hopeful the two of you will get along.**

Connor: **We will. I have a plan.**

Until recently, Angelina would have needed to know what the plan was. She would have dissected it, mentally listed every reason why it might fail, and likely had a nightmare or two about it as her subconscious visualized worst-case scenarios.

But I'm not going to torture myself like that.

I'm going to keep saying, "Everything will work out."

The more I say it, the more I believe it.

And I really want to believe it.

Angelina: **See you tomorrow at eleven.**

His response was an emoji of a gorilla.

That's good.

Right?

Chapter Sixteen

THE NEXT MORNING, after packing the trunk of his car, Connor started the drive to Angelina's apartment then remembered something he'd meant to do the night before. Via the phone in his car, he called Clay. Surprisingly, he picked up.

"You're going to love what I have planned. The car should be there to pick you up in about an hour," Clay said.

"I love you for wanting to do this, but Angelina and I are already working things out."

"I know. I heard. Because of your lack of patience I had to change today's itinerary. It was going to start with a helicopter ride. I'll admit, though, filling one with white rose petals was a nice touch I didn't consider."

"Clay, I'm not even going to ask you how much you do or don't know about that ride. Later we'll discuss having healthy boundaries. Right now, you need to hear what I'm saying. I'm not home. I won't be home until later tonight. If you send a car no one will be there for it to pick up."

Almost without missing a beat, Clay asked, "So, where do you want it to retrieve you and Angelina?"

And people think I'm slow.

"Clay, I made my own plans for the day. I don't need your help. I've got this."

"Oh."

"I'm grateful for everything you've done. You've been wonderful to me. It's just that—"

"Don't worry about it. I'll cancel the car."

"Don't be mad at me."

"Dogs with rabies get mad. I'm not mad."

"Angry then."

"That would require being emotionally involved, which I'm not. My intention was to do something nice for you. If you can do this all on your own, that's better for everyone."

The problem with Clay was that rather than hugging him, or spanking him, his parents had raised him to believe money was the way people showed they cared. Someday Clay would see that people would love him just as much if he showed up in a Jeep with a case a beer. The private jet? The endless gifts? They were nice, but they weren't why Connor considered him a friend. More than anything else, Clay didn't just say he wanted to be involved—he showed up. Like when he'd bought a new wardrobe for Connor. The only reason Connor had accepted it was because Clay had been right there, picking out each item with the care of a proud parent sending his child off to school for the first time. It had been so touching Connor hadn't been able to say no.

He didn't like that he was disappointing Clay, but one thing Connor had learned recently was that while he still wanted to make others happy . . . he had to do it in his own way. If he and Clay were going to remain friends, Clay would need to respect that.

"I'm on my way to Angelina's right now. I planned two separate dates. I'm going to let her choose which one she wants."

"I don't care one way or the other."

Yes, he did. Otherwise they wouldn't still be having this conversation. "If it goes the way I hope it does, I'll call you later to tell you about it. My biggest goal for the day is to get her kid to like me. I have to tell you, meeting him is a little intimidating. This kid is smart. Brilliant. I'm not even going to pretend I know big words around him. I can't fuck this up. I see a future with Angelina."

"You'll do fine."

"I can't badass this. That's not who I want to be in her life. I also don't want to be a joke to her son."

"You won't be."

"I know everyone calls me a meathead. Hey, Fairy God-father, do you have an intelligence wand you can wave? Because that's what this Cinderfella needs. Or am I Prince Charming? See, I don't even fucking know. I thought I had two great dates planned, but now that I'm talking it out, I don't know if either is a good idea."

Clay sighed. "Meathead. I wish that had been my nick-name growing up. My boarding school was a cesspool of negativity. Money and 'big words' don't insulate a person from ridicule. In fact, sometimes they're a magnet for it. I don't know what Angelina's son is like, but I know you. You play the idiot, but you're not one. Be yourself with Angelina's son and you'll be fine. I've never met a kid who didn't adore you."

"I am kind of likeable."

"You are."

"So are you, Clay. You're a good friend. I have an idea. Don't waste the date you planned for me. Take your wife on it. I bet Lexi would love that."

Sounding much happier, Clay said, "That is a fabulous idea. I haven't surprised her with anything in a while."

"See. It all worked out. I'm going to let you go now because I'm almost at Angelina's apartment, but let's talk tomorrow."

"Good luck, Connor."

"Thanks, Clay."

Connor parked in the garage of Angelina's New York apartment and smiled. Ever since he'd asked his father if he'd been happier before meeting the Barringtons, he'd been asking himself the same question. What he'd realized was it wasn't a simple yes or no.

Since meeting them, he'd learned to doubt himself.

But he'd also grown because of the experience.

Like a pendulum, his life had swung back and forth between extremes.

If he hadn't met the Barringtons, he wouldn't know that where he wanted to be was somewhere in the middle. He got out of his car and opened the trunk. He also wouldn't know the bonding power of board games. Video games were fun—he enjoyed them as much as anyone, but there was something magical about going old school. Monopoly. Battleship. UNO.

They were the perfect icebreakers.

No one could remain reserved while gleefully telling another person that they sunk their battleship. He didn't know how Angelina would feel about him suggesting a game day rather than a romantic one, but he had a plan B just in case.

And if everything went as he was hoping, there would be a lifetime of romantic days ahead.

AFTER ANGELINA BUZZED Connor up, she paced nervously back and forth to the door of her apartment. Whitney was sitting on the couch playing a violent video game he knew she didn't approve of. It was a show of defiance that didn't bode well for how this was about to go.

On a normal day she would have reminded him that such games were banned from their home. She also would have reminded him to watch his manners with Connor.

There was nothing normal about introducing Whitney to a man he knew she'd slept with. She took ownership of the part she'd played in making this introduction awkward.

Whitney didn't look up from his game when there was a knock on the door. Angelina took a deep breath, forced a brave smile, and let Connor in.

"Hi," she said breathlessly. Each time she saw him felt as exciting as the first. Would that zing always be there? She hoped so.

"Hi, yourself." His arms were laden with at least ten board games, but he leaned in to kiss her on the cheek.

"Where should I put these?"

"On the dining table, I guess." She referenced a table behind the couch. "That's a lot of games. Whitney, stop and say hello."

Whitney continued to play his video game.

While Connor was occupied with putting the games down, Angelina leaned over the back of the couch and said softly, "Whitney Timothy Kroll, I respect how you feel about meeting Connor. You need to remember that respect goes both ways. I care about this man."

Whitney ended the game and stood. Angelina wasn't sure what to expect when Connor joined them.

Connor held out a hand to Whitney. "Nice to meet you, Whitney. I feel ridiculous because I was imagining you as a child, but you look old enough to drive."

Whitney didn't shake his hand. He looked him over and asked, "Did you know you wanted to date my mother before you hired her?"

Connor lowered his hand. "I did. It's complicated, but I'm telling myself it's not morally an issue because she seems to like me as well."

Angelina stood awkwardly between them. "Did you see the games Connor brought? You used to love to play board games, remember? We'll have to try them out."

Whitney frowned and directed his next question at Connor as well. "What's the deal with all the games?"

Connor didn't seem bothered by Whitney's cool tone. "I thought they'd be a fun way for all of us to get to know each other. I kick ass at Parcheesi, am a formidable opponent in

UNO, but—full disclosure—I've been known to cheat at RISK."

"So, you're a cheater?" Whitney latched onto the word like a prosecutor in a courtroom.

"Only at the end of RISK. I think everyone should. Who really enjoys that last part? Maybe the same people who claim losing at Monopoly is still fun? RISK is a war game. You can't convince me if you were losing a war you wouldn't find a way to get a few extra soldiers behind enemy lines. Like a Trojan ram."

Ram? Angelina didn't correct Connor.

Whitney wasn't as kind. "Don't you mean horse?"

Without missing a beat, Connor said, "I only read the Iliad as a graphic novel so I could be wrong, but I think Homer exaggerated the details a bit for effect. Think about it—you've been at war for about ten years. All of a sudden, the other side gives up and sails away? Yeah, because that happens. And one guy who says he's no longer with the losers who left wants to give you an enormous gift—one that no one fucking needs. A big, hollow wooden horse. A story that doesn't make sense isn't likely to be true. First, you don't make shit like that overnight or by yourself. It takes time and that means people knew about it. And people talk. Second, let's pretend it's possible to keep a huge wooden horse a secret . . . I challenge you to gather up a bunch of your friends and tell them to quietly hide in a wooden horse. Have you ever gone hunting with a bunch of guys? How long were they in there? More than five minutes? Guaranteed one of them had to take a piss. Because no matter how many times you tell someone there won't be a bathroom, they don't get it. And those soldiers would have been nervous. Their backup buddies just left on a boat. Yeah, so there's no chance there wouldn't have been leakage out the hooves of that Trojan horse. The only version of that story that makes sense is if the Greeks had built the horse as a battering ram. They broke down the damn door then decided to not only slaughter everyone inside but also perpetrate a smear campaign so good we're still talking about it today."

Angelina watched her son's expression. He cocked his head to one side, then the other as he seemed to be trying to decide what to make of Connor. "There are theories that the Trojan horse was a battering ram."

Connor smiled. With one hand he did the motion of an explosion. "Bam. I knew it. I should write history books."

A slow smile spread across Whitney's face. "I'd read them." After a short silence, his expression turned serious. "What are your intentions regarding my mother?"

Oh my God. Angelina started to say something but held back when she saw that Connor wasn't uncomfortable with the question.

"My *intentions?*" Connor scratched his chin. "Today? Or in general?"

"In general." Whitney held his gaze like two men in a standoff. Despite their significant size difference, Angelina was proud that her son didn't seem at all intimidated by Connor.

Connor pocketed his hands and let out a slow breath. "I really like her. I don't have anything after that figured out."

Giddy warmth spread through Angelina. She wanted to throw herself in Connor's arms and announce that was enough for now. She didn't, though, because Whitney was as important to her as Connor would ever be. "That's as far as I've gotten as well," she said. Connor shot her a quick smile.

She melted.

Whitney looked from Connor to her. "Instead of taking my mom out, you'd really want to stay here and play board games all day?"

Connor shrugged. "That depends."

"On what?" Whitney asked with another frown.

"On how much you'll cry when you get your ass kicked at those games. Dylan is a sore loser. He whines like a five-year-old an hour past bedtime. Sometimes I let him win just so I don't have to hear it."

"I can't imagine *Dylan Sutton* whining," Whitney said.

"You saw our movie?" Connor's tone held real delight. "Trust me, I'm not brilliant and Dylan is a pus—wussy."

"No way." Whitney's eyes rounded.

"Way. Next time he's in town you and I will tag team and take him down in a game of UNO. As soon as he gets too many cards, I'll bet my left testicle he'll throw down his hand and quit."

Angelina winced at his choice of phrase.

Whitney's mouth dropped open. As far as Angelina knew, adults in her son's world didn't swear. They definitely didn't reference their genitalia.

Connor seemed to sense the mood change. His smile turned sheepish. "I shouldn't have said testicle, huh? Too much? I was going to say I'd bet my left ball, but thought that was a little crude so I upgraded to testicle at the last second." He sighed. "Listen, Whitney, I'm going to be honest with you. I'm not the brightest guy you'll ever meet and I get myself in trouble every time I try to be someone I'm not. I'm a simple man. I wanted to go to college, but there was never enough time or money for it. I'm really good at fixing machinery. After a significant amount of instruction, I'm not bad at acting. I'm not rich, but I'm not poor either. I like to laugh a lot more than I like to fight, but when it comes to the people I love there's nothing I wouldn't do for them. Your mom could do a lot better than me, but on the upside, she could also do a lot worse."

"Stop," Angelina said with a laugh. It was hard to tell whether Connor was being entirely serious or not.

Whitney took a moment then said, "I don't know if I cry when I lose—because it never happens."

"Yeow," Connor exclaimed with a chuckle. "Let's test that shall we? To be nice, I'll let you choose the first game."

"I'd say winner chooses the next game, but I'd hate for you to never have a chance to." Whitney's bravado was accompanied by a lighthearted smile that had Angelina's heart singing.

"Go pick a damn game," Connor said, shaking his head.

When Whitney walked over to the table, Angelina hugged Connor. In a low tone, she said, "Thank you."

He looked down at her and for a moment she knew exactly how it felt to be in love with someone who loved her back just as passionately. Exciting. Terrifying. Wonderous.

He winked then said, "Whitney. Look at your mom trying to soften me up so I'll let her win. Not. Going. To. Happen. Sweetheart. Everyone. For. Themselves." He set Angelina back from him.

For effect, Angelina put her hands on her hips and said, "You'll eat those words. I wasn't the captain of Reemsly's chess team for nothing."

The next few hours were filled with laughter and a variety of board games. Angelina was too distracted to pull in a win, but Connor and Whitney took turns taking victory laps around the table.

They paused the games to eat a late lunch. Angelina cooked, Connor and Whitney cleaned up afterward. As they gathered around the table again, Connor surprised Angelina by saying, "This may sound corny, but I'd like to teach you a game Viviana taught me and Dylan. One person starts a sentence and the other finishes it as honestly as they can."

Angelina placed her hand over his on the table. "That sounds like a beautiful game."

Connor shrugged. "After my mother died, Viviana said trying to get men to talk was like trying to teach a goldfish to sing. She didn't give up on us, though. And some of her ideas weren't half bad. Okay, I'll start with you, Angelina. I didn't win a single game today, but—you finish."

She cocked an eyebrow at him. "But winning isn't everything?"

Connor made a face. "You're supposed to say something meaningful or insightful."

"Oh, sorry. Let me try again. I didn't win a single game

today, but I loved watching the two of you get to know each other."

Connor smiled. "That's more like it. Now you try it."

Angelina considered several options, then said, "Connor, I wasn't able to go to college when I was younger and now—"

His cheeks turned pink, but he said, "I'm too scared to try. College is for—"

Angelina's hand tightened on his. "Dammit, stop. Don't you dare say anything about not being smart enough. I hate that someone made you feel that way."

Whitney whistled. "She means it. She never swears."

Connor raised her hand to his mouth and gave it a kiss. "I know I'm not stupid, but I'm a slow reader. I didn't pay much attention in elementary school, or middle school, or high school really. It didn't feel important at the time. Now there's just a lot of shit I don't know. I'd like to change that, but . . ."

"Colleges have online courses now," Whitney said in a tone so supportive, Angelina nearly gave in to proud mama tears. "If you ever need help with them, I took several academic courses online recently and I could show you how it works."

"Seriously?" Connor asked.

"Seriously," Whitney answered. "You could learn at your own pace."

Connor smiled. "I'd like that. I don't need the degree, but I do like learning new things."

"Me too," Whitney said.

"Me three," Angelina added. She turned to her son and

said, "Whitney, I'm happy with my new school, but—"

Whitney hunched his shoulders forward and looked down at the table without answering at first. Finally, he said, "I don't want to be in the technology club. I want to be on the soccer team."

Angelina reached over and took her son's hand in hers. "Oh, honey, then let's get you on that team."

He pulled his hand away. "It's not that easy. I'd have to try out."

"Okay. So, you try out." She didn't see the problem.

Whitney stood. "I'm going to my room." He waved once at Connor. "Nice to meet you."

Angelina raced to intercept him. "Wait. Talk to me, Whitney. Are you afraid you wouldn't make the team?"

"I don't want to talk about it, Mom," Whitney said between clenched teeth.

Connor moved to stand with them. "If you'd like, Whitney, you and I could practice kicking the ball around."

"You played soccer?" Whitney raised his eyes to Connor's.

"A few times and I totally sucked at it. Apparently, you're not supposed to tackle anyone," Connor admitted.

Whitney looked down again. "Thanks anyway."

"But I'd be glad to learn with you. Hell, I know this guy who is so good at it he could probably teach your mom how to score goals."

"Who?" Whitney challenged.

"Ever heard of Ronaldo Torres?"

"The Brazilian World Player winner three years in a row?

You're shitting me."

"Whitney, watch your language," Angelina said automatically.

"I'm serious," Connor said. "He's probably crazy expensive, but I have a fairy godfather who is itching to pay for something and this would be perfect. That is, if you're interested."

"Is this all about impressing my mom?" Whitney challenged.

"One hundred percent. Work with me here, Whitney. After I get you on that team, she'll totally forget about how I nervously discussed my testicles the first time I met you."

Angelina covered her mouth with her hand. Connor was hilarious even when she wasn't sure he was trying to be.

Whitney pressed his lips together as if holding back a similar smile. "She might forget sooner if you stopped mentioning them."

"Good point," Connor said so seriously, all three of them burst out laughing. "So, should I set up a lesson for us this week? All three of us. Your mom and I will just be on the field to make you look good."

"Yes, if you're serious," Whitney said, his tone full of wonder.

"I am. I used to practice football with my dad and Dylan. Those are some of my favorite sober teenage memories." He raised a hand. "Not that I condone drinking. Not at your age, anyway. And not at mine. Really, I think they have the age limit backward, though. At thirteen if you got drunk, no one should care. You can't drive anyway. The young are expected to be stupid. Now me, I'm almost thirty. I have to be more responsible. I have to keep down a job, maintain a certain public reputation. There's a lot of pressure when you're an adult."

"He's joking," Angelina said.

"Is he?" Whitney countered with a smirk.

Angelina elbowed Connor. "He is. Connor, you're not suggesting it would be okay for my child to start drinking early, are you?"

"No, not until he's like eighteen."

"Twenty-one is the legal age limit," she reminded him. "And by 'drinking' Connor's talking about consumption with moderation. A beer once in a while."

Connor nodded obediently. "Couldn't have said it better myself. Don't touch alcohol until you're much, much older and then only like half a beer once a year."

Whitney laughed. "Whatever. I'm going to my room. I approve, Mom."

After Whitney's door closed, Angelina linked both hands with Connor's. "He approves."

Connor kissed her lips lightly and asked, "Did you ever doubt it?"

"Honestly? I did worry. It wouldn't have been a deal breaker, but it would have made things . . . complicated."

Pulling her in for a hug, Connor tucked her beneath his chin. "I worried a little too. Not much makes me nervous anymore, but this was important to me. Which might explain why I babbled on about the Trojan war and my body parts."

Angelina chuckled then hugged him tightly. Never had she imagined she could find a man who fit her as perfectly as Connor did. On the surface they might not appear suited, but he filled a place she hadn't known anyone could. "You were perfect."

"I'm far from that, but I'm becoming more comfortable in my skin. I am serious, though, about signing up for college classes. For me, not for anyone else."

She smiled against his chest. "I love that about you. Socrates once said, 'The only true wisdom is in knowing you know nothing.'"

"He was a pretty smart guy."

"Yes, he was. And mostly he just asked questions. Here's another good quote, 'Aha, universe, we have solved all of your mysteries—said no scientist, ever.' We're all learning, Connor. At least, we should be."

He set her back a little and met her gaze. "What are you learning?"

She considered the question, then said, "That it's okay to not want to be alone. That being too proud cost me more than being foolhardy ever did."

He ran a hand through her hair. "With your family?"

She nodded. Connor would make a good counselor. He saw through layers of defenses right to the heart of a person. "I miss them. I hate that Whitney doesn't have a relationship with them, and it's my fault."

Connor nodded then hugged her to his chest again. Another man might have lied and said it wasn't her fault or told her there was nothing she could do about it. Connor did neither. He saw her . . . the good and the bad . . . and accepted her as she was.

She stood there, listening to the even thud of his heart, and didn't have to chant to herself that things would be okay. She knew they would be.

She raised her head and asked, "Hey, today was perfect, but I have to ask—what did you plan for the alternate date?"

He smiled down at her. "I'd signed us up for a cooking class."

"You cook?"

"Nothing beyond pasta, but that's why a class would have been fun. Actually, I can't imagine a day with you that wouldn't be amazing."

She blushed. "You always know the right thing to say."

He kissed her breathless, then said, "Only with you."

Chapter Seventeen

S IX WEEKS LATER, Angelina was seated on the bleachers of
a soccer field with Connor at her side. Clay Landon and
his wife, Lexi, were seated beside Connor, standing and
cheering every time Whitney got the ball. At first the idea of
having a fairy godfather hit Angelina as strange, but the more
time she spent with Clay the more she saw him the way
Connor did—as a man seeking connections. Lexi was a
spitfire, but she seemed to be yearning for the same. Angelina
had invited her out for a girl's night with Aly and Joanna,
and Lexi had gushed with gratitude. They'd stayed in touch
since.

Apparently being the wife of one of the richest men on
the planet made it difficult to make friends. Thankfully, no
one was more down to earth when it came to wealth than
Aly and Joanna. For all the jokes they made, Angelina's
friends were both living their best lives and that came across
in their confidence and open natures.

From one seat back, Joanna said, "So, is anyone else
wondering if the soccer coach is single? No? Just me?"

Aly leaned forward between Angelina and Connor.

"Connor, quick, cough up a single friend for Joanna. I don't want to diagnose the coach without ever seeing him in my office, but the way he shifts his weight back and forth makes me think he's itchy down under . . . it's not a good sign. Please, offer her a better alternative."

Connor looked over at the coach. "Oh my God, you're right. Hey, for someone who looks at vaginas all day, you're observant of the concerns of the cock."

"Thank you." Aly laughed. "I consider that a compliment."

Joanna broke out laughing as well . . . then Angelina joined in. "Connor, have we told you lately how much we adore you?"

"A man can never hear that too much," Connor said with a thick British accent.

"Don't encourage him." Angelina rolled her eyes. "He's practicing for a role he just accepted. It's a comedy set in England, which means he thinks everything he says in that accent is hilarious now."

"Isn't it?" Connor joked, sitting up straighter and looking down his nose at her with a fake stern expression. "I would have bet my left scone it was."

This time Angelina gave up and laughed along. "You're a goof, you know that?"

He hugged her closer. "But I'm your goof."

"Yes, you are." They kissed briefly then turned back to the field just in time to see Whitney score a goal. Everything else was temporarily forgotten as they cheered.

When they settled back to their seats, Angelina realized

her hand was still laced with Connors and she smiled. This was really happening. She and Connor were a thing. When he'd first said he wanted to teach Whitney how to play soccer, she'd imagined him doing it once. He'd said it was a ploy to impress her, but all it had taken was watching him on the field once with her son to see that it was about so much more. Connor invested in people and, in turn, they tended to invest in him.

Despite her protests that she wanted to pay, Clay Landon had flown in Ronaldo Torres. Three times a week, Angelina, Connor, and Whitney had attended his after-school boot camp.

Together they'd struggled.

Failed.

Laughed.

Tried again.

Grown.

Connor had been at her side in the stands the day Whitney had tried out for the team. Afterward, they had celebrated with pizza and the Fetters in Queens.

And just like that the three of them had become a family.

"I love you," Angelina said spontaneously.

He grinned down at her. "Of course you do. I'm fucking amazing."

She socked him in the arm. "Jerk. You're supposed to say you feel the same."

"So bossy." He brought a hand to his upper arm as if she'd hurt him and turned to Aly and Joanna. "Did you see that smack? And now she says she wants me to tell her I love her. She wants to see me get all sappy and say that before her I didn't know what love was. Hell, that I didn't know who I was. She's looking for me to proclaim that I can't imagine my life without her in it."

Aly and Joanna were all smiles. Aly said, "You might want to say it then, before she kicks your ass."

Joanna brought her hands to her heart. "If she doesn't know how you feel by now, dump her and marry me. I'd never smack those beautiful, perfectly sculpted arms of yours." When Aly's eyebrows shot up, Joanna announced, "Kidding. Unless it doesn't work out between you, then after an appropriate grace period . . ."

With a laugh, Angelina jumped in, "He'd still be off-limits."

"Even his calendar?" Joanna asked with a grin.

"Yes," Angelina, Aly, and Connor said in unison.

"Damn." Joanna was such a little shit. No one took her seriously. "Well, back to the drawing board. Can I have his brother?"

Connor snapped his fingers. "I'm glad you said that. I forgot that Dylan wanted to see the game." He brought his brother up on video chat. "Dylan, say hi to everyone." He turned the phone to those sitting around the bench. "Everyone, say hi to Dylan."

"Hi, Dylan," the group said in unison.

"Hi, everyone. Has the game started?"

"Yes, and you missed a score by Whitney, but he's on fire out there. He'll score again."

"Awesome. Angelina, you must be so proud of him."

"I am," Angelina said. Although she had yet to meet Dylan in person, Connor had included her in on so many phone conversations with him that she felt as if she had. "He'll be thrilled when I tell him you watched the game as well."

"Looking forward to meeting him next week."

"Next week?" Angelina asked. "I didn't know you were coming for a visit. Connor, you didn't say anything."

Connor turned the phone toward his face. "Because it's a secret and the key to a secret remaining one is to not blurt it out the first chance you get."

"Oh, fuck," Dylan said. "I forgot. Sorry, Connor."

"Shut up and watch the game." Connor turned the phone toward the field and propped it up against Angelina's handbag. "Can you see?"

"Yep. What number is he?"

"Twenty-seven."

"That was your football number."

"Cool coincidence, huh?" Connor asked.

Angelina leaned forward so Dylan could hear her as well. "Actually, Whitney looked up old photos of Connor playing football and requested the same number."

"He did?" Connor's mouth dropped open.

"He looks up to you." It was true. Connor had an easygoing confidence that Whitney was drawn to. Since meeting him, her son had begun to stand taller, speak louder, and laugh more. Angelina had fought to hold back happy tears the day he'd told her that he no longer felt invisible.

Invisible?

I never knew he felt that way. There was so much he never felt he could tell me that he shares with Connor.

Two weeks after meeting Connor, Whitney had told him that an upperclassman had started shoving him in the hallways of the school. Angelina had wanted to call the school, but Whitney had asked Connor what he'd do.

Connor had asked Angelina for permission to show Whitney how to handle it. Since it had been important to Whitney, she hadn't felt she could say no.

"Does the kid pick on anyone else?" Connor had asked.

"Yeah, Travis, a boy in my history class. He gets teased a lot because he's ridiculously tall and still close to a hundred pounds."

"Invite him to come over Saturday morning. I'll invite Bradford. We'll show you what to do."

That Saturday would forever stand out as the day she knew Connor was the one for her. They'd gathered at Joanna's house for privacy and Connor asked Bradford to kick his ass. "Just don't mess with the face in case I need it for my next movie," had been his only stipulation.

Although Bradford had seemed reluctant at first, Connor had encouraged him until—*Ouch*, the first punch he'd given him had sent Connor stumbling back and hunching over. Winded, Connor had turned to the boys and said, "What do you do when you get knocked down?"

Wide-eyed, they'd shaken their heads.

Angelina hadn't known what he'd expected them to say either.

Connor had added, "You get back up. That's how you

win." Then he'd said, "Bradford, hit me again."

The second hit had come as a roundoff kick that had sent Connor to the ground. He shook his head and rose back to his feet. "Again."

Each time he was hit, he stood. When he became shaky on his feet, Bradford stopped. "I think they get the point."

Connor turned to the boys and said, "I don't have to punch Bradford for him to know he hasn't beaten me. I'm not suggesting you let anyone hit you. I just want you to see that fear hurts more than pain. That's what I learned from football. If you're afraid of the hit, you've already lost. Now, Travis, shove Whitney to the ground. Then Whitney, shove Travis to the ground. Do it like you mean it. Punch like you have something to defend. It's going to hurt like hell, but not as bad as that dick thinking he can scare you feels."

With Connor's encouragement, two formerly peace-loving kids beat the crap out of each other then ended the session with smiles and high fives—oh, and a black eye Whitney congratulated Travis for giving him.

It shouldn't have worked. It was the opposite of how Angelina believed conflicts should be handled. However, when she picked up Whitney at school a few days later he told her the upperclassman had sought him out and had been about to knock the books out of his hand when he'd growled, "Don't fucking touch me."

"It worked, Mom. Just like Connor said it would. I didn't care if he hit me because I knew I'd get back up. I wasn't afraid and he knew it."

And what had Connor done when Whitney had told

him? He'd suggested they celebrate with dinner at the Fetters. Loving Connor was that easy—that wonderous.

Now Dylan had spilled the beans about a surprise Connor was planning, a surprise that included a visit from his brother, and she was dying to know what it was. "Is there anything you want to tell me?" she asked Connor.

He laced his fingers with hers then kissed her knuckles. "Nope."

Angelina turned and asked her friends. "Do you guys know what Connor is planning?"

They were both horrible at lying. "No. No idea."

Angelina leaned forward so she could see Clay's face when she asked, "Clay, how about you? Any idea what Connor's secret is?"

Clay smiled. "Only that it's going to be so incredible I hired a film crew for it."

"A film crew?" Angelina studied Connor's face. Normally, he couldn't keep a secret either, but she had no clue what he was up to. "Does Whitney know about it?"

There was a twinkle in Connor's eyes. "Everyone knows, they're just all better at keeping their mouths shut than Dylan is."

"Wow, sounds like a big surprise. How about a little clue? Just a hint?"

Connor's response was a kiss so tender Angelina nearly forgot what she'd been asking him. She was melting against him, when he surged to his feet and yelled, "Go, Whitney. You've got this. Yes. Yes. He's wide open."

Angelina turned toward the field in time to see her son

kick the ball to a teammate who scored the goal. She cheered beside Connor. Whitney looked up from the field with a huge smile on his face as his other teammates cheered as well.

The road to where they were had been a rocky one. There were still parts of her life that needed addressing, but the past no longer had a hold over her. Names no longer had the power to affect how she saw herself. Like punches, they'd been used to knock her down. With Connor, she'd learned that getting knocked down and getting back up felt a whole lot better than running from the pain.

She didn't know how she'd do it, but she knew it was time to patch things up with her family back in Oklahoma. It probably wouldn't be easy at first, but nothing worthwhile usually was.

As she settled back down beside Connor, he leaned down and said, "I love you, Angelina Kroll."

"Of course you do," she said. "I'm fucking amazing."

He threw his head back and laughed, then bent to give her a warm kiss. Against her lips, he murmured, "Yes, you are."

CONNOR WAS ON his feet again, cheering Whitney on when he spotted his sister, Viviana, little Sean in her arms, standing off to the side with her husband, Grant. When he waved to her, she motioned for him to join her. "I'll be right back," he told Angelina.

She nodded.

When he reached his sister's side, he hugged her, took Sean from her for a cuddle, then shook Grant's hand. "Hey,

I didn't know you were coming today."

Viviana's expression was somber. "Can we talk?"

"Sure." He scanned Grant's face but found little there to help him determine what this was about. Still holding little Sean, Connor followed Grant and Viviana several feet away from the bleachers.

Once out of earshot of everyone, Viviana said, "We haven't seen you at game night lately."

"I've been kind of busy." He kept his voice light and his eyes on his nephew's smiling face. Little Sean pinched at his cheeks and squealed with delight.

"I received your invitation for the Barringtons to join you in Oklahoma next week," Viviana said.

Connor's mood took a quick dive. If his sister was there to say he was once again an embarrassment to her, it was time to set her straight on a few things. For over a year he'd done everything he could to appease her. He didn't want to live that way anymore. If that meant pulling back from the Barringtons, that was a path he was okay with. He wanted his sister to be happy, but he'd found a way to be happy also. "And?"

Viviana's eyebrows rose at his curt tone. He felt bad, but he was also beginning to think he should have pushed back long before this. "I understand why you invited them through me, but I don't feel good about it."

"Then don't pass the invitation along to them." Really? What did she want him to say? As if sensing his mood, Little Sean began to fuss. Grant offered to take him, but Connor settled him onto his hip and made a silly noise to him that had the little one smiling again. He understood kids, they didn't overthink things the way adults did.

"No," Viviana said in a rush. "You don't understand. I don't feel good about what that says about how I've been behaving. My whole life you and Dylan have done nothing but support me. No matter what I wanted to do. When I went to the city, you told me I could do anything I set my mind to. When I came home pregnant, you tracked down Grant to threaten him . . . but you never judged me. I didn't see I wasn't doing the same for you until Sophie took me aside and opened my eyes." She reached out and laid a hand on her son's head as she spoke. "I never meant to make you feel like you needed to change. I was so worried about not fitting into Grant's family that I couldn't see how much they love you too. I'm here to say I'm sorry."

"Thank you." At his mother's touch, Sean decided he wanted her back, so Connor handed her back. "Not all the changes you asked me to make were bad. My movie career is taking off—Claire helped make that possible. I'm taking my first college class because I've learned it's never too late to better yourself. You helped me see that."

Grant put an arm around Viviana and son. "Your sister cares about you more than you know. So do I. My family had forgotten how to be silly and laugh together. You reminded us that life doesn't always need to be serious. I'm grateful Sean will have an uncle like you. When I see Asher allowing his son to tackle him to the ground, I credit you for reminding us how lighthearted love can be."

Connor smiled. "Little Sean is awesome. I love my Big

Man, too. Asher cracks me up as well."

Viviana pursed her lips before saying, "You have your own relationship with Asher, with Sophie and Dale, and all the Barringtons. You shouldn't feel that you have to run an invitation through me. They're your family as well. I hate that I ever made you feel like they weren't."

It was almost enough to bring tears to a man's eyes. Instead, Connor hugged his sister, then her husband. When he stepped back, they were both smiling and Sean was clapping happily. "We're good," he said.

Viviana wiped the corner of her eyes. "I'm glad. By the way, I told everyone about the invite and they're all planning to be there."

How could he not smile at that? "Any of them going to participate?"

Grant said, "Andrew and I are in."

Viviana tucked herself against her husband's side. "Are you sure?"

"I am," Grant said, flexing his hands in the air. "Who knows, a scar or two might be good for my image."

Connor chuckled. "We'll make sure you're safe."

Viviana added, "Lance is bringing Willa and the twins, but he's just going to watch. He's anti-anything that might involve snakes. Asher said he'd do it, but he has a thing against standing in water where he can't see his feet. Dax was a hard no. Ian said he'd rather be shot at."

"Kade and Dylan said they'd team up, though," Grant said. "Although I wonder which one will be the spotter and which will be brave enough to use his hand as bait."

"My guess is not Dylan," Connor said. "Although, he says he's doing his own stunts now, so maybe."

A cheer erupted from the bleachers. Connor turned and scanned the field. Whitney was high-fiving another player, but it was impossible to know which had scored. "Hey, I don't want to be rude, but let's get back to the stands. I don't want to miss another moment of this."

"Mind if we join you?" Viviana asked.

Connor offered to take Little Sean back. His nephew went to him happily. "I'd be disappointed if you didn't."

As they walked toward the bleachers she said, "We don't want to miss another moment of this either."

She didn't say it, but he knew that 'this' wasn't just the soccer game. He and his sister had been closer before she married Grant. For a while, she'd seemed to need boundaries between Connor and her new family. He'd done his best to respect that. She was saying something different now. "When we get back from Oklahoma, I'd like to start bringing Angelina and her son to game night at the Barringtons."

Viviana hugged his arm then smiled at her husband. "If you hadn't said that, we were going to suggest it."

They all sat back down on the bleachers. Viviana chose to sit next to Angelina. A moment later they were laughing and chatting about something and Connor felt another piece of his happiness puzzle click into place.

When he'd met Angelina he'd been confused about more than just how to talk to people. He'd lost sight of who he was. She'd helped him find his way back to himself.

He hoped his surprise did the same for her.

Chapter Eighteen

A WEEK LATER, Angelina gripped the arms of her seat and tried to calm her nerves as their small plane circled the airport. Her stomach had been doing somersaults ever since the pilot had announced they were about to touch down at a private airport outside of Tonkawa, Oklahoma.

Connor was taking her home—to her home.

Whitney appeared remarkably calm about the whole thing considering it was his first trip back. It wasn't the first time he'd meet his uncles and grandparents, but he'd been much younger the last time they'd come to New York for a visit.

Connor leaned down and gently asked, "Nervous?"

"I want to lie and say no, but I might vomit and reveal the truth," she answered.

He kissed her cheek. "Don't throw up. It's going to be great. I guess I can tell you now that your parents and brothers are meeting us at the airport. They're really excited."

"You've been talking to them?"

"Twice a week since you told me you missed them.

They've missed you too."

Angelina covered her face with her hands. "Oh my God. I don't even know what to say to them. I feel so bad about not contacting them myself. So bad about—" She stopped and swallowed hard. "So many things."

Connor nuzzled the side of her head. "So do they, Angelina. They've spent a lot of years beating themselves up for not protecting you when you found out about Whitney, for not knowing how to show you it was safe to come home. They love you. Whitney's biological father never became a man he should meet, but he and his family have moved away. Those who stood with him against you—well, they've had time to grow up and regret how they behaved. When you get off this plane, you do it with your head held high . . . and you go give your mother the hug she's hoping you will. Cry if you want to, but know that they'll cry right along with you if you do."

Angelina sniffed and wiped tears from her cheeks. "I'm not going to cry."

"Uh-huh."

From across the cabin, Whitney said, "Don't ruin your makeup, Mom. There's a film crew documenting all this."

Angelina let out a shaky breath and met Connor's gaze. "Why?"

He smiled and shrugged. "Clay says we'll want to remember this day. I tried to refuse the offer, but you know how he is."

Angelina nodded then asked her son, "How are you feeling about seeing everyone again?"

Just like Connor, he shrugged and smiled. "I've been talking to them too. They needed to know all the things you've done right and who better to tell them than me?"

Looking back and forth between the two most important men in her life, she shook her head in wonder. "I should probably be upset with you two for keeping this all a secret, but I'm so damn grateful to have you both in my life. How did I get so lucky?"

Puffing up and donning a British accent, Connor said, "Albert Einstein said, 'In the middle of every great difficulty lies opportunity.' I didn't understand what he meant when I first read that, but I think I get it now. If the people in your town had never mistreated you, you would have never left Oklahoma. You wouldn't have known your aunt Rudi or Aly or Joanna." He smiled. "Or me. Before Viviana met Grant I was perfectly happy with my small town life. I had to be pushed, shoved really, out of that comfort zone to see that I could be so much more. I don't regret trying to be the man I thought I had to be. I'm a better man because of it. I probably should have asked you if you wanted to take me home to meet your parents, but I hope you see an opportunity in how difficult I made it. Hang on, that sounds bad when I say it like that. What I mean is—"

She laid two fingers lightly over his mouth. "I get it. And I love that you did this."

The plane touched down with a bump that brought the conversation to an end.

Just as Connor had said they would be, her family was right there waiting for them as they stepped out of the plane.

There was a heavy awkwardness to the meeting when she first stood before them, but she took a leap of faith and followed Connor's advice.

There was something powerfully healing about a good hug. She stepped into her mother's arms and simply held on. There was so much she wanted to say, so much pain, so many regrets, but instead of spilling them out, she held on and hoped her love came through in that hug.

When she stepped back, there were tears in her mother's eyes, but she was smiling. Angelina found herself doing the same. She turned to her father and gave him the hug she'd yearned to for so long. "I'm so sorry, Daddy," she whispered.

"We all are, baby. We all are," he murmured. "Don't you trouble yourself with none of that anymore."

Her brothers were next and her heart was bursting with love and gratitude. She turned in time to see her mother give Whitney a warm hug and Connor lift her father off his feet in a bear hug. A laugh burst out of her. She was glad his sister had never succeeded in changing him.

"So, what now?" she asked.

Whitney trotted over to her. "I'd tell you, but you'd never believe it."

Still dabbing tears from the corners of her eyes, Angelina's mother said, "It sounded crazy when Connor first suggested it, but the whole town has come out to welcome you home and be a part of this." She nodded toward Connor. "He's a keeper. You could have done a lot worse."

With a laugh, Connor said, "I tell her the same thing."

Angelina slipped beneath his arm and hugged him. "Definitely a keeper."

Her father cleared his throat. "We should probably head over. Everyone is already there."

They began to make their way toward where her family had parked their trucks. Whitney chose to ride with his grandparents. Angelina and Connor climbed into the front seat of her brother Jared's truck. She took the middle spot as she had so many times in the past. The smells were familiar. The country music was as well. For a moment it felt like no time had passed since she'd left.

And for once, that wasn't a bad thing.

She looked from her brother to Connor and back. "So, which one of you is going to give me a hint about what's going on?"

She shouldn't have asked because to avoid her question they both started singing along with the radio, and neither of them had much skill with it. Given no other choice, she joined in and found herself feeling younger, freer, and not at all embarrassed that she also couldn't carry a tune.

She wondered what Aunt Rudi would have thought of her in that moment. It might have been her imagination, but she would have bet her left scone her aunt was smiling down in approval.

As they drove along, Angelina kept trying to guess where they were going. They didn't take the road to her parents' home. They weren't headed toward downtown.

When she saw the sign for a pond she'd spent most of her childhood swimming in, she was confused. What were they doing there that the town all wanted to be part of? A barbecue? The road leading to the pond was lined with cars. The parking lot beside the pond was full.

And just as Whitney had said, there was a cameraman filming their arrival. When she climbed out of the truck and looked around, she swayed on her feet and clutched Connor's hand. Everyone she loved was there.

Aly and Joanna.

Kimmie, Javier, and Linda.

Clay and Lexi.

Bradford.

Most of the town—so many familiar faces and all of them smiling.

She greeted each of them, introducing Connor as she went. Some were excited to be meeting a celebrity. Some seemed more excited to simply see Angelina again. It was a better homecoming than she'd ever dared imagine.

Connor introduced her to a few of his friends from his hometown. She couldn't help but think he'd only gather everyone they knew for one reason. One magical reason.

When several black SUVs pulled into the parking lot, a hush fell over the crowd as all eyes turned toward the arrivals. The first ones out looked like well-dressed, paid security. They fanned out over the area then the door of the second SUV opened and Sophie Barrington stepped out, accompanied by her husband. After that, Barringtons of all ages streamed out of the other vehicles.

"Ready to meet more of my family?" Connor asked.

Angelina nodded and walked over to them with him. Sophie held out her hands in greeting. Angelina took both of them in hers.

Sophie said, "Look at you. Absolutely stunning. I knew you would be. And you're glowing."

Angelina glanced at Connor. "I have a lot to be happy about."

Sophie's smile was so welcoming Angelina saw why Connor adored her. "You take good care of him, Angelina. I love that boy."

"I will," Angelina promised before greeting Dale politely.

Connor gave Sophie a hug that swung her up into the air and had her laughing. "It means a lot to me that you're here, Sophie."

She laid a hand on his cheek. "I wouldn't have missed this for the world. Now, promise me none of my sons will drown today."

"We're keeping to shallow ground because there are so many newbies," Connor answered.

"And the snakes?"

"Ian had the area swept clean of anything that the locals say make this exciting, but it'll still be entertaining."

"I'm sure it will be," Dale said in a dry voice. "I can't say there's enough money on the planet to get me to put my hand in a hole for a fish to swallow."

"Hang on," Angelina said with a gasp. "We're noodling today? That's what we're doing here?"

"Of course," Connor said. "What did you think we were doing?"

Angelina tried not to give in to the disappointment nipping at her heels. For a moment there she'd started to think

Connor had gathered everyone together to propose to her. She shook her head to clear that thought out. Just because it wasn't what she thought it was about, didn't make it a less-amazing day.

Connor had found a way to smooth things over between her and her parents.

He'd done what she'd thought was impossible . . . brought her home in a way that was actually not painfully awkward. After that day, she could see herself being able to easily return to see her family. Holidays. Vacations.

Angelina wrapped her arms around Connor and hugged him with all the love welling within her. So what if the day didn't end in an engagement? It was already life changing in a wonderful way.

And this man had given her that gift.

He is definitely getting oral sex as soon as we're alone.

"What did you say?" Connor asked.

Angelina's chest clenched. "Did I just say something out loud?"

"I think so," he said in her ear. "But you were mumbling. Still I thought I heard the word sex."

Oh my God. She forced a smile and said in a loud voice, "I said six. That's how many times I've gone noodling. Six times. So, watch out. I know what I'm doing."

If Sophie or Dale had heard differently, they didn't say a word. Either way, the rest of their clan came over and soon Angelina was being introduced to so many Barringtons she worried she'd never remember all their names.

A short time later, most of the people attending were

gathered on the shore of the pond. Everyone who had paired up with the intention of noodling was waist deep in the water listening to Angelina's brothers give instructions on how to not only catch a catfish, but also how to survive a possible violent underwater tussle with one.

Grant and Andrew were the first to go. Jared led them over to a hole beside a large rock. "Andrew, stick your hand in there. Go real slow. Being that this is your first time and all, we did our best to make sure there's no snapping turtles or poisonous snakes in there, but it ain't like any of us got X-ray vision. Anything could have swum in there while we weren't looking. Don't worry, most body parts can be sewn back on."

"Thanks for the pep talk," Andrew said. "Let's just get this done."

From the sidelines, Asher called out, "You sure you trust Grant to pull you out if there's trouble?"

Andrew chucked a nervous looking Grant in the shoulder. "Always."

Only because Grant was looking a little queasy, Angelina said to Connor, "Get a little closer just in case they need you. If the catfish is big enough it can pull a man under."

"On it." Connor hovered where one might have thought he just wanted to see what was happening, but close enough to dive in and help if he needed to.

Without fanfare, Andrew bent down so the water was shoulder high and stuck his arm inside a hole. He made a face, but didn't move. A moment later, he pulled out an impressively large catfish like he'd been doing it his whole life.

Out of the water, it thrashed around. He called out, "Catch." And tossed the fish to Grant.

Grant hugged the fish to his chest for a moment, looked hilariously horrified, then released it back into the water. "That was a squirrely one," he said in a calm voice that was completely opposite of how he likely felt.

Applause and laughter rang out from the shore. "It's all good," Angelina's father said. "Although, when it comes to fishing, the ones you hold on to make better eating."

"I'll keep that in mind for the next time," Grant said as he made his way back to shore.

Viviana was right there to greet him with a towel. "Will there be a next time?"

"Hell no," he said with a laugh. "But at least I tried it."

"You sure did, honey," Viviana said in sweet support.

Jared announced the next group should step up. This time it was Dylan Sutton and Kade Thompson-Barrington.

Kade said, "Want me to do it, Dylan? It can't be worse than gator hunting back home. Every once in a while one of them would try to move into a neighborhood pool. Never intentionally put my hand into any of their mouths though."

Dylan looked around and puffed out his chest. "I've been doing my own stunts. How bad can this be?"

"Okay, I've got your back," Kade said in agreement.

Andrew lingered nearby. Without saying so, it was apparent he did as well.

Dylan stuck a hand in, swore profusely, but stayed bent over. "Holy hell, what's that?" he asked. Just then he was spun underwater and disappeared from view.

There was a split second of shock then the men began to dive to retrieve him. Collectively no one above the water moved.

Waist deep in water herself, Angelina wrung her hands as Connor dove after Dylan. No one she knew had ever died doing this, but it did happen. She sent up a prayer and scanned the crowd for her child. He was standing beside his grandparents looking just as scared as she felt.

Dylan resurfaced with Connor holding one arm and Andrew holding the other. Andrew was the first to speak. "You are one crazy bastard, Dylan."

With that, Dylan raised both arms, he had a wildly thrashing catfish attached to each of his hands, one significantly larger than the other—so big, her brothers rushed in to pull it off him and hold it up for the crowd. It was the largest Angelina had personally ever seen pulled from the pond.

Dylan was beaming as the other fish was retrieved from his hand. He called out to Sean Sutton. "Dad, did you see that shit? That is how noodling is done."

"I saw," Sean called back. "Just glad you survived."

"Me too," Dylan said as he made his way to shore. Joanna met him with a towel and a smile.

Oh, she's good.

When the cheering died down, Connor announced, "Looks like it's our turn." His hair was already plastered to his head and he stunk like the bottom of the pond. God, she'd never loved him more.

They stood before a hole Jared said they'd confirmed a good-sized catfish resided inside. "You ready?" Angelina asked.

"I was born for this," Connor boasted and stuck his hand in. "Holy crap, it's a huge one. Oh, no. Are those teeth? Ow. Ow. Holy shit that hurts." He pulled his hand out. "I can't do it."

"That's okay," she said. Really, the whole sport was insane. That he couldn't was actually a good sign. "You don't have to prove anything to anyone."

"Oh, we're getting that fish. I just think you should do it."

"Me?" Her voice came out as a squeak.

"You're a six-time noodler, remember? You can do this."

"I believe in you, Mom," Whitney called out from the shore.

Angelina turned to face Connor. "Hold on. That fish is too big for you to want to catch, but you think I can do it?"

His grin was all challenge. "I believe in you too."

The crowd began to chant for her to do it.

Angelina considered refusing, but this was her town—her sport. And dammit, she'd once pulled a fish out that had weighed more than her. No way was she going to back down now. "Fine," she said, squared her shoulders, and stuck her hand inside the hole.

Nothing.

No bite.

No thud of warning.

"You sure there was something in here? Doesn't seem to

be anything now."

"Try near the bottom," Connor said.

Catfish could hide low. Angelina ran her hand along the bottom then stopped when she came across a small box. "I found something, but not a catfish." She straightened out of the water and held the box out. It was small like a—ring box.

Her breath caught in her throat. She opened it with shaking hands.

"Easy there," Connor said, bringing his hands around hers to steady them. "Drop it now and we'll never find it."

There in a wet velvet display was a round diamond set simply on a platinum band. Connor retrieved the ring and said, "I would kneel but honestly it's disgusting down there."

"No need," Angelina said in a voice just above a whisper.

"Angelina Kroll. I have fallen in love with you over and over again since the day we met. Every time I'm with you I think I can't possibly love you more, then you do something that shows me I can. Marry me so I can spend the rest of my life showing you how good life can be with someone who loves all the sides of you."

"Yes," she said, slipping the ring on her finger before he had a chance to drop it. "Connor Sutton, you make me laugh every day. You brought back parts of me I thought I'd lost forever. You bet your ass we're getting married."

He swung her up and around, then down for a deep kiss.

When they broke the kiss off, they took a moment to simply stare into each other's eyes. Just when she began to relax, Connor called out, "Whitney, get on in here. You and I are catching a catfish."

Angelina opened her mouth to say no way in hell was her son doing any such thing, but he was already hopping into the water. She didn't need to tell anyone to spot him. Connor moved to stand beside him. Dylan, Andrew, Kade, both of her brothers, and even Bradford joined them to make a half circle behind him.

Her eyes filled with tears when she saw her father shed his shoes and join them. Her baby was far from alone in the world and no longer a baby at all. The fish he pulled from the water wasn't the biggest she'd ever seen, but the triumphant smile on his face was.

From the shore Clay Landon looked on with pride, part of the moment yet also above it, as all good fairy godfathers are.

Epilogue

A WEEK LATER, flushed and smiling, Angelina and Connor arrived at their offices an hour late. They came to a skidding stop when they saw Kimmie standing on her desk with Linda on a crate beside the desk.

Connor shook his head and thumbed in their direction. "Are you sure you'll be okay with them while I film on location?"

"I'll be fine." Angelina laughed and put her hands on her hips. "What's going on, ladies?"

"Hang on," Kimmie said as if her behavior were perfectly normal. "What if you bend at the waist?"

Linda shook her head. "Look at him, he's even taller than I am right now and you're too low for this to be comfortable." She climbed off the crate. "Just have her lay across the desk."

"I wanted to spice the scene up a little."

Connor stepped closer. "What you're not taking into account is how strong I am." Without touching Kimmie he motioned how he'd pick her up by her waist. "I'd toss those legs right over my shoulders, lean Angelina back a little against the cabinet and take my time."

Angelina blushed, but put that on a mental list of what she wanted to try with him.

"That's perfect!" Kimmie exclaimed then jumped down from her table and wrote it on a sticky note. "Thanks, Connor."

Linda gave Connor a pat on the arm. "We're going to miss you."

"It's only a few weeks. The rest of the filming is happening stateside," Connor assured her. "And you'll have Angelina. She's covering for me while I'm gone."

Kimmie returned to her seat behind her desk. "That can't be easy—to be apart right after you get engaged."

Angelina walked over and linked hands with Connor. "Before I met Connor I would have agreed with you. I wasted a lot of time worrying about every way things could go wrong. Now I focus on how they're going right. I found a man I can be myself with. My son goes to school now without complaint. I love my job. And that movie he's making? It allows us to afford two secretaries who don't actually get much work done, but are amazing anyway."

Linda took her spot behind her desk as well. "Don't worry Angelina, we're writing you into the next book—the one with the reluctantly alpha prince."

Angelina temporarily lost herself in Connor's smiling eyes. "I don't need a prince, I've already found my happy ending."

"Quick," Linda said, "jot that line down. I like it."

Kimmie sighed audibly. "I'd rather describe how he's

looking at her. Love is a beautiful thing, isn't it?"

"It sure is," Connor said with a lustful twinkle in his eyes. "Ladies, why don't you take the morning off? Angelina and I have some work to get done in my office."

As soon as the door closed behind them, Connor swept Angelina up into his arms and carried her into his office, kicking his door closed behind him.

Best job ever.

THE END

Not ready to say good-bye to these characters? Sign up for my newsletter via my website ruthcardello.com/newsletter and stay informed about releases.

To get a complete list of all my books to to:
www.Ruthcardello.com

About the Author

Ruth Cardello was born the youngest of 11 children in a small city in southern Massachusetts. She spent her young adult years moving as far away as she could from her large extended family. She lived in Boston, Paris, Orlando, New York—then came full circle and moved back to New England. She now happily lives one town over from the one she was born in. For her, family trumped the warmer weather and international scene.

She was an educator for 20 years, the last 11 as a kindergarten teacher. When her school district began cutting jobs, Ruth turned a serious eye toward her second love– writing and has never been happier. When she's not writing, you can find her chasing her children around her small farm, riding her horses, or connecting with her readers online.

Contact Ruth:
Website: RuthCardello.com
Email: Ruthcardello@gmail.com
FaceBook: Author Ruth Cardello
Twitter: @RuthieCardello

Printed in Great Britain
by Amazon

45912901R00169